A QUIET LIFE IN THE COUNTRY

A QUIET LIFE IN THE COUNTRY

A Lady Hardcastle Mystery

T E KINSEY

THOMAS & MERCER

The characters and events portrayed in this book are fictitious. Any similarity to real persons, living or dead, is coincidental and not intended by the author.

Text copyright © 2016 by T E Kinsey

Published by Thomas & Mercer, Seattle

www.apub.com

ISBN-13: 9781503938267
ISBN-10: 1503938263

Cover design by Lisa Horton

Printed in the United States of America

1

'Good heavens!' said Lady Hardcastle as we stepped down from the dog cart. 'This is rather larger than I had expected.'

The driver of the faintly dilapidated cart handed me Lady Hardcastle's Gladstone while she fished in her purse for her customarily generous tip. With an astonished 'Thank you, m'lady', he flicked his whip. The cart clattered off, back towards the station in Chipping Bevington where it had picked us up.

I stood beside her in the bright summer sunshine and looked at our new home. She was right, it was rather large.

'When you suggested we move to the country, my lady,' I began slowly, 'I confess that my imagination conjured up images of a rose-covered cottage, perhaps with a small kitchen garden and an apple tree. It was quaint and old-fashioned, with low doors that you could bump your head on while I passed through unharmed. "Charming" is, I believe, the word people use.'

'This has charm, Flo,' she said. 'And it's new, and clean, and excitingly modern. And it has all the space we'll ever need.'

I couldn't argue with her there. It was all of those things and more; it's just that it wasn't what I'd been expecting. Built from red brick, it looked nothing like the houses we had passed on the road from the railway station to the village of Littleton Cotterell. The good folk of Gloucestershire favoured stone for their housebuilding – fat, rustic stones with contrasting quoins and jambs. We hadn't passed anything like this imposing family home with its red bricks, its gabled porch and its symmetrical bay windows.

The house was set back from the lane that led back to the village, and its boundary was marked by a low wall of similar red brick. Entrance to the neat front garden was through an ornate, wrought-iron gate, painted green to match the sturdy-looking front door of the house. The gate creaked as I opened it.

'We might have to find a chap from the village to grease the hinges,' said Lady Hardcastle as we walked up the path. 'Having that thing creaking every time someone comes to the door will drive us barmy.'

'"Barmy" isn't a frightfully long drive for you, my lady,' I said. 'But shall we be endlessly beset by visitors? You don't know anyone. I thought your plan was for a quiet life in the country.'

'Oh, it is, but we're certain to have visitors. At least I hope so. I want a quiet life, not a cloistered one.'

She tried the door handle and found the door unlocked. We walked in.

Our footsteps on the wooden floor echoed as we drank in our new surroundings. The hall was panelled in dark wood and the hall table and hatstand from the London flat didn't look at all out of place.

'This will do very nicely,' she said. 'Very nicely indeed.'

'We'll not be living in squalor, that's for certain,' I said with a smile. 'If I get the range lit, it can be warming up while we explore, then we can have a nice cup of tea before we settle ourselves.'

'A sterling plan, Flo. I'd like to check that the removal men followed my instructions. You know how these chaps can be. They promise to put everything in its place, but then you move in and find that they've put the aspidistra in the bedroom and the piano in the kitchen.'

'You've never had an aspidistra,' I called from the kitchen.

'Good thing too,' she said, 'if that's the way removal men treat them.'

There was a stack of wood beside the range and I had it lit in no time.

'I thought we'd left the piano behind,' I said as I came out of the kitchen. She was nowhere to be seen, so I tried the door to the right of the hallway. It was the drawing room and she was fussing with the placement of the chairs and the small table between them.

'What was that, dear?' she said.

'I said I thought we'd left the piano behind.'

'We did,' she said, a puzzled frown crinkling her brow.

'You were saying you were expecting to find it in the kitchen,' I persisted.

'Was I? It certainly sounds like the sort of thing I might say, but we definitely left it. I never liked it – horrible tone. I've ordered a new one.'

'Right you are, my lady.'

'So far, so good,' she said, indicating her old chairs and occasional table, which entirely failed to fill the spacious room. 'They even managed to put the books on the shelves.' She looked closer. 'I'm not sure I'd have put Charles Dickens next to Isaac Newton except at a dinner party, and then only if Nellie Melba hadn't turned up, but they've done their best.'

'What happened to the lovely comfy armchairs?' I said.

'They should be in the sitting room.'

'Gracious, we have a sitting room, too? How very decadent.'

'And a morning room. Jasper and his wife have four children so they'll need plenty of room if they ever get back from India.'

'Did he say when that might be?'

'No,' she said. 'He was a bit vague about it all, to be honest. "Business, blah, blah, have to stay out here for a while, blah, blah, rotten luck, blah, blah, don't suppose you want to rent a house in the country, old girl?" You know the sort of thing.'

We moved across the hall and through the opposite door, which led to the dining room. The walnut dining table could seat eight and had always seemed a little large in the flat, but here in this spacious, high-ceilinged room it was much more at home. Lady Hardcastle cast about the room to make sure that everything was in its proper place.

'They've done a much better job than I had feared,' she said, opening one of the doors on the sideboard. 'Look, they've even managed to remember to put the dinner service away.'

Before I could look as instructed, she had breezed out and was heading towards the back of the house and the kitchen. Instead of turning left, though, as I had done to find and light the range, she turned right into a small square room. There, we found her desk, which had been positioned so that it looked out of the window onto the spacious walled garden and the fields and hills beyond.

'This will do very nicely indeed,' she said again, resting her hand on the back of her chair. 'We might need to redecorate at some point – I do rather find these pale colours a little insipid – but it shall do for now. Upstairs next, I think.'

'Just one thing, my lady,' I said as we completed our survey of the upper floors and headed for the kitchen.

'Just one?' she said.

'For now. You are planning to hire some more staff, aren't you?' I said. 'I'll not be able to look after this place on my own. The apartments in London were simple enough, especially with being able to send the laundry out, but here . . .'

'Fear not, tiny servant,' she said. 'When Jasper rented me the place he put me on to the local landowners and they've sorted out some people for me to interview. It's all in hand.'

'Well, that's a relief,' I said, and put the kettle on to boil.

'Of more pressing concern,' she said, looking about, 'is what shall we eat? The Great Western Railway offers a punctual service but a lacklustre lunch. I shall be somewhere beyond starving by dinner time.'

'Fear not, ageing employer,' I said. 'I ordered some supplies before we left London and asked that they be delivered to the house. If all is well, there should be plenty in the pantry.'

I opened the larder door and indicated the shelves, chock-a-block with groceries.

'Well done, you,' she said. 'We shall have our tea, and then I'll leave you to practise your culinary witchcraft while I make sure that my equipment has been safely stowed in the orangery.' She pointed to the door beside the large sink. 'Is that the way out to the garden?'

'Through the boot room, yes,' I said.

The kettle soon boiled and I filled the pot and joined her at the table.

'Lamps!' she said suddenly.

'What?'

'Have we got any lamps? I've grown so accustomed to having electricity in the flat that I completely forgot.'

'All taken care of, my lady,' I said. 'Lamps, oil, candles, matches . . . all in that tea chest over there.'

'What would I do without you?'

I thought for a moment. 'Starve to death, my lady. In the dark.'

I awoke early the next morning and got to work. New staff would be a boon, but there was little chance of us even interviewing applicants within the next couple of days, much less actually employing them. And I confess that I felt myself better qualified to handle the important matter of settling in than would hired help from the village, no matter how eager they might be.

I woke Lady Hardcastle with tea and toast on a tray and it wasn't long before she came down to breakfast, which we ate together in the morning room.

'What are your plans today, my lady?' I asked as I poured her another cup of tea.

'I need to get things properly organized in the orangery,' she said. 'But other than that, I think we ought to take our leisure. It's been a hectic couple of months since that awful business at the Bulgarian embassy and I think we deserve a rest, the pair of us. What shall you be doing?'

I outlined my main tasks for the day and hinted at some of the minor ones.

She laughed. 'So much for taking your ease,' she said. 'Well, don't overdo it. We'll have a housemaid and a cook by the end of the week and we must leave them something to do.'

I raised my eyebrows sceptically. 'I'll do my best to make sure they're kept busy, my lady,' I said, though I remained unconvinced that we'd manage to find anyone quite so quickly.

We finished our breakfast amid more chit-chat and she left to find her overalls. By inclination she was an elegant dresser, favouring fashions that flattered her tall, graceful figure. She often chose dark blues to bring out the blue of her eyes, or deep, rich purples, which made her dark hair seem to glow. Dun-coloured engineer's overalls did nothing for her, but did at least make the laundry easier after a day in her studio.

I returned to a list of chores that would have made Hercules blanch.

During the course of the morning my labours were interrupted no fewer than half a dozen times by the ringing of the doorbell. In London a lady might just about manage to make the acquaintance of her nearest neighbours after a few years if she were particularly gregarious. Out in the West Country it seemed that everyone and his dog wished to find out more about the stranger in their midst.

The Reverend James Bland, vicar of St Arild's Church, was the first to call, bearing a rather formidable fruitcake baked in Lady Hardcastle's honour by his wife who, he assured her, would be calling on her own account within a day or two. A butcher's boy from Spratt's called with a note introducing his employer's shop, followed closely by lads from the baker's and the grocer's bearing similar introductions. I couldn't help thinking that the three establishments might have saved themselves a few pence by employing just one of the lads to run the errand for all of them, but the boys were delighted – Lady Hardcastle gave them each a few coppers for their trouble.

The village policeman called next. Sergeant Dobson said he couldn't stop. Nevertheless he wanted to pay his respects and reassure Lady Hardcastle that he and his assistant (whose name went in one ear and out the other) were there to keep us safe. Not, he insisted hastily, that we would need it. His village was the safest in the district. If we needed anything, we had only to ask.

True to his word, he didn't press us for a cup of tea as our friends on the London force might have. Instead, he bade us both good day and strolled back down the garden path whistling a music hall song.

Lady Hardcastle invited the sixth caller, Dr Fitzsimmons, into the drawing room. I made up another tray of tea and pondered the wisdom of inflicting the vicar's wife's cake on the poor chap. On the one hand it seemed the very opposite of hospitable to subject the man to such a terrifying fruitcake, but on the other it was all we had. I felt sure that he would have been exposed to Mrs Bland's baking before and would be inured to it by now. I cut small slices and served it to them.

From the kitchen I could overhear snippets of their conversation and it seemed that Lady Hardcastle had tried to explain her new obsession to him.

'. . . all very interesting,' he said, and I heard the clink of cups and saucers being replaced on the tray. 'I don't imagine many of the villagers will take to it – I sometimes suspect that many of them regard my own simple talents as witchcraft . . .'

She laughed. 'I'll bear it in mind.'

'Well, I shall bid you good day,' he said, and their voices reverberated in the wood-panelled front hall. 'I'm sure you have much to do. Moving in is such a busy time.'

Yes, I thought, it really rather is. For some of us.

'Thank you, doctor,' she said.

'It's all go, isn't it?' she said, joining me in the kitchen.

'It certainly does seem to be,' I said. 'It seems my doubts about the frequency of callers were entirely misplaced.'

'Your assumptions have been proved wrong so far, yes. What's for lunch?'

'Lunch, my lady?' I said. 'After all that cake?'

She groaned. 'I'm afraid I didn't eat any of Mrs Bland's cake. It seems like the sort of thing they'd load cannons with when the ammunition had run out. Luckily Dr Fitzsimmons correctly guessed its provenance, so your reputation as a *pâtissière* remains untarnished, but we both agreed to give it a miss.'

'I don't blame you,' I said. 'In that case, you'll be ready for a slice or two of the gala pie I ordered before we left London and which lurks, e'en now, in our extraordinarily well-stocked pantry.'

'It'll not be as good as yours, but I'm sure it'll do nicely. Is there chutney? Tomatoes?'

'All that and more, my lady. Will you be changing for lunch?'

She laughed. 'I might wash my hands – I seem to have become rather grimy. The vicar and the doctor looked a little taken aback by my appearance, I must say.'

'I suspect that was less to do with the grimy hands and more to do with the engineer's overalls.'

'Hmm, perhaps,' she said. 'Ah well, that'll teach them to call on a lady unannounced. I can't be expected to be dressed for visitors all day – I have work to do.'

'Quite so, my lady. Lunch in ten minutes?'

The afternoon passed with only one further interruption, in the form of a message delivered by a uniformed chauffeur. He insisted upon waiting for a reply, but declined the offer of a seat in the kitchen and remained on the doorstep.

The message was from Sir Hector and Lady Farley-Stroud, the local landowners. They lived at The Grange, a large, comfortably dishevelled manor house, which we'd seen on the hill as we drove through the village the day before. The Farley-Strouds apologized for the short notice but wondered if Lady Hardcastle might like to come to dinner that evening 'to meet a few people', an invitation that, of course, she had readily accepted. Bert – for that was the chauffeur's name – took her note and assured me that if her answer was 'yes' he'd be back at half past seven to collect her and drive her to The Grange.

I helped Lady Hardcastle dress. Then, once she was gone, I settled into one of the comfortable chairs in the sitting room with a book and a sandwich. She had suggested that I open one of the bottles of wine we'd brought from the London flat, but I made do with water. Wine was for sharing.

Time passed quickly as I lost myself in my book. My journal doesn't record what I was reading, but I do recall enjoying it, so it probably wasn't Thackeray. I never could get on with Thackeray.

Shortly before midnight Lady Hardcastle breezed into the sitting room.

'What ho, Flo,' she said. 'I didn't expect to find you still up.'

'You know how it is, my lady,' I said, waving the book.

'Ah, yes. You and your books.'

'Just so. How was dinner?'

'Really rather more pleasant than I expected. I thought I was in for a dull evening in the company of the pompous country squire and his frightful wife, but they turned out to be really rather splendid.'

'How so?' I said, sitting up more comfortably.

She caught sight of herself in the mirror above the fireplace. 'Do you think these pearls go with this blue dress?'

'As if the ensemble were designed by the finest Parisian *couturiers*, my lady. You have the attention span of a wasp. What was so splendid about the Farley-Strouds?'

'Oh, yes, sorry. Not only are they the most charming old buffers ever to draw breath, it turns out that Gertie Farley-Stroud knew my mother. I walked in and she said, "Now tell me, dear, before we carry on, was your maiden name Featherstonhaugh?" So I said, "Ye–es." And she said, "And do you have an older brother, Harry?" And I said, "Ye–es", again in that exact same drawn-out, puzzled way, thinking she must have looked me up in *Who's Who* or something. And then she said, "My dear, I knew your mother."'

'Apparently she and Hector met my parents when Daddy was in India and they kept in touch. She said the last time she saw me was in the family home in London. I was four years old and recited Newton's Laws of Motion to her and then played *Frère Jacques* – quite badly, she says – on the piano before announcing that when I grew up I was going to be a polar bear.'

'You were ambitious, even then,' I said.

'Always, dear, always. Evidently she and Mummy wrote to each other for years and Gertie followed my progress: up to Cambridge, marrying Roddy, all our postings abroad, everything. When Jasper's agent introduced me as the new tenant of this place, she wondered if I might be the same Emily Hardcastle she knew of old and, as it turns out, I am.'

'Surely there can be only one, my lady,' I said.

'Well, quite. But they were sweet and charming and quite as barmy as a sack of gibbons and I had a lovely time. The only oint in the flyment was that they insisted I should meet the local "people" so that I might be properly introduced to Gloucestershire society. I could have done without it, to be honest, but it seemed churlish to make a fuss so I mucked in as best I could. What I'd expected to be an intimate supper with the local landowners turned into some manner of formal introduction to the Great and the Good. Or the local equivalent, at least. The Moderately Significant and the Well-Intentioned, perhaps. Still, they think themselves frightfully important and that's what counts, I suppose.'

'Any juicy gossip?'

'None whatsoever, I'm afraid. The only thing happening of note at all is that the Farley-Strouds' daughter has become engaged to the scion of a local commercial family. They're in shipping or something. It's all anyone can talk about. I confess I paid little attention.'

'Still, it could be worse. You could have been called upon to foil the assassination of the Bulgarian ambassador. Again.'

'That was a lark, though, wasn't it?'

'A lark indeed, my lady. I think we're better off without all that, though.'

'You're probably right. How was your evening?'

'Sandwiches and a good book – I can't imagine better.'

'An evening with me, of course. Do you fancy a nightcap? I could do with a brandy before bed.'

I fetched the brandy and a couple of glasses. Life in the country wasn't so bad, after all.

2

I had been assured that our new life in Gloucestershire would be peaceful and uneventful. A train from the nearby market town would take us north to Cheltenham or Gloucester, or south to Bristol or Bath, and we could be in any of those bustling cities in 'no time at all'. We'd not be entirely cut off from civilization, but I'd been promised that there would be calm after the years of adventure (and occasional terror). Lady Hardcastle and I would finally be able to relax. And to rest. To take it easy. Away from the violence.

And so it was that we were up and eating breakfast together in the morning room shortly after dawn on our second full day in the village.

'You promised me a life of ease,' I protested as I put another sausage on her plate.

'And you'll get one,' she said, spearing the sausage with her fork and waving it in the air before her. 'Gertie has arranged for two promising potential servants to call on us tomorrow, so you'll soon have so much time that you'll not know what to do with yourself.'

'And yet here I am at the breakfast table while even the birds are thinking it might be a bit early and are contemplating another half an hour in their nests before they have to face the day.'

'You'll thank me later,' she said. 'We shall go for a walk to explore our new surroundings. Perhaps make a few sketches. Then we'll pop into the village and place some orders with the shopkeepers – it's nice to show one's face. I wonder if there's a tea shop – we could stop for a cuppa and a sticky bun.'

'And all before lunch,' I said.

'Exactly so. We can do all that and still have the best part of this glorious summer's day ahead of us.'

'You make a good case, my lady,' I said as I made a start on clearing away the breakfast things. 'But I'm reasonably certain that I'd have preferred an extra hour in bed and then still have all those things to look forward to.'

'I'll be back to my sluggardly ways in no time. I think it's the change of air.'

'That's definitely something for me to look forward to.'

She rose to leave.

'I've put your outdoor boots by the front door,' I said.

'You're a marvel,' she said. 'Ready to leave in ten minutes?'

Ten minutes later we were indeed almost ready to leave. Almost.

'I say, Flo, you couldn't be the absolute sweetest of sweethearts and pop out to the orangery for me? I should like to take some drawing things with us. The bag is in there somewhere.'

Lady Hardcastle was an inveterate sketcher. She kept pencils and a sketch pad in a canvas bag, always packed and ready for adventure. Always packed, at any rate. The bag was never actually ready for the adventure because she could never remember where she had left it.

I took the opportunity to take a look at what she had done with the orangery. Her ceaseless sketching was a symptom of a much broader obsession with the visual arts. While we had been living in London she had been introduced to the exciting new world of moving pictures. She had seen an exhibition of the work of several experimental moving-picture artists. She had been particularly taken with the photographic trickery of Georges Méliès, who had been using various techniques to produce magical effects.

She was so taken with it all that she had thrown herself into the study of the art and science of moving pictures with her customary zeal. Ideas tumbled from her imagination and she began to experiment with making films of her own. When she decided to move to Gloucestershire, one of her principal requirements for our new home had been a large, well-lit space where she could set up her photographic equipment. The orangery had proved ideal.

It took me several minutes of energetic searching amid the arcane tools of the film-maker's art to locate the canvas sketch bag. Eventually I found it beneath a pile of miniature clothes and some designs for what looked like animal mannequins. Or should that be animallequins?

I was still pondering this vital question as I locked the orangery door and returned to the house.

We turned right out of the gate, away from the village and off into the wilds. I'd seen a fair bit of the country as a young child as we travelled from one end of the island to the other. We'd always stopped near towns and villages, though, and so to me, as much as to any native city dweller, the countryside was something one passed through on the way to the next bit of civilization. Seen from the driving seat of a wagon, the British countryside is beautiful, but it was never somewhere I'd hankered to be. There were no libraries or museums in the countryside, only cows, sheep, and thousands of unidentifiable trees.

I'd travelled the world with Lady Hardcastle, but parts of our homeland were like a foreign country to me. So this simple act of turning right, away from the houses and shops, was as much of an adventure as trekking across the Chinese heartland. The hedgerows were rustling with life as we passed and the air was full of the sounds of birdsong and the smells of . . . It's always struck me as slightly odd that people complain about the smells of the city – the smoke, the waste, the factories, the breweries – as though the countryside is a perfumed garden in Paradise. If that's the perfume they prefer in Paradise, I think I might look into what I might do to furnish my immortal soul with some sort of face mask.

As we rounded a bend, Lady Hardcastle decided that we should leave the lane and venture instead across the fields.

On the other side of the enormous field I could see a farmer driving his herd of cattle out of another gate and towards the farm buildings in the distance, perhaps for milking. He appeared to notice us and, after a moment's indecision, abandoned his cows and started towards us.

The cows, indignant at this interruption to their routine, began lowing irritably. Some plodded towards their usual morning destination, drawn on, presumably, by the promise of the relief of milking. The others milled around, leaderless and lost. I never let on to Lady Hardcastle but I'd always been rather afraid of cows. I was glad they remained at a safe distance and appeared to be heading away from us.

'Look out,' I said. 'We're for it now.'

'What?' said Lady Hardcastle, who hadn't noticed the farmer.

'One hundred and fifty yards off the port bow,' I said. 'Closing fast.'

She turned to look. 'Gracious,' she said. 'He can move pretty smartly for such a plump little chap.'

We slowed our pace and waited for the red-faced farmer to draw alongside.

'Mornin', ladies,' he said, as he came within hailing distance. He tipped his cap.

'And good morning to you,' said Lady Hardcastle, genially. 'Beautiful morning, isn't it?'

'That it is, ma'am,' he said. 'Out for a walk, I see.'

'We are, yes. I do hope we're not trespassing.'

'You are, as it 'appens,' he said.

'My dear chap, I am most dreadfully sorry. But it's such a beautiful day it seemed a shame to be stuck on the lane, walled in by hedgerows, when we could be enjoying this glorious country-side.'

'Ah, well,' he said, the wind taken out of his sails somewhat. 'Just you mind you shut the gates and don't frighten the beasts and we'll get along fine.'

'Thank you, Mr . . .?'

'Thompson, ma'am, Toby Thompson.'

'How do you do, Mr Thompson? I am Lady Hardcastle and this is my maid, Miss Armstrong.'

'Ahhh,' he said, knowingly. 'You'll be the lady from up London as has taken the new house on the lane, then.'

'That's right.'

More pleasantries were exchanged but I heard nothing of their conversation. My own attention was entirely held by the confused and disgruntled cows until I saw Mr Thompson pointing to the woods about half a mile distant and saying, in his unfamiliar West Country burr, 'I reckon they woods'll be a nice walk this time o' the mornin', m'lady. Like you says, it's a beautiful day. I often goes into the woods for a bit o' peace and quiet of a summer's mornin' once the milkin's done.'

'Thank you, Mr Thompson,' said Lady Hardcastle, 'I believe I shall do the same.'

'Right you are, then. You 'ave a good day, m'lady.'

Lady Hardcastle expressed her thanks and we set off across the pasture towards the dense stand of trees.

'That ended better than I expected,' I said as we altered course. 'I thought he was going to shoot us.'

'He was just curious,' she said. 'And he didn't have a gun. I don't think they get many strangers round here, that's all, so we're bound to be something of a curiosity.'

'Pity you and I didn't meet when I was younger. If they'd known what a draw you'd be, my mam and dad could have put you in a sideshow tent and charged people a tanner to gawp at you.'

'Nonsense,' she said. 'I'm worth two bob of anyone's money. Sixpence, indeed. Tch.'

As we entered the woods, I looked back across the field we had just crossed, and at our tracks through the dew-damp grass. I had a sudden jolt of panic at leaving such an obvious trail, but just as quickly I remembered that we no longer had to worry about such things. No one had wanted us dead simply for being English for a number of years now. Indeed, here in Gloucestershire 'English' was rather a desirable thing to be, but 'old habits' and all that.

Ahead of me, Lady Hardcastle stepped nimbly over a patch of mud and turned back to me. 'Keep up,' she said with a smile, 'and watch out for the mud.'

'Yes, m'lady,' I said in my best approximation of the local accent as I hopped across the miniature mire. I checked behind us again as we made our way further into the dimness of the wood.

'For goodness' sake,' she said, 'do stop acting like a blessed bodyguard, you'll upset the natives. You've been looking for pursuit since we left the house.'

'Sorry, my lady. It's just—'

'I know, dear.' She reached out and touched my arm reassuringly.

The morning sun was struggling to have much of an influence on the world beneath the canopy of rich green leaves. The dark ground beneath our boots was soft and damp and the air was surprisingly chill. I began to wish I'd thought to put on a jacket, or at least to have brought my shawl.

Lady Hardcastle resumed her enthusiastic descriptions of the local plant and animal life. She had a passion for the natural sciences, which she never tired of trying to share with me, but I confess that despite her best efforts I was still unable to tell a beech tree from a beach hut. There were the obvious difficulties one might have in getting into a bathing costume in a beech tree, of course – at the very least there would be issues of balance and of being poked by errant limbs. Though thinking about it, an errant limb can be a problem in a shared beach hut, too. My laugh brought a questioning look and I was about to share my observations when we broke through into a beautifully sunlit clearing.

'And in the centre of the clearing, my dear Florence,' she was saying, without apparently having broken her conversational stride, 'we have . . . I say!'

'A dead body, my lady?' I said.

'I was going to say, "a magnificent English oak",' she said, somewhat distractedly, 'but the body is definitely the more arresting sight.'

We stepped forward to take a better look. There, in the centre of the clearing, was a magnificent oak tree. A rather old one to judge from its girth. Hanging by its neck from one of the elderly tree's lower limbs was the body of a man.

We approached. It was a youngish man, perhaps in his late twenties, dressed in a neat, dark-blue suit of the sort that might be worn by a clerk. And he was most definitely dead. Even without Lady Hardcastle's scientific education I knew that being suspended by the neck on a length of sturdy rope wasn't conducive to long life.

A log lay on its side beneath his feet. I immediately had the image of the poor despairing fellow teetering on it with the rope around his neck before kicking it aside and bringing an end to whatever troubles had tormented him.

Lady Hardcastle interrupted my thoughts. 'Give me my bag, dear, and hurry back to the village. Rouse the sergeant and tell him we've found a body in the woods,' she said, calmly but firmly. 'We're not too far from the road,' she said, pointing. 'That way, I think.'

I took the canvas bag from my shoulder and passed it to her. 'I'll be as quick as I can, my lady,' I said, as I struck out in the indicated direction.

Lady Hardcastle was right: the road back into the village was just a few hundred yards through the trees. My sense of direction has never been the best but I managed to make the correct choice when I reached the road, turning right and heading at a brisk trot down the hill.

I crossed the village green to the baker's shop, which was the one place I was certain would be open at this hour. Mr Holman, the baker, directed me to a cottage a few doors down and told me that I'd be certain to find Sergeant Dobson there. I hurried back out into the morning sunshine.

A few moments later, perspiring gently, and slightly out of breath, I reached the two cottages on the village green which belonged to the Gloucestershire Police. One of them served as both the village police station and the home of Sergeant Dobson. The large, cast-iron knocker on the dark-blue door made a pleasingly loud bang as I rapped it firmly, and soon there were sounds of activity from within. The portly sergeant recognized me as soon as he opened the door and his gruff rebuke for disturbing the constabulary slumbers died on his lips when he saw me standing there.

'Why, Miss Armstrong,' he said solicitously, 'whatever's the matter? You look all of a pother.'

As succinctly as I could, I told him what we had found. Within just a few moments he had fetched his hat, finished fastening his tunic and was leading me to the door of the smaller cottage, which adjoined his own.

'Young Hancock will be fast asleep like as not, so just you keep knocking till he wakens. Tell him what you told me, then say I said he's to fetch Dr Fitzsimmons. They're to come up to the old oak in Combe Woods in Dr Fitzsimmons's carriage so we can bring back the body. Begging your pardon, miss.' He blushed slightly at speaking of such things in front of a woman, then turned hurriedly away and mounted his black, police-issue bicycle.

He turned and waved as he rode off towards the woods, and I began knocking on the door.

It was, as Sergeant Dobson had suggested, something of a task to awaken the sleeping constable. Almost five minutes had passed before a bleary-eyed young man in a long nightshirt opened the door.

'What the bloomin' 'ell do you—' Once again coherent speech was extinguished by the sight of an unexpected woman at the door. 'Sorry, miss, I thought you was . . . No matter. Miss . . .?'

'Armstrong,' I said. 'I'm Lady Hardcastle's lady's maid.'

'So you are, so you are,' said the tall young constable. He yawned impressively and scratched at his beard. 'What can I do for you, miss?'

'Lady Hardcastle and I were walking in Combe Woods and we found a man hanging from the old oak in the clearing.'

'Dead?'

No, I thought to myself, he was in remarkably fine spirits, actually, despite the rope round his neck. His face was purple and his breathing a little . . . absent, but he seemed frightfully well, considering. I decided not to say that, though. Be polite, Flo, I thought.

'Yes, Constable, quite dead. Sergeant Dobson asks that you fetch Dr Fitzsimmons and bring him and his carriage to the clearing. He wants to bring back the body but I imagine the doctor might want to certify death, too.'

'He might at that,' he mused. He stood awhile in thought before making up his mind what to do, then stepped brightly out of the door. But when his bare feet touched the cold, dewy grass, he became suddenly aware of his state of dress. 'Oh. Oh,' he said, slightly flustered. 'Give me a few moments to make myself decent and I'll be with you.'

'Thank you. Might I prevail upon you for a lift back to the woods? It was quite a run to get here.'

'You ran?'

'I did indeed.'

'But you're a—'

'Yes, I'm one of those, too. It's remarkable the things we can do when we think nobody's looking.'

He looked briefly puzzled before hurrying back inside and slamming the door. I heard his footsteps running up the stairs and waited patiently for his return.

Dressed, behelmeted and ready for duty, Constable Hancock reappeared at his front door a few minutes later. We made our way across the green to Dr Fitzsimmons's house.

'Might I ask you a question, Constable?' I said.

'Certainly you may, miss.'

'This seems like a very small village to me. Why does it have two policemen? And such luxurious accommodation?'

Hancock laughed. 'We're not just here for Littleton Cotterell, miss. This is just where we have our headquarters. We serve several villages for miles around.' He seemed to inflate with pride as he said it. 'It's quite a responsibility, and one that the boys in the towns tend to underestimate.'

'Well, I'm glad we have you to ourselves this morning. I don't know what I should have done if I'd had to get all the way to Chipping Bevington for help.'

21

'You'd'a been disappointed when you got there, an' all, miss,' he said. 'Them's idiots over there. You could have used the telephone, mind. We've got one now.'

I'd been wondering about that. We took the telephone for granted in London, but I had no idea if such conveniences had made it all the way out here. It seems that the police stations had them, at least.

We reached the doctor's house and knocked at the door. It was answered very promptly by a middle-aged woman dressed from head to toe in black.

'Hello, Margaret, is the doctor in?' Hancock said.

'Whom shall I say is calling?' she asked.

'It's me, Margaret, Sam Hancock.'

'I know who you are, you fool, don't be so impertinent. But the . . . lady?'

Hancock was losing his patience. 'Is he in or not? We are here on urgent police business and I don't have time for your tomfoolery. I've a good mind to—'

Dr Fitzsimmons appeared behind the suspicious housekeeper. 'Thank you, Mrs Newton, I'll take care of this.'

Margaret reluctantly shuffled back into the hall and went about her business.

'My apologies for the welcome, Constable. How may I help you?'

Hancock introduced me and I ran once more through my brief account of the finding of the body.

'I'll get Newton to harness the horse and we'll be off in no time. Do come in in the meantime. Can I offer you anything while we wait? Tea, perhaps? Have you eaten, Constable? I'm sure Mrs Newton could find an extra helping of something.'

By the time we reached the clearing, more than an hour had passed since we'd made our grisly discovery. We found Lady Hardcastle deep in conversation with Sergeant Dobson some way from the dangling body. They seemed to be looking at some sketches.

'Look at this, Hancock,' the sergeant said with glee. 'Lady Hardcastle has sketched the scene for us.'

Hancock inspected the drawings and nodded gravely with what he imagined was professional approval. 'Very good,' he said. 'Very good indeed.'

'They'll be a great help at the inquest, Lady Hardcastle,' said the sergeant. 'Thank you. Oh, and where are my manners? Lady Hardcastle, may I introduce Dr Fitzsimmons?'

'We met yesterday, thank you, Sergeant. How are you, doctor? It's a shame our second meeting couldn't be under more pleasant circumstances.'

'It is indeed, my lady, it is indeed. Now what have we here? A suicide, it seems. Do we know who it is?'

'Not quite yet, sir, no,' said Dobson. 'I've got the queerest feeling I've seen the gentleman before somewhere, but I just can't place him. I can't quite reach his pockets, neither, or else I'd have seen if he had a letter or something that might have identified him.'

Constable Hancock had been staring at the body. He didn't look too comfortable and I wondered if he'd seen many bodies in circumstances like this rather than laid out neatly in a coffin ready for the last respects of their loved ones.

'I knows him,' said Hancock slowly. 'That's Frank Pickering. He's from over Woodworthy but he's played cricket for us since their club folded last season. He worked in Bristol. It cost him to get in on the train every day from Chipping Bevington but he always said he'd rather that and live out here than live in the city. Nice bloke.' His voice drifted off as he looked on, still mesmerized by the body.

'That's it, young Hancock,' said the sergeant with a jolt of satisfied recollection. 'Well done, boy. Yes, I seen him playing against Dursley a week ago last Sunday.'

'Was he a melancholy fellow?' the doctor asked Hancock.

'No, sir, that's just it. He was the life and soul, he was. Bright and bumptious, always had a joke.'

'It can often be the way that a jovial exterior masks the pain within,' mused the doctor. 'Shall we cut the poor fellow down? Then we can take the body back to my surgery and we can make the arrangements for the inquest.'

Lady Hardcastle had been slightly distracted throughout all this. She was looking at the ground beneath the body and checking it against her sketches. 'Might we test one or two of my ideas before we do, please, gentlemen?'

'If we can, m'lady,' said Dobson. 'What troubles you?'

'Would you say the ground was soft, Sergeant?' she asked.

'Passably soft, m'lady, yes.'

'And so one might expect that this log, which had borne the weight of quite an athletically hefty man, should have left an impression in the ground beneath the tree.'

'That seems reasonable, m'lady.'

'And yet . . .' She indicated the ground immediately below the body. It was trampled and bore one or two odd impressions, but there was no obvious large indentation from the end of the log. 'I wonder if I might trouble you to stand the log on its end, Constable, just as it would have been before poor Mr Pickering met his unfortunate end.'

'Certainly, m'lady,' Hancock said, stepping forwards and lifting the log. He positioned it on its end with its top some six inches below the toes of Frank Pickering's boots.

We looked at the newly created tableau for a few moments before Constable Hancock slowly said, 'Wait a moment, if his feet don't touch the log, how can he have been stood on it before he topped hisself?'

'Upon my soul,' said Dr Fitzsimmons.

'Well, I'll be blowed,' said Sergeant Dobson.

'And there, gentlemen, you see what's been troubling me,' said Lady Hardcastle. 'I'm not an expert in these matters, but I'd say the odds were somewhat against this being suicide.'

'It does seem unlikely,' said Fitzsimmons, looking up at the body. 'But how the devil did they get him up there? He's not a featherweight, is he?'

'Cruiserweight at the very least,' said Dobson appraisingly.

'They could have just hoisted him up,' said Hancock.

'I thought that,' said Lady Hardcastle, 'but take a look at the rope. See where it's wrapped around the branch there? If one had hoisted him up from the ground, how would one then manage to wrap the rope five times round the branch and tie it off so neatly? It was made to look like Mr Pickering had prepared the rope before standing on the log, and if he'd been hauled up, the rope would have to be tied off down here somehow, by someone standing on the ground.'

'But,' said Hancock, still trying to puzzle things out, 'why would he be out here in the woods in the middle of the night? And who would have wanted to kill him?'

'Luckily,' said Dobson, 'that's soon to be someone else's problem. We need to get him down, get him to the surgery, and then telephone the CID in Bristol. Murder makes it their case.'

'Just one more thing I noticed before we go,' said Lady Hardcastle. 'There are ruts in the ground running from the road to the tree, along the line you all walked to get here. Maybe two inches wide, about a yard apart. My guess, and I don't want to be seen to be interfering in any professional work here, is that they might be from some sort of handcart. It would be an ideal way to get a body here.'

'If he were killed somewhere else, you mean?' said Hancock.

'As I say, gentlemen, none of this is within my area of expertise. I wouldn't want to step on any toes.'

'Course not, m'lady, and we appreciates your help,' said Dobson.

'You're most welcome, I'm sure. Gentlemen, it's been quite a morning for me. Would you mind awfully if I excused myself? You know where to reach me if you need me.'

'Certainly, m'lady. You get yourself home and get a nice cup of hot, sweet tea for the shock. We'll take care of things from here.'

'Thank you, Sergeant. Come along, Armstrong, let's get home.' And with that, she strode off towards the edge of the clearing and I followed. Once we were on the road and safely out of earshot she said, 'Hot, sweet tea, indeed! We shall have a bracing brandy and the devil take the blessed tea.'

We set off for home.

3

We had found Mr Pickering's body on Wednesday and had both been interviewed by the detective in charge of the case on Thursday afternoon. Inspector Sunderland had been an easygoing and affable fellow. His quiet confidence in his authority and abilities left him free to treat everyone around him with calm respect. Nevertheless he seemed unimpressed by Lady Hardcastle's questions and suggestions. We had been dismissed as soon as he had taken our statements.

On Friday morning I ventured into the village to place some orders with the local shopkeepers. The village green was in the most splendid condition. It was obviously a very important part of village life and was currently in use as the cricket pitch so I was extremely careful not to walk across the pristine 'square' of the wicket at its centre.

My first call was to F. Spratt's, the butcher's shop. Mr Spratt was cutting chops from a loin of pork as I entered. Hearing the bell, he stopped what he was doing and wiped his hands on a cloth hanging from his apron.

'Mornin', miss,' he said jovially. 'How can I help you this fine morning?'

'Good morning,' I said. 'I have Lady Hardcastle's meat order. I wonder if you would take care of it for her, please.'

'Certainly miss,' he said, reaching across the counter to take the paper I offered him. He looked at it carefully. 'Hmm,' he said, with evident disapproval. 'I a'n't got *Lincolnshire* sausages. Not much call for 'em round here. I got me own *Gloucestershire* recipe. Will that suffice?'

'That will be fine, I'm sure.'

'Would you care to try some faggots?'

'Oh, that would be lovely,' I said. 'I haven't had faggots since I left home. I'm sure Lady Hardcastle would love them if she hasn't already experienced them.'

'Where's home, then, miss?' he said, making a note on the order.

'My mother is from South Wales. Aberdare.'

'Sorry to tell I've never heard of it, but if they has faggots, they can't be bad people. How are you settling in up at the new house?'

'Quite well, thank you. I think we shall be happy there. And everyone in the village has been so charming and friendly.'

'They's mostly a friendly bunch. One or two bad uns, mind, but that's like anywhere, really, i'n't it?'

'It is indeed.'

He looked at the order once more. 'I can get the boy to bring this lot round this afternoon if you likes, though you might have to wait till tomorrow for the sausages – I'm making some fresh tonight.'

'Tomorrow will be fine, Mr Spratt, thank you,' I said. 'Good day to you.'

Before I could turn, he spoke again. ''Fore you goes, like. I heard tell it was you and your mistress as found young Frank in the woods.'

'We did,' I said.

'He was hanging from a tree, they says.'

News always travels fast in a small place. 'Yes, that's right. The poor fellow.'

'I heard tell it was made to look like suicide, but that he were murdered.'

News travels very fast indeed. 'I'm not at all certain what the official police view is,' I said, 'but it certainly looked that way to us.'

He nodded sagely. 'Bad business, that. Bad business. Nice lad, young Frank. Bad business.' He stared pensively at his blood-stained butcher's block for a few moments. I felt uncomfortable about leaving him in the middle of this rumination on the badness of the business but then he suddenly brightened. 'Still, don't do to dwell on it, eh? Things was getting right cheerful round here what with news of the engagement and all.'

'Ah, yes. I gather it's causing some excitement,' I said. I wasn't entirely certain it was but Lady Hardcastle had said something about it.

'Ar. Young Miss Farley-Stroud from up The Grange. She's going to be marrying Mr Seddon's son from over Chipping Bevington. Your mistress will be going to the party, I 'spect?'

'I'm not certain,' I said. 'She hasn't mentioned anything.'

'She's bound to get an invite, important lady like her. It's going to be quite a do. I've got an order long as your arm from Mrs Brown, the cook up at The Grange.'

'It sounds like good news all round, then,' I said. 'I look forward to hearing more about it. Good day to you, Mr Spratt.' This time I managed to get out of the door without being called back.

Holman, the baker, proved to be no less well informed.

'. . . hangin' up there all night, they said. A night in the pub with his pals, and then murdered 'fore he could get home. Hung up out in the woods. Addin' insult to injury, that was, makin' it look like suicide.'

'I gather he was quite well liked,' I said, trying to turn the conversation back to the man himself rather than his tragic demise.

'Lovely chap,' said the baker. 'Terrifyin' bowler, mind. Frightened the life out of many a visitin' batsman, that lad.'

He rattled on for quite a while as he bagged the rolls and buns I'd bought for the afternoon. His enthusiasm for cricket in general, and for the skills of the late Mr Pickering in particular, was seemingly boundless. As he chattered, I actually began to wish I'd seen this prodigy in action, though I knew I'd have understood little of what was going on.

I extricated myself from his cricketing talk as politely as I could and made my last call of this trip. So far both the butcher and the baker had buttonholed me about the murder and if there'd been a candlestick-maker in the village I'm sure he'd have done the same. As it was I had to make do with being interrogated by Mrs Pantry who ran the grocer's shop. She did sell candles, though, so I decided that was good enough.

She made the same comments as the others had about what a well-liked chap Frank Pickering had been but then her conversation took an entirely different turn.

'What did the body look like, dear?' she asked. She leaned forwards and spoke more quietly. 'Was his face bloated and blue? Was his tongue lolling out?' She performed a grotesque mime to represent her idea of what a hanged man might look like.

And then I thought about it. 'Actually, no,' I said, after a few moments. 'No, he didn't look too bad at all. His face was a little purple, I suppose, but nothing gruesome.' Perhaps that should have given us our clue that he was already dead when he was hanged from the tree, I thought.

She looked disappointed. 'Ah, well,' she said. 'We don't get much excitement round these parts, so you were lucky. Most thrilling thing to happen round here is the engagement. Load of old nonsense.'

'You disapprove?' I asked. 'I heard about Miss Clarissa and Mr— I'm sorry, I've forgotten his name.'

'Teddy Seddon,' she said, with a sneer. 'Useless article. All them toffs is useless if you asks me.' She looked up at me sharply. ''Cept your mistress, of course. I'm sure she's all right. But the rest of 'em? I wouldn't give you two farthings for the lot of 'em.'

She enumerated the many shortcomings of the moneyed and titled classes in colourfully explicit language for a while longer before I was able finally to bid her good day. I found myself back on the pavement without several of the things I had intended to buy, but I couldn't face a renewal of the tirade so I resolved that we could do without them for another day.

It was a pity the conversation was so strongly biased towards violent crime and the inadequacies of the bourgeoisie. I had been desperate to find out if Pantry was really her late husband's name or if she'd changed it for business reasons. I might never find out.

Lady Farley-Stroud's interview candidates were due at eleven o'clock. I had a long list of all the things that needed to be done to get the place shipshape before we hired the new staff.

In the fourteen years I had been working for Lady Hardcastle I'd had plenty of time to learn her ways. I decided it would be easier to get the house the way we liked it and then just to instruct the new servants on how to keep it that way. This seemed like a splendid idea at the time, but for every item crossed off at the top of the list I seemed to add two more to the bottom. I began to despair of getting things done in time.

Lady Hardcastle had more or less settled into the orangery, so she was 'helping' around the house. When there was a knock on the side door on the stroke of eleven o'clock, I was more than ready to take a break.

I answered the door to see two women, plainly dressed and clearly nervous.

'Edna Gibson and Blodwen Jones,' said the older one. 'We've come about the jobs.'

'How do you do?' I said. 'I'm Miss Armstrong.'

'How do you do, miss. Lady Farley-Stroud said you were looking for a cook and a maid.'

'Yes,' I said. 'Yes, we are. Do come in.'

I stood aside and ushered them through into the morning room where we had decided to conduct their interviews.

'Do sit down,' I said. 'Would you care for some coffee? I was just making some for Lady Hardcastle.'

'Thank you, Miss Armstrong,' said the older woman who had clearly assumed the role of spokesman. 'That would do lovely.'

I finished off the coffee while the two women sat in awkward silence. By the time I returned from taking the tray through to Lady Hardcastle, they still hadn't moved or spoken. I judged the older one to be in her fifties. She was a little below average height, though still a shade taller than me. She was a good deal rounder, though, to the point of plumpness. She had a genial face topped by greying hair and I presumed that she was the cook. The younger was tall, almost as tall as Lady Hardcastle I should say, but that was where the similarity ended; this young girl was beanpole thin with mousy hair that poked untidily from beneath her hat. Clearly the maid.

I sat at the table opposite them and poured us all cups of coffee.

'Well, then,' I said, 'let's get acquainted. Which of you is which?'

'I'm Mrs Gibson,' said the older woman. 'And I've got plenty of experience as a housekeeper. But I'm getting on a bit now and my knees i'n't what they used to be, so I'm lookin' for lighter duties.'

So much for appearances, I thought. 'So you must be Blodwen?' I said to the other.

'That's right, miss,' she said timidly. 'And I've been working as a kitchen maid these past four years. Learned a lot, I have. And Mrs

Cooper – she was the cook at the house I was at last – she reckons I'm ready to take over a kitchen of my own. I got references.'

She passed an envelope across the table. I glanced through the letter from her former employer to which was attached a note from her mentor in the kitchen.

'If anything,' I said, looking up, 'you're rather too well qualified. This is quite the most enthusiastic reference I've ever seen. Your Mrs Cooper thinks the world of you. We're just a small household – are you sure you wouldn't be bored? You really ought to be working in a much grander house. Or a hotel. Or one of the restaurants in London if Mrs Cooper is to be believed.'

The girl blushed. 'Thank you, miss,' she said. 'Trouble is, our Ma's not well and I can't leave her now, so I thought the position here would suit very well.'

'That's the attraction of it for me too, mind,' said Edna. 'I don't want to have to live in, and what you're offerin' sounds ideal.'

'I see,' I said. 'Do you have your references?'

The older woman produced a more battered envelope containing a collection of creased and stained notes from a number of local employers who all seemed to think quite highly of her.

'These seem to be in order,' I said at length. 'Why don't you both tell me a little about yourselves? Lady Hardcastle and I have been biffing along on our own for quite some while now, so it's important to us both to have people in the house that we can get along with.'

'Quite understand that, miss,' said Edna.

For the next half an hour I was treated to a retelling of their life stories and by the end of it all we were properly acquainted. I was reasonably sure that I, at least, would be able to stand having them in the house for several hours a day.

I asked them to wait while I went to the study to confer with Lady Hardcastle.

'What news from the scullery?' she asked.

'Two reasonable women,' I said. 'A maid with bad knees called Edna—'

'She has knees called Edna?'

'Must you, my lady? A maid called Edna who has bad knees, and a cook who doesn't look old enough to be allowed to use a knife on her own. But their references are impeccable and they seem like decent sorts.'

'Splendid,' she said, looking up from the letter she was writing. 'Would you employ them?'

'I would, my lady,' I said.

'That's good enough for me. Offer them the jobs at the rate we agreed.'

'You don't want to see them first?'

'If you say they're right for us, then they're right for us. I'll see them tomorrow when they start work. I want to go out for a walk now.'

'Right you are,' I said, and returned to tell our new cook and maid the good news.

'Good morning, my lady,' I said, placing her coffee tray on the bed.

'And good morning to you, too, Flo, dear,' she said sleepily. 'How kind of you to bring me a tray.'

'I always bring you a tray.'

'Yes, and it's always very kind. Are the serfs here?'

'Edna and Miss Jones arrived about half an hour ago,' I said. 'And please don't let them hear you calling them "the serfs". It's the twentieth century now. We servants will be rising up and overthrowing you lot before you know it.'

'Righto, dear. You will keep an eye out for me if there's a rebellion, won't you?'

'I shall do my best, my lady, but I'm only little.'

'I knew I could count on you.'

'Do we have plans for the day, my lady?' I said, as I opened the curtains.

'I rather thought that a Saturday morning promenade around the village might be in order. Show my face and all that. See what's what. I've not had a proper explore yet.'

'Watch out for Mrs Pantry in the grocer's. She doesn't like your sort.'

'I shall have you with me as guide and protector.'

'Very good, my lady. Would you like breakfast soon? I'll get Miss Jones going if you do.'

'Yes, please, dear,' she said. 'In the morning room, and you should join me if you've not eaten. Can you find something tweedy for me to wear, too.'

'If you're going to dress for the country all the time, you're going to need to go shopping,' I said, as I rummaged in the wardrobe. 'You're a bit of a town mouse at the moment.'

'Dash it, then. I shall dress as always. Conventions can be so boring, don't you think?'

'The blue?' I said, holding up my favourite dress of hers.

'That will do splendidly.'

This being a stroll rather than a shopping expedition, we chose to walk around the village green rather than across it. An early shower had cleared but the roads, and especially the well-kept grass of the green, were still wet with the summer rain. As we drew near the row of shops, a lady and gentleman in country clothes emerged from Holman the Baker's in the company of another couple in more citified dress. The country lady caught sight of Lady Hardcastle and hailed her at once.

'I say, Emily! Over here, m'dear.'

Lady Hardcastle leaned in close and whispered, 'Gertrude, Lady Farley-Stroud.' Then she waved a greeting and increased her pace towards the waiting group.

'Emily, m'dear,' said Lady Farley-Stroud as we approached. 'Allow me to introduce Mr James Seddon and his wife Ida. Mr and Mrs Seddon, Emily, Lady Hardcastle.'

'How do you do?' they all said together. The Seddons looked out of place in the village. Mrs Seddon's unusually powerful frame was wrapped in a fashionable and fussy day dress. She would have been overdressed for lunch at Claridge's. Even Mr Seddon, whose suit was of a more sober cut, stood out as someone who was unused to being outdoors.

The two couples were making a great show of chumminess – in-laws who realized that for the sake of form, at least, they were going to have to appear to the world to be the best of pals.

I smiled a greeting but hung back. Lady Farley-Stroud and Mrs Seddon seemed to make a great display of ignoring me. Mr Seddon made a more natural job of it, seeming genuinely oblivious to my presence. Sir Hector, though, gave me a mischievous smile and a little wave of the fingers. He rolled his eyes before recomposing his face and pretending to pay rapt attention.

'I knew Emily's mother, you know,' said Lady Farley-Stroud. 'Splendid woman. Met her when Hector and I were in India.'

'How charming,' said Mrs Seddon. Her accent was hard to pin down. She seemed to be trying hard to sound like a lady, but traces of her Bristol accent poked through the veneer, making her sound like a music hall artist playing a lady for a satirical skit. Or Mrs Elton from *Emma*, perhaps.

'I've known Emily herself since she was very young,' continued Lady Farley-Stroud. 'It's so wonderful to have you here with us, m'dear. Are you settling in? Not missing London at all?'

'We're enjoying ourselves immensely,' said Lady Hardcastle, including me as she always did. Lady Farley-Stroud's eyes flicked casually towards me but Mrs Seddon maintained her steadfast denial of my existence. It was as though she was continually having to remember to pay the likes of me no attention. The ability to ignore 'the lower orders' came naturally to those born into the gentry, as did an easy affability when circumstances allowed. Mrs Seddon was trying far too hard.

'You've moved here from London?' said Mrs Seddon. 'I don't blame you at all. I could never live in London.'

'No?' said Lady Hardcastle.

'No. James is senior partner in a shipping firm, you know. Family business. They've been an important part of business life in Bristol for several generations. London holds no attraction.'

'I've heard many people say that. We shall have to venture into town one day and explore Bristol properly.'

'You should,' said Mrs Seddon. Her championing of Bristol over the nation's capital was starting to seem a little defensive.

'Do you enjoy the theatre?' asked Mr Seddon. 'We have the Prince's Theatre and the Theatre Royal—'

'I'm sure Lady Hardcastle doesn't want to hear you wittering on about the theatre, James,' interrupted Mrs Seddon.

Lady Hardcastle would almost certainly have loved to hear all about it, but with her customary grace and tact, she navigated them to calmer conversational waters. 'Would you be kind enough to convey my congratulations to your son, Mrs Seddon. I wish him and Clarissa a long and happy life together.'

'Thank you, Lady Hardcastle. It makes one think of medieval times, doesn't it – two important noble families coming together to form a powerful alliance.'

Domestic servants are required at all times to maintain an air of respectful discretion. It was only my years of experience that prevented me from laughing out loud at this pompous nonsense.

Sir Hector, on the other hand, felt no such professional obligation to tactfulness. He rolled his eyes again but this time was caught in the act by his wife. Her own eyes narrowed in warning as she saw him. He grinned sheepishly at her before winking at me.

'Yes,' said Lady Hardcastle, with an earnestness that must surely be put on. 'It really does, doesn't it?'

'You'll come to the party, of course, m'dear? I'm sure we mentioned it at dinner,' said Lady Farley-Stroud. 'Invitations have already gone out, but we didn't know you were going to be among us.'

'Oh, you really must,' said Mrs Seddon. 'Everyone who's anyone will be there.'

'I should be delighted, I'm sure,' said Lady Hardcastle graciously.

'Good show, good show. Well, we mustn't keep you, m'dear. Sure you've got lots to do. We're only halfway through our tour of the village ourselves.'

'Have fun, Gertie, dear,' said Lady Hardcastle. 'Good day, Mr and Mrs Seddon. I'm glad to have met you at last.'

We left them to their 'tour' and resumed our own meanderings.

'I may be wrong,' said Lady Hardcastle as we passed Mrs Pantry's grocery shop, 'but I get the impression from what I've heard so far that Mr Seddon is very, very important indeed.'

'Quite the most important businessman in Bristol by all accounts,' I said. 'Well, by his wife's account, at any rate.'

'Doesn't say much, for such an important chap, though, eh?'

'I'd be afraid to say anything at all if I were him,' I said.

4

Lunchtime that day was a source of some amusement. For me, at least. When I explained to Edna and Miss Jones that I usually ate with Lady Hardcastle, it had caused them some consternation. I could see in their faces all the phrases I'd heard before over the years. 'Who does she think she is?' 'Ideas above her station.' 'She ought to know her place.'

'Don't tease them, dear,' said Lady Hardcastle, when I told her about it. 'You know how people get when you ignore the rules.'

'They're stupid rules,' I said, almost petulantly.

'I can't say I wholly disagree with you, but don't antagonize the staff or we'll lose them.'

We ate and chatted as we usually did, and I soon forgot the narrow-eyed disapproval of the new housemaid and cook. When we were finished, I cleared the table and returned to the kitchen, expecting more mute disapprobation. I found, instead, Edna and Miss Jones behaving as if nothing were the matter. It was a rapid change of course, but I decided not to question it. For all I knew they were still clucking disapprovingly behind my back, but as long as we were able to rub along in person without any direct antagonism, life would be pleasant enough. Things were certainly easier for me with the cooking and cleaning taken care of, so I decided I could probably endure some mild disapproval.

A few minutes later Constable Hancock rang the front doorbell.

'Good afternoon, Miss Armstrong,' he said amiably, as I answered it. 'Is Lady Hardcastle at home?'

'She most certainly is, Constable,' I said. 'Won't you come in? I'll tell her you're here.'

'Thank you, miss, most kind.'

I left him in the hall and announced his arrival to Lady Hardcastle.

'I heard, dear,' she said. 'Bring him in and you can join us with that pot of tea you were making.'

'Oh,' I said, 'the tea. I'd forgotten all about that.' I led Constable Hancock into the dining room and left them to talk. I went through to the kitchen, leaving the doors open the better to hear their conversation as I prepared the tea tray and made a separate pot for Edna and Miss Jones.

'Well, then, Constable, to what do I owe the pleasure of this unexpected visit?'

'It i'n't nothin' to worry about, m'lady, I just thought you might be interested to know what was happening in the Frank Pickering case. You remember Inspector Sunderland?'

'I do. He seemed intelligent enough, but not very . . . interested. No, that's not quite fair. But he gave the impression of having more important things to be getting on with.'

Constable Hancock paused for a moment, as if uncertain whether to voice his thoughts. 'He gave me that feeling too, m'lady, to tell the truth. But, anyway, I thought you'd like to know he's arrested the man who done it.'

'I say, really? That was quick work.'

'We don't hang about in the modern force, m'lady,' he said with some pride.

I arrived with the tea tray at this point and poured tea for them both.

'Thank you, dear. It seems not, Constable. But tell all, dear boy, how did he solve it?'

'Well, m'lady, he started interviewing people on Thursday after he'd spoken to you and Miss Armstrong. He went to the Dog and Duck and talked to old Joe Arnold there. It seems Frank Pickering had been in the pub on Tuesday night. He got in a fearful row with Bill Lovell, one of the lads from the village, about a girl they was both sweet on. Seems all the cricketers was there, havin' some sort of meeting, when Frank and this other lad started a terrible to-do. This lad Lovell said he was engaged to Daisy Spratt and how dare Frank be taking her out for a walk. And Frank said he could walk out with whoever he liked and Lovell could go hang. And Lovell had said he'd be the one who got hanged if he had anything to do with it and stormed out.'

'Sorry, Constable, let me just check. Lovell was engaged to Daisy. Pickering walked out with Daisy. Lovell found out and threatened violence?'

'In a nutshell, m'lady. So the inspector has arrested Bill Lovell for murder and he's holding him in a cell down in Bristol.'

'Gracious me. Did he speak to anyone else?'

'No, m'lady, he didn't need to. Clear case of jealous murder, he says, and lays him by the heels. Another victory for justice if you asks me, so there's no need for you to be worrying yourself.'

'Thank you, Constable, that was very thoughtful. What do you know of these two chaps? Our victim, Mr Pickering, for instance. Who was he? What did he do? Who were his friends? Where did he work?'

'I can't say I knows much about his private life, m'lady, 'cept to say he was a fine and well-liked fellow. Calm and quiet for the most part, jovial company and a demon on the cricket pitch. Finest pace bowler the village has ever known, by all accounts.'

Lady Hardcastle and I exchanged confused glances.

'Sorry, m'lady, I forgets not everyone enjoys their cricket. He could bowl the ball very fast. Very useful for taking wickets.'

'Thank you, Constable. Roddy – Sir Roderick, my late husband – used to talk about cricket all the time and I tried so hard to be interested. The game lacked excitement for me though, I'm afraid, and I never really picked up the argot.' She paused in wistful contemplation as she often did when something reminded her of her husband. And then, just as suddenly, she came back to herself. 'I'm so sorry, do carry on.'

'Yes, m'lady. I made some enquiries, spoke to a few people and it seems there weren't nothing remarkable about him apart from that. He grew up at Woodworthy, about three miles east of here, and when he left school he got hisself a job with a big shipping agents at Bristol: Seddon, Seddon and Seddon. He moved on down to the city and found hisself cheap diggings nearby the office. He worked hard. Damn good at his job, they say, and he done very well for hisself. But he was homesick, see, so when he got his latest promotion last year to chief clerk, he come back out to Woodworthy to be with his friends and family, like. Like I said t'other day, he rode his bicycle into Chipping Bevington every morning and caught the train into the city.'

'I see,' she said. 'We met James and Ida Seddon earlier. Are they the same Seddons?'

'That's them, m'lady. Their son's marryin' Miss Clarissa from up The Grange.'

'I had no idea they already had links with the area.'

'Quite strong uns. They lives over near Chipping Bevington.'

'Do they, by Jove? Well, I never,' she said. 'And what about the chap who's been arrested—'

'Bill Lovell, m'lady.'

'Yes, Lovell. What sort of chap is he?'

'Nice lad, I always thought. Boisterous, you know, like lads are, not afraid of a bit of a punch-up on the green to settle an argument—'

'But not the sort to hang someone from a tree?' she asked.

'I would never have said so, m'lady, but it just goes to show that you can never tell what murderous impulses might lurk in the minds of the young these days.'

I smiled to myself at this; the constable looked no older than five-and-twenty years himself.

'I see. Well, thank you very much, Constable. It's certainly reassuring to know that we no longer have a murderer lurking in our midst.'

'My pleasure, m'lady. As I said, reassurance was most definitely the purpose of my visit. I shall bid you good day. I'm sure you have plenty to be getting on with, what with bein' in a new house and all.'

'And good day to you, too, Constable. Armstrong will show you out.'

I took the smiling constable to the door and wished him well, thanking him again for his thoughtfulness in coming to let us know.

I returned to the dining room yet again.

'What did you make of that, dear?' asked Lady Hardcastle, as I sat back at the table and finally poured a cup of tea for myself.

'As you said yourself, it's nice to know that there's no longer a murderer in the village.'

'But . . .' she said, thoughtfully. 'Did it all seem entirely satisfactory to you? Would your mind leap instantly from a bit of snarling and yapping in the pub over a girl to a murder in the woods?'

'When you put it like that,' I said, 'I don't suppose it would. It's a clear enough motive, though, don't you think?'

'People have been murdered for far less, certainly. But . . . I don't know . . . it's as though this Inspector Whatshisname—'

'Sunderland, my lady.'

'As though this Inspector Sunderland just arrested the first person with a motive so that he could return to whatever more important matter was waiting for him back in the city. It just doesn't seem altogether right.'

'It's not really our concern, though, is it? We've given our statements and now it's time for the wheels of justice to do whatever it is they do.'

'They turn slowly but they grind exceedingly fine is what they do,' she said. 'And that's rather apt. The quality of the flour is still entirely dependent upon the quality of the corn, no matter how thorough the mill. If the courts don't have all the facts, they can never grind out justice.'

'It's out of our hands now, though, my lady.'

'Is it? Is it, though? I wonder if we might not gain some entertainment – and possibly save a young man from the gallows – if we took matters back into our hands and poked our noses in them.'

'Other than it being a faintly disgusting image,' I said, 'I do tend to agree. I suppose it might be fun, too. I just worry that it might make us rather unpopular with the police if we start our own investigation.'

'They'll be happy if we manage to solve the case for them.'

'But, as far as they're concerned, they've already solved it.'

'Yes,' she said. 'But the more I think about it, the less convinced I am that they really have. Oh, oh, we can be detectives. You can be Watson to my Holmes.'

'But without the violin and the dangerous drug addiction, my lady,' I said.

'As soon as the piano arrives from London that will make an admirable substitute for the violin. And I'm sure we could both have a tot of brandy from time to time to grease the old wheels.'

'The slow-grinding ones?'

'No, ours shall be lightning fast.'

'Steam powered?'

'Brandy powered, at least. But we can't leave poor Whatshis-name in gaol—'

'Lovell, my lady.'

'Lovell, yes. If he's not the guilty man, we must find out who is and set him free. It's our duty.'

'Very well, my lady,' I said. 'But we're going to need another pot of tea.'

I returned to the kitchen to make a fresh pot of tea. Edna had finished her work for the day and Miss Jones had put a stew on the range for our dinner, so I said they could both go. They were delighted and I hoped this small gesture might make them warm to me a little.

Edna hung back while Miss Jones was fetching their coats.

'Was that young Sam Hancock who come callin'?' she asked.

'Constable Hancock? Yes. Do you know him?'

'I knows his mother. Lovely lad, he always was. Was he here about the murder up Combe Woods? It was you who found him, wasn't it? Young Frank Pickering?'

I smiled. 'You knew him as well?'

'I knows his mother. She's from over Woodworthy. She used to walk out with our Dan's brother till she met her Nathan.'

'I see,' I said, trying not to let my smile get out of control.

'Terrible business about Frank, though. We was in the Dog and Duck that night, me and our Dan. Just a quiet drink, mind. All they cricket lads was in there larkin' about. I said to our Dan as how young Frank had better watch out for hisself. Looked like he was spoilin' for a fight, mind. First he has a row with Bill Lovell, then he goes and has another row with Arthur Tressle—'

'With who?'

'Arthur Tressle,' she said, with a hint of impatience, as though I should have known. 'Captain of the cricket team.'

'Oh,' I said. 'Was he given to rowing with people?'

'Frank? No, lovely boy. Did Sam say if they know who did it?'

'Bill Lovell has been arrested,' I said.

'He's never! Blimey.'

'Do you know him at all?'

'I knows his mother,' she said.

Miss Jones returned with the coats.

'Well, we'd best be off,' said Edna. 'Our Dan will want to know the news, I'm sure. Good day, Miss Armstrong, and thank you for letting us get away early.'

'Yes,' said Miss Jones. 'Thank you.'

'Are you sure about this, my lady?' I said, as I set the tray down on the small table in the sitting room. Lady Hardcastle had decamped there and had settled into one of the chairs by the unlit fire. I sat in the other.

'Sure about tea?' she said.

'Sure about poking our noses into the matter in our hands.'

She laughed. 'When you put it like that . . . But, yes, I think it will be fun. You can be my eyes and ears among the lower classes, just like in the old days. You can start by making some discreet enquiries in the village. It will be fun to be working together again. Won't it? Say it will, Flo.'

She usually tried to remember to call me 'Armstrong' in company, but alone in the house she tended to call me by my first name. Somehow, despite my disdain for 'the rules', I could never quite bring myself to call her anything but 'my lady'. I think I only ever called her Emily once, in China, when we were sure we were about to die.

'I've said it before, my lady, more than once, but I distinctly remember being promised a quiet life in the country. Yet here I am about to equip myself with thumbscrews and cosh and slink into the murky village underworld on your behalf.'

'"Murky village underworld" indeed! You do have an over-developed sense of the melodramatic, dear. And when have you ever needed a cosh to protect yourself?'

'It's just for show, my lady, just for show. But I really thought we'd left all the skulduggery and intrigue behind us. And, be honest, what do we really know of detective work? It's not as though we have any experience. We were always involved in more . . . direct action.'

'It's true, it's true, but I really think we need to try to do something to help. Neither of us would be happy to see a lad hanged for something he didn't do.'

'Surely it would never come to that,' I said. 'I still think the truth will come out during the trial, at least. And if we mess things up, we might make it worse for him.'

'Oh, we shall be most circumspect, pet, don't worry. Perhaps Inspector Thingummy would have come to the truth in the end. But, just in case, let's have a dig around and see what we can come up with. What can it hurt? And poor Constable Hancock is so sweet. Think how much it would help him in his career if we were able to point him in the right direction.'

'I think Edna might be quite excited, too.'

'Oh?'

'She was asking me about it before she left. Apparently she was in the Dog and Duck on Tuesday night and saw Frank Pickering's arguments.'

'Arguments? Constable Hancock mentioned only one.'

'Evidently he argued with another chap later on. The captain of the cricket team, she said.'

'Well, there we are, then. What more do you need to persuade you to stick our beaks in? Inspector Whiffwhaff knows about only one argument and he's arrested the chap. What if it were the other one? We'll be doing everyone a service.'

'Hmmm,' I said. 'Very well. Let's imagine, then, that we really are detectives and that we have even the first idea how to conduct a murder investigation. Where shall we start?'

'We need to be methodical. We must start at the beginning; we must start with our victim. We need to find out all that we can about him—'

She was interrupted by the ringing of the doorbell.

'Excuse me, my lady,' I said, and went to answer it.

It was the boy from the local post office with a telegram.

'Telegram for her ladyship,' he mumbled quickly, holding it out for me to take.

'My lady doesn't sail,' I said.

He looked blankly at me.

'She doesn't have a "ship".' I tried to explain. 'She's a knight's widow so she's "Lady Hardcastle" or "my lady".'

'Eh?' he said, bewildered.

'Never mind,' I said. 'Thank you for bringing it.' I made to close the door.

He stopped me. 'I'm to wait for a reply,' he said.

'Very well. Wait here and I'll see if there is one,' I said and took the telegram through to Lady Hardcastle who was sitting at the dining table, sketching.

'What is it, Flo?' she asked. 'News?'

'Telegram for you, my lady,' I said, handing it over.

She opened it and read it. 'Aha,' she said, 'another invitation to dine.'

'You're quite the popular one these days.'

'And justifiably so. This one might not be up to much, but I do rather think that it could be useful to our investigation.'

'It could?'

'It could. It's an invitation to dine with James and Ida Seddon.'

'Of course,' I said. 'Our Mr Pickering's employer. Which Seddon is he, do you think?' I asked.

'The second one, I should imagine.'

'How can one tell, I wonder?'

'I believe they have it stamped on the bottom. But anyway,' she said. 'Tomorrow I am to pay a call on the Seddons where I might learn more about our victim, and you shall accompany me.'

'I shall?'

'Of course you shall. I need to win them over and impress them if I'm going to get anything useful from them, and nothing impresses the commercial classes more than a title and turning up to lunch with a personal servant in attendance. It'll give you a chance to snoop around and talk to their own staff, too.' She scrawled a reply on the form and gave it to me with some change for the boy.

He was kicking stones on the path and looked up guiltily when I opened the door. I handed him the reply and the money.

'The ha'penny's for you,' I said. 'Don't spend it all at once.'

He grinned and scampered off towards the village. 'Tell her ladyship I says thanks,' he called over his shoulder as he disappeared from view.

5

On Tuesday morning I had everything nicely under control. The same could not be said of Lady Hardcastle.

I set Edna to work on the laundry and her morning was spent soaking, washing, wringing, mangling and hanging. It was perfect drying weather – sunny and with a good breeze – and Edna herself was sunny and breezy, too. I wondered if she and Miss Jones had talked things over on their way home the day before. Perhaps they had come to some agreement about accepting our ways because the cook was in fine spirits, as well, and they both chatted amiably with me as we went about our duties.

By eleven o'clock everything was well in hand. There was tea in the pot and I still had an hour to make myself presentable for Lady Hardcastle's lunch at the Seddons'.

Until, that is, Lady Hardcastle appeared at the kitchen door, evidently in some sort of panic. 'There is a trichological crisis of disastrous proportions,' she said.

'I beg your pardon, my lady?'

'My hair, Flo, my hair. Look at it.'

I looked at the wispy mess of long dark hair, inexpertly piled on top of her head. 'It does look a little . . . untidy,' I suggested.

'It looks as if squirrels are nesting in it. Squirrels, Flo!'

'If you'll forgive me for pointing it out, my lady, it's your own fault for being so impatient. I did say I'd help as soon as the laundry was done.'

'Hang the laundry. Isn't that what we hired Edna for?'

'We did, but I was helping. I've finished now, though, and we have plenty of time to make you beautiful for your appointment.'

'I'll settle for "presentable", but thank you. But where are my new stockings? And have you seen my small handbag? And are my patterned boots clean? And—'

'I'll take care of it all, my lady. Sit down and drink this tea. I'll be with you as soon as I've changed into something less . . . domestic.'

She sat at the kitchen table, heaved a great, frustrated sigh, and drank her tea.

By five minutes to twelve we were both dressed for lunch and ready to go. That's to say, Lady Hardcastle was dressed for lunch and I was dressed in my smart 'going out' uniform – I'd get lunch with the servants if I was lucky. I was helping her with her hatpins.

'It strikes me, Flo, that this fashion for huge hats might have its advantages. What do you think of hiding a Derringer in there?'

'A pistol, my lady? In your hat?'

'Quite so.'

'Wouldn't that open you to the danger of shooting yourself accidentally in the head?'

'I had a sort of holster in mind,' she said, 'concealing the gun inside, perhaps covered by a flap.'

'I see. And wouldn't that open me to the danger of you shooting me accidentally in the head as I walked beside you?'

'You could walk a pace or two behind like a proper servant and then you'd be well clear.'

'I could indeed. Do you think you need a Derringer?'

'A lady should always be prepared for any eventuality.'

'Like Lord Baden-Powell's Boy Scouts, my lady?'

'Similar, but with skirts on.'

'I shouldn't think there was anything in *Scouting for Boys* about skirts, my lady. The newspapers portrayed it as a very manly work. Perhaps he should write something similar for girls.'

'Most definitely he should,' she said. 'As long as he places the same emphasis on being prepared.'

'One would certainly hope he would. I doubt he would encourage the carrying of small-calibre pistols, though.'

'I suppose it does seem rather reckless,' she said thoughtfully.

The doorbell rang.

'A timely interruption, my lady. I believe you're ready, and I'll wager that's the car.'

I answered the door. There on the step was a handsome young man in a chauffeur's uniform of fine grey wool. Behind him, on the road, was a similarly grey, similarly handsome Rolls-Royce Silver Ghost.

'I'm Daniel, miss,' said the chauffeur, 'come to take Lady Hardcastle to Mr Seddon's house.'

'Thank you, Daniel,' I said. 'I'm Armstrong and my mistress will be with you presently.'

'Shall I wait in the car, Miss Armstrong?'

'Thank you, that will be fine. She'll be a minute or two longer, no more.'

'Yes, miss.' And with that he turned smartly and returned to the beautiful car.

I made to return to the kitchen but Lady Hardcastle was already on her way into the hall. 'Ready, my lady?' I said, as she inspected herself in the mirror.

'I believe I am, dear, yes. Let's go snooping.'

It was a perfect driving day as well as a perfect drying day. The half-hour journey was exhilarating and all too short. The Seddons lived in a grand Georgian house on the main road into Chipping Bevington and as the Rolls scrunched onto the broad gravel drive, Mr Seddon himself appeared at the door to greet his guest.

'My dear Lady Hardcastle,' he gushed, as Daniel helped her from the car. 'How wonderful of you to come.'

'Good afternoon, Mr Seddon. It was charming of you to invite me.'

Daniel was sweet enough also to help me while this pantomime continued and I was out of the car in time to see Mrs Seddon greeting Lady Hardcastle with equal effusion. Daniel winked at me.

'Leave the car there, Daniel,' said Mrs Seddon brusquely, 'and take Lady Hardcastle's maid—'

'Miss Armstrong, madam,' said Daniel quickly.

'Quite. Take Armstrong to the kitchen. Cook has some lunch for her, I believe. Does that suit, Lady Hardcastle?'

'That will be fine, Mrs Seddon,' she said. 'Enjoy your lunch, Armstrong. I'll ring through to the kitchen if I need you.'

'Yes, my lady,' I said with a slight curtsey. I followed Daniel round to the rear of the house where I was warmly invited into the kitchen by the cook, Mrs Birch.

The house, though spacious, was too small to have a proper servants' hall, so the staff ate at one end of the kitchen at a large, oak table, which had already been set for a lavish lunch. It seemed I was to be treated as the guest of honour and they seated me at one end of the table, in a wonderfully comfortable chair.

In private Lady Hardcastle and I usually ate well and had shared some splendid meals. When she was staying away from home and I was dining with the household servants, the best I could usually hope for was 'hearty and satisfying'. 'Meagre and grudgingly served' was more common, but this lunch was utterly magnificent. Pies, cold meats, poached salmon, Scotch eggs, fresh salads, fresh breads . . . all prepared with exquisite skill. It was like the most wonderful picnic. There was even a bottle of champagne. I sat down and tucked in.

'I must say,' I said, as I grabbed a slice of pie, 'it really is astonishingly generous of you to treat a stranger to such a splendid lunch.'

'We were eating anyway, my dear,' said Mr Langdon, the butler. 'And it's always a pleasure to have company.'

'Proper company,' said Daniel.

'Who works for a proper lady,' said the lady's maid.

There were murmurs of agreement around the table. The atmosphere was friendly to the point of rowdiness but there was a definite undercurrent of dissatisfaction and resentment. At first I was a little embarrassed by their frankness, but as lunch progressed and the wine flowed, I decided I was fulfilling a vital service as a sort of safety valve. One by one the cook, lady's maid, housemaid, kitchen maid and chauffeur each shared with me their joy at meeting the servant of a 'real lady' and their dismay at their own *arriviste* employers.

'Blimmin Lady Muck and her airs and graces,' said Mrs Birch through a mouthful of pie. 'She was a shop girl when she met him. A blimmin shop girl. And now she swans round here like the Duchess of Blimmin Lah-di-Dah, treatin' us like the dirt on her shoe. That's not proper class. She don't know how to behave.'

The others nodded their agreement, and one by one added their own descriptions of their employers' shortcomings. I'm not at all sure I would ever have complained about my employer to anyone, much less a complete stranger, but as they told their tales of extravagance, rudeness and generally gauche behaviour, I realized that they felt besieged and just needed to tell someone who might understand. I let them talk.

Mrs Birch also seemed to need to explain the extravagance of the meal. 'We might as well treat ourselves, my dear,' she said. 'She don't know what goes on, nor care overmuch, I'm sure. She don't deign to come into the kitchen and talk to the likes of me. I gets summoned to her study to discuss menus, then sent off to crawl back to my proper place. She pays the bills without looking at them. I overheard her talking to one of her friends once. "If one has to worry about the bills," she says, "one can't afford them anyway." So if that's the way she sees it, I makes sure to slip a little treat in for us now and again. Nothing too much, mind – I i'n't no thief – but a nice treat once a month is only what we deserves after putting up with her.'

As our eating slowed in pace and the savoury course drew to a natural close, the bell from the dining room rang. The housemaid slipped out, carrying a tray of cakes and pastries.

They asked me about Lady Hardcastle, where we'd come from, how we were settling in, and what we were up to now. I answered truthfully as much as I could, but not fully. I did let them know we were trying to find out about the murder of Frank Pickering, though.

'Ah, yes,' said Mr Langdon. 'Poor Mr Pickering. He worked for Seddons, you know. A fine young man. More of a gentleman in manner than his employer if you ask me.'

'You met him?' I asked.

'Yes, once or twice. I usually accompany Mr Seddon on business trips as his valet and Mr Pickering was sometimes there or thereabouts. He came to the house once.'

'To the house? Isn't that a little unusual?'

'It was, rather. It was quite recently, too.'

'Have you any idea why?'

'None at all, I'm afraid. Opportunities for eavesdropping aren't quite what they were in some of the houses I've worked in. Thick walls and doors, you see. He didn't seem in the best of spirits when he arrived and he saw himself out, slamming the door as he went, so I can't presume it was a joyful meeting.'

I was about to try to press him for more details when the bell rang from the dining room again.

'I expect that'll be for me,' he said, getting up. 'Please leave me a piece of trifle if you can spare it. I'm rather partial to trifle.'

He went off towards the dining room and our conversation lightened once more, turning to stories about the antics of the younger servants.

When he returned, we were still laughing at a story told by Doris the kitchen maid – with actions and comic voices. He came over to my chair and spoke discreetly in my ear. 'It was for you, actually, my dear. Lady Hardcastle asks if you'd take her her pills.'

'Of course. Thank you,' I said, rising from my chair. 'Please excuse me, everyone. Duty calls.'

I found my bag and rummaged inside. Lady Hardcastle didn't take 'pills' but she clearly wanted me in the dining room for some reason. I carried a box of aspirin, which would suffice, and I took out two of the little pills and went towards the door I'd seen Langdon use.

'Straight up the passage, turn right and it's the second door on the left,' said Mrs Birch. 'Follow the sound of self-important bragging and you won't go far wrong.'

The panelled passageway was hung with watercolours of ships and the harbour at Bristol, interspersed with polished-brass nameplates. There was a binnacle beside the dining room door, complete with compass, with a brass ship's bell mounted on a shelf above it. If I'd been asked to identify the theme of the decor I should definitely have plumped for 'nautical'.

The room was large, high ceilinged and decorated in fashionably pale shades of blue. It might have been elegant but for the continuation of the clumsily nautical theme. Around the wall were more items of memorabilia: polished portholes; another bell, this one slightly dented; framed bills of lading; an intriguingly asymmetrical display of blocks and lines from a ship's rigging; more paintings of ships; and there, in pride of place above the fireplace, a large portrait in oils of Mrs Seddon in regal pose.

My experience of the houses of the gentry was that their decor tended towards the chaotic. Inherited items jostled for space with treasured mementoes. Knick-knacks were collected capriciously and displayed haphazardly. Themed rooms, where there were any, tended to be bedrooms: 'The Chinese Room', 'The African Room'. There was something altogether too staged about the Seddon home. Someone, I thought, was trying just a little too hard. If the servants were to be believed, it wasn't difficult to guess who it was.

The dining table was large enough to seat ten but there were only six for lunch. Mr Seddon sat at the head of the table with his wife to his right. Lady Hardcastle sat opposite her, with a chubby, red-faced gentleman I didn't recognize to her left. The man bore a vague familial resemblance to Mr Seddon – his younger brother, perhaps. A similarly plump lady that I presumed was his own wife sat opposite him.

A dreary-looking man in his early twenties sat next to the plump lady. 'I say, Aunt Margaret, would you mind passing me the butter?'

'The what, dear?' said the lady.

'The butter.'

'Where is it?'

'By your elbow,' said the young man. His tone had acquired an arrogant impatience which seemed at odds with his dreary, vapid appearance.

The young man rolled his eyes as he buttered a last piece of bread roll.

Mary, the housemaid, was pouring tea. Their lunch, the remains of which were piled on the sideboard, appeared to have been a more modest version of the one I had just enjoyed. I smiled to myself.

'Ah, Armstrong,' said Lady Hardcastle beckoning me over. 'Thank you so much.'

I gave her the aspirins and she swallowed them down. She thanked me again and waved me away. Instead of leaving, though, I made full use of the mystical powers of invisibility possessed by all household servants and slipped unnoticed to the corner of the room.

'You poor thing,' said Mrs Seddon. 'Are they for nerves? It must be the shock of talking about that terrible business.'

Mrs Seddon was in her early fifties, I judged, slim of figure and blond of hair. Pretty, I thought, but not truly beautiful. Her clothes were on the gaudy side of elegant, but undoubtedly expensive.

She spoke again. 'We were simply horrified to hear of his death,' she said. 'How much more awful it must have been to actually find his . . . body. Was it suicide, do they think?'

'That's certainly how it was intended to appear,' said Lady Hardcastle, 'but the police weren't convinced. They've arrested a local man for the murder.'

'Murder? Did you know about this, James?' she asked her husband sharply before turning back to Lady Hardcastle. 'He used to work for James, you know,' she explained.

'I . . . er . . . yes, my dear. I think I heard something about it,' he stammered nervously.

'You never said anything.' Her tone was distinctly icy by now.

'I . . . I . . . didn't want to vex you unduly, my sweet. Nasty business. Nasty.'

Mr Seddon might have been the senior partner of a successful shipping agency, but it was becoming clear who was the senior partner in the Seddon household.

'Don't want to speak ill of a chap when he's lying on the slab at the mortuary and all that,' said the red-faced man, slightly drunkenly, 'but it's dashed inconvenient his dying like that. Left us in the lurch, what?'

'Oh, Percy, don't,' said the unknown lady. 'You speak as though he got himself murdered on purpose.'

'Unless he was the victim of a lunatic, m'dear,' he said, 'he must have upset someone. Could say he brought it on himself, what?'

'No, one couldn't,' she replied sternly. 'And I think you've had altogether quite enough to drink.'

There was an embarrassed silence during which everyone but the red-faced man sipped at their tea; he mutinously carried on with his wine. The silence dragged on for almost a minute before Mrs Seddon said, 'Oh, my dear Lady Hardcastle, you do look quite ill. Are you sure you're all right? Should I call a doctor?'

Lady Hardcastle looked absolutely fine to me, but it was an elegant way of giving her a reason to excuse herself early. She took it. 'Thank you, Mrs Seddon, I'm sure I'll be fine. But might I impose upon your generosity a little further and ask your chauffeur to drive me home?'

'Of course you may, of course,' said Mrs Seddon, with barely concealed relief. 'Mary, please go back to the kitchen and tell Daniel to ready the Rolls. You can clear this up later.'

'Yes, ma'am,' said Mary and made for the door.

As unobtrusively as I could, I followed her out and we walked to the kitchen together. As soon as I thought we were safely out of earshot, I said, 'That all got a bit frosty.'

'It had been heading that way for some time, miss, that's why your mistress sent for you, I reckon. Wanted to get out of there. The missus don't like being shown up, see. What with the other Mr Seddon being a little tipsy, and him and our Mr Seddon joking about, then all that talk of Mr Pickering, our Mrs S. was just about ready to knock some heads together. There's going to be skin and hair flying when the guests have all gone, I'd put money on it.'

By now we were back in the kitchen and Mary indicated to Daniel that he was required.

'Do they fight often?' I asked, as I put on my hat and gloves.

Mrs Birch laughed. 'Now "fight", dear, that's a tricky word. See, for a fight you needs two, and their fights is a bit one-sided. She screams and shouts and throws things and he stands there meekly and takes it.'

'Crikey,' I said. 'Well, I hope we've not made your lives any worse by our coming. Thank you so very much for your hospitality. That was quite the most enjoyable lunch I've ever had.'

'It was our pleasure, miss,' said Langdon. 'And I hope we have the pleasure of your company again soon.'

'Well, Flo,' said Lady Hardcastle as we took off our hats and gloves in the hall, 'that was . . . bracing.'

'An unusual experience, to be sure,' I said.

'Disappointing not to get anything helpful about Mr Pickering. And lunch was lacklustre.'

'That's a shame, my lady,' I said with a grin. 'Still, it does mean we're home somewhat earlier than planned. Perhaps I should use the opportunity to try to talk to some people in the village? Fetch out those thumbscrews?'

'A splendid notion. I rather think your first task will be to get to the Dog and Duck and speak to the landlord.'

'Joe Arnold, my lady.'

'"Old" Joe Arnold, yes. Talk to him and see what he's got to say for himself. Perhaps he saw something of the fracas between Pickering and Tressle. Or perhaps even something else.'

'Right you are, my lady.' I was secretly warming to the idea of poking our noses into the murder. I wasn't used to all this rusticating.

The life of a circus child was lived in cheerful chaos. When my parents gave up the performing life and returned to look after my grandmother in Wales, we lived in a riotous house of boisterous noise and endless activity. When I left home to go into service, I never once had a quiet employer. There were dinners, parties, and endless toing and froing. Lady Hardcastle was quite the worst offender, always in the middle of something tangled and dangerous. Now, though, I was beginning to find the lack of mortal danger disorientating. Perhaps sleuthing was an acceptable compromise.

'But first I want a cup of tea; there'll be time for thumbscrews later. And you must tell me everything you learned from the Seddons' servants.'

I nipped through to the kitchen and found Edna and Miss Jones taking their ease at the table. They looked slightly guilty.

'Hello, ladies,' I said. 'Is everything under control?'

'Fine, thank you, Miss Armstrong,' said Edna. 'To be truthful with you, there i'n't that much for us to do with only Lady Hardcastle to look after. I've done the cleaning and you gave a hand with the washing. Young Blodwen here has baked you a ham in case you fancy some sandwiches for your supper – you did say you probably wouldn't be eating, didn't you?'

'I did, yes.'

'So that's us pretty much done,' she said with a shrug.

'In that case, I don't see any point in your hanging about for the sake of it. Why don't you both toddle off home? I'll make sure Lady Hardcastle doesn't mind.'

'Thank you, Miss Armstrong,' said Miss Jones. 'Our Ma does like a bit o' company in the afternoons.'

I thought for a moment. 'How would it be if perhaps we made the arrangement more formal, set it so that you were expected to work only half-days? I can see what Lady Hardcastle says.'

'So long as it's the same wages,' said Edna, quickly.

She put me in mind of Euphemia Gilks, who looked after the monkeys in the circus and never gave a moment of her time for free. Ask her for so much as a hand holding a rope and she'd force you into a bargain for it. It was something in the set of Edna's eyes.

'Of course,' I said, remembering this was Edna not Euphemia, and I held the purse strings. 'But it would save you sitting about here wondering what to do with yourselves.'

They both thanked me and bustled about getting their hats and coats while I put the kettle on. By the time they were ready to leave, I'd made the tea and we said our goodbyes as I carried the tea tray through to the morning room.

'How are they getting on?' asked Lady Hardcastle when I returned.

'Not too badly,' I said. 'I think they've got over their initial shock at seeing you treat me like an old chum. Neither of them actually said anything, but I could tell that they thought it more appropriate for a companion than a lady's maid.'

She laughed. 'I always thought "companion" was a rather odd job title – a little humiliating for both sides. On the one hand you have a lady who is so friendless that she has to employ someone to keep her company, while on the other there's a servant who is paid to pretend she likes her employer. I much prefer "lady's maid". More dignified.'

'Hmm, yes, my lady.'

'It's been so very useful over the years at getting you below stairs for snooping and skulduggery. Like today, for instance.'

'I suppose so,' I said. 'Though most of the time I'd much prefer to be upstairs in a fine gown with the nobs.'

'Only most of the time?'

I told her about the delicious lunch, and Mrs Birch's reason for it.

'You got champagne, you lucky thing? I didn't get any flipping champagne. I had to make do with an indifferent white burgundy.'

I went on to describe the servants' general contempt for their employers and Mrs Seddon's stern ruling of the Seddon roost.

'I definitely got the impression that he's slightly in awe of her,' said Lady Hardcastle. 'She has a taste for the more expensive things in life, too, I noticed, white burgundies notwithstanding.'

'Not perhaps the most elegant or refined things, though,' I added.

'Oh, Flo, you snob,' she laughed. 'But yes, you're right. Opulence without elegance seems to be her motto. I'm glad to know the "shop girl" history, though. Her accent is atrocious.'

'Who's the snob now, my lady?' I said.

'*Touché.*'

'What happened before I arrived?'

'Nothing of note. They twittered on about people they knew, dropping names and titles at such a pace that even I couldn't keep up. As soon as I mentioned Pickering's death, the whole mood of the table changed. Mrs Seddon feigned an air of delicately swooning propriety, but it sounded to me as if she wanted to avert a scandal.'

'She does seem the type that wouldn't want that sort of attention. Not quite the elegant sophistication she aspires to.'

'Not at all,' she said. 'To be fair, I don't think any of them wanted the firm to be dragged into a murder investigation. Understandable, I suppose. Reputation is everything in the business world.'

We drank our tea together in the morning room and it was with some reluctance that we left the table, with me still feeling far too full from lunch. But we hauled ourselves up, put hats and gloves back on and walked the half-mile into the village together. I left Lady Hardcastle to call upon Constable Hancock in search of new developments, while I made my way round the green to the village inn.

6

To judge from the architecture, the Dog and Duck had been serving food, ciders, ales, wines and spiritous liquor to the people of Littleton Cotterell for at least four hundred years, possibly longer. It was a small country inn with a yard to one side filled with barrels and crates awaiting the drayman's next visit. There was also a stout handcart, tipped up and propped against the wall of the building.

I went into the snug and coughed delicately to attract the attention of the landlord. Old Joe Arnold was, indeed, rather old, but he was spryly alert and fairly skipped across the bar to greet me.

'I was wondering when we might see you in here, my love,' he said toothlessly.

'Good afternoon, Mr Arnold, it's a pleasure to meet you.'

'And you, my dear. What can I get you? A nice glass of sherry? A small cider? On the house, of course. It's not often we get new folk in the village, and you and your mistress are the talk of the town.'

'You're very kind, Mr Arnold, very kind. What a charming inn.'

'Family business, my love. My old dad ran it afore me and his dad ran it afore him, back four generations.'

'You must see all the village life in here. Everyone must come in sooner or later.'

'We're the heart of the village, miss. The very beating heart of it. I'n't that right Daisy?'

Daisy, the young barmaid, was wiping the public bar with a dirty rag. 'The beating heart, Joe,' Daisy agreed, with only the tiniest trace of weary sarcasm.

I recognized the name. 'Daisy Spratt?' I asked.

'That's right,' she said suspiciously. 'How'd you know?'

'You're engaged to Bill Lovell.'

'What if I am?'

'It's just that I'd heard both your names recently. What with the . . . er . . . the goings on.'

'I bet they're all talking about us now. Well, he didn't do nothing and neither did I and don't you go thinking we did. He didn't do for Frank. Not my Bill.'

I hadn't fully thought through how I was going to go about questioning Mr Arnold, but both bars were empty so it seemed as good a time as any for my interview. I still wasn't sure quite how to broach the subject but, with Daisy there too, I thought I might have an opening. I didn't want to create false hope but I wondered if I might start with a little bit of openness to see if I got any in return.

'Would you both mind talking about that night a little?' I asked. 'Lady Hardcastle and I aren't completely convinced that Mr Lovell is guilty, either, but Inspector Sunderland is going to need a little more to convince him than the opinion of a newcomer and her lady's maid.'

They looked briefly at each other before Mr Arnold said, 'I never seen a copper in such a hurry to get gone. We usually has to chase old Sergeant Dobson out with the brush and bolt the door behind him to get him to stop talking once he gets going, but this feller from Bristol was in and out afore I could tell him anything. He heard what he wanted to hear and was off to collar young Bill afore you could say ninepence.'

Mr Arnold's toothlessness made it very difficult for him to convincingly say 'ninepence' at all, but I suppressed my smile. He led me over to a table in the corner of the bar and beckoned to Daisy to join us.

As we sat, he continued talking. 'See, I told him about the argy-bargy 'tween Frank and Bill, but that weren't the only row Frank got into that night.'

Daisy interrupted. 'No, it weren't. Arthur Tressle near started actual fisticuffs right there in the public,' she said, indicating the other bar.

'What about?' I asked. 'Was Mr Pickering walking out with his fiancée, too?'

Daisy glared at me. 'No one,' she said indignantly, 'was walking out with anyone, most 'specially not me, and I'll thank you to keep your insinuations about my character to yourself. Frank was sweet on me, that was all, and I walked out with him once – in public, mind – to set him straight about me and Bill.'

'My apologies,' I said. 'I didn't mean any offence. But your Mr Lovell got to hear about it?'

'Well, yes. He's protective is all. He just wanted to set Frank straight. He wasn't even going to hurt him, much less kill him. He just has this way of talking. He can be a bit—'

'Fiery?' I suggested. 'Hot tempered?'

'I s'pose you could put it like that. But he didn't do for Frank. He wouldn't. He wouldn't.' She was close to tears.

Mr Arnold looked slightly embarrassed and carried on quickly, trying to defuse the situation. 'Arthur, see, he's the captain of the cricket club. They was all in here that night for a meeting and Arthur, well, he's a prickly sort, and he's got it in his head that young Frank was trying to take over. He was only a fair batsman, was Frank, but he had a fast ball as could take a man's arm off. He was keeping that team going, I reckon, and Arthur had taken a notion that he was angling for the captain's cap.'

'And was he?' I asked.

'Couldn't say, my love. All I can tell you is that they squared off in the public bar and I had to get a couple of my regulars to separate them.'

'They threatened each other?'

'No, young Frank was one of they gentle-giant types. Calm as you like normally. He could stand his ground, mind, but he wasn't the sort to go shouting the odds. No, it was Arthur. Seething, he was, fair ready to boil over. Said he'd never let Frank do it. Said he'd do for him if he tried it.'

'All that over a cricket team?' I asked incredulously.

'We takes our cricket very serious round here, my love, very serious.'

'Then what happened?'

'I was trying to calm Arthur down and Daisy saw to Frank.'

'There weren't much for me to see to, to be honest,' said Daisy. 'I went over to him and asked him if he was all right. He said he was, then he gets out his watch, takes a look at it and says, "Yes, well, I'd probably best be going anyway", and walked out.'

'And what time was it?' I asked.

'Just 'fore eleven, I think,' she said.

'And that was the last you saw of him?'

'Last time I ever spoke to him,' she said with a sniff.

'Was Bill still there? And what about Arthur? Did he stay?'

'Bill left soon after, but Arthur sat back down with the rest of the cricket lads and they finished their drinks,' said Joe. 'They didn't stay long, mind, maybe another quarter of an hour. They was the last in here so I shut up after that, sent Daisy home and went to bed.'

'Did you see anything on your way home, Daisy?' I asked.

'I saw the cricket lads on the green, still larking about.'

'But nothing else?'

'No,' she said. 'I walked straight home. I lives with my ma and dad round the corner. Our Dad's the butcher.'

'Yes, I've met him. You live above the shop?'

She looked affronted. 'We most certainly do not. We've got a house up behind the church a way.'

'Ah, I beg your pardon,' I said. 'What about you, Mr Arnold? Did anything else happen here?'

'I should say it did, my love, but I can't see as how it's connected. Must have been getting on for half past when I hears this commotion outside in the yard. Banging and crashing and laughing. Our bedroom's round the back and I looks out the window but I couldn't see nothing, so I puts on me boots and a coat and goes down in me nightshirt to see what's what. They'd had me bloomin' handcart away, 'a'n't they?'

'Who had?'

'Cricket lads, I reckon.'

'But it's back there now. I noticed it when I arrived.'

'That it is, my love, that it is. We found it next morning over outside the cricket pavilion. Arthur Tressle was asleep inside on the dressing room floor.'

'Sleeping it off?' I said.

'Or hiding out, racked with guilt,' said Daisy venomously.

'You think he murdered Frank Pickering?' I asked.

'Well, it certainly weren't my Bill. There's no way he could do an awful thing like that. No way on earth. And that Arthur Tressle . . . well, I don't trust him is all. He's too . . . he's too . . . prim. That's what it is. I reckon he thinks he's a cut above the rest of us. And he loves being in charge of the cricket club. I reckon he'd do anything to protect that.'

Like everyone else in the village, they were keen to talk about Clarissa Farley-Stroud's engagement. Joe was dismayed not to have been asked to supply beer and cider.

"T'i'n't a party without a few barrels of cider,' he said.

'Different world, Joe, different world,' said Daisy affectionately.

We chatted for a few moments longer before I rose and said my goodbyes.

I walked off towards the main road and home. I'd gone a few yards before I had a sudden thought and went back to the yard to take a look at the handcart. It was old and weathered, but sturdy enough, with large, iron-bound wheels about two inches wide and set about a yard apart. It was about six feet long, easily big enough to accommodate a man, but it showed no obvious signs of having carried one recently. To be truthful, I wasn't sure what form such signs might take – a fragment of torn cloth, perhaps, or a smear of earth from the victim's shoe – but I thought it only right and proper that I take a look and report my findings, or the lack thereof, to my mistress.

I set off once more for home.

Lady Hardcastle was in the hall, taking off her hat.

'Ah, splendid, it's you,' she said.

'It is I indeed, my lady,' I said, closing and bolting the door.

'I do wish you'd relax a little,' she said. 'I'm quite sure there's no need for bolts and bars out here.'

'One can never be too careful, my lady,' I said, unmoved. 'When I'm certain there's no danger, then I'll leave all the doors and windows open as much as you like. Until then, the simple act of sliding a bolt will make me feel much safer.'

'Very well, have it your way. But come. Make tea. Tell all.'

Removing my hat and gloves, I went through to the kitchen and began to make a pot of tea. As I worked I recounted my conversation with Mr Arnold and Daisy Spratt as closely as I could.

'You're terribly businesslike,' said Lady Hardcastle when I had finished. 'No small talk? No gossip? No servants' chatter to tease out the sordid secrets of the village? I thought you'd have been hours yet.'

'No, my lady. I'm not completely sure they trust me yet. But I thought I was under instructions to collect facts, anyway.'

'Facts, dear, yes. But what about your impressions? Who are these people? What do they think? What are they like?'

'Well, then. From her manner, I suggest that Daisy is an attention-seeking little tease who had been stringing Frank Pickering along and is devastated to have been caught out. I don't trust her further than I can spit your piano – is there any word on when that's being delivered, by the way? – but beyond desperately trying to cover her tracks and make out what a pure and wholesome girl she is, I don't think she's hiding anything important. Her belief in Bill Lovell is genuine.'

'Gracious. Remind me never to ask you for a character reference.'

'"Emily, Lady Hardcastle, is a bossy, overbearing, flippantly glib woman with a fine mind, a remarkable education, a breathtaking talent for music and drawing, and absolutely no common sense, nor any sense of self-preservation whatsoever. Without me to look after her she would have long since starved to death, been strangled by her own corsets (the fitting of which continues to baffle her, despite her advanced years), or have been set upon by thugs, footpads and garrotters as she made her giddy way about town." Will that suffice, my lady?'

'You're a cheeky wench and I shall have the carpet beater to your backside,' she laughed. 'What of Joe the publican?'

'Mr Joe Arnold,' I continued in the same style, 'is a charming and toothless old soul of indeterminate years. He's honest, hardworking and rather too fond of the locally brewed cider, which is the preferred tipple in these parts. He likes to avoid arguments when he can and is slightly intimidated by women, most especially

Miss Daisy. I suspect there's a Mrs Arnold waiting upstairs of whom he is inordinately fond and profoundly afraid. He seems to have a keen sense of justice and, like Daisy, is steadfast in his belief that Bill Lovell is not the murderer.'

'No, indeed, they both seem to favour this Arthur Tressle fellow.'

'They do, and I'll allow that the case against him is stronger than against Bill Lovell. But I can't quite shake the feeling that they're charging in as blindly as Inspector Sunderland. They don't want it to be Lovell so they're pointing the finger at the next person they can think of. But there doesn't seem to be any proof for either of them beyond a bit of shouting.'

'I say, you do seem to have picked up something of the scientific method, my girl. My giddiness hasn't prevented me from passing that on, at least.'

I curtseyed.

'That handcart,' she went on, 'seems to be just the sort of thing to have made those tracks in the clearing. And the cricket lads seem like just the sort of fellows to have pinched it for a lark.'

'I'd not be out on the street proclaiming their innocence if they were banged up for that, my lady. But pinching a handcart and doing a chap to death are two completely different matters. Joe and Daisy don't seem to have linked any of the goings-on to the handcart, though. I think he was aggrieved that it had gone missing, that's all.'

'Then we shall have to see what proofs we can come upon.'

'Even if that means proving it was Bill Lovell all along, my lady?'

'Even so. I'm more than happy for a guilty man to hang, but as yet I remain unconvinced that Bill Lovell is guilty of anything more than being humiliated by that flighty girl, Daisy.'

'Did the constable have any more news?'

'Not really. We talked about the events of that night in the pub as he understands them. I came to much the same conclusion as you did about Daisy; she's well known around the village for being something of a flirt. I expect she thought she might be able to paint herself in a more flattering light to a newcomer.'

'Anything else?'

'I confirmed my initial impression that Constable Hancock is an absolute poppet.'

I laughed. 'Yes, I suppose he is.'

'Like a big, eager puppy.'

'You could keep him in a kennel in the garden and he could guard the house for us. Maybe that would make you take security seriously.'

'I'll keep you in a kennel in the garden if you keep going on about "security". But I had a delightful little chat with the good constable; he's been quite diligent in his researches.'

'Anything more of our victim? Any rivals? Any other romantic entanglements?'

'No, sadly, despite his heroic efforts he knows nothing more.'

'We're really not very good at this, are we, my lady?'

'We have to be, Flo, we have to be. But let's leave it for now. I confess I'm not really in the mood for dinner. Would you be a dear and make some sandwiches?'

I made the sandwiches with the ham that Miss Jones had cooked for us. We ate them together in the sitting room, reading until bedtime.

On Wednesday it rained, a beautiful summer downpour that made me thankful we'd had time for the laundry on the previous day. Confined to the house, Miss Jones and I instead rearranged the freshly stocked pantry.

Thanks to the mischievous whim of whatever malevolent gods are responsible for the security of bags of flour, one had split just as I was transferring its contents to the flour jar. I was still covered in the stuff when the doorbell rang. Wiping my hands on my pinafore and trying to brush the worst of the mess away, I went through to open the door to find a man in overalls and cap.

'Begging your pardon, miss. Is this the right house for . . .' he said, consulting the scrap of paper in his hand, 'Lady Hardcastle?'

'It is,' I replied.

'Bloomin' 'eck – begging your pardon, miss – but you're hard to find. We've got a delivery for you.'

'A delivery of what?'

'A piano and a blackboard, miss. You starting a school?'

'Starting a school?' I said, incredulously. 'Why on earth . . . We're expecting a piano, but—'

'It's all right, Armstrong, it's for me.' Lady Hardcastle had appeared silently behind me. 'Bring them in, would you. I want the piano against the back wall in the drawing room and the blackboard by the fireplace in the dining room. Would you care for some tea? And there's cake. I should expect delivering things is quite thirsty work.'

'Tea would be most welcome, madam, yes. Thank you. I'll get my lad to start shifting a few things around in here if you don't mind – give us a bit more room to get the piano in.'

I looked outside and parked in the lane was a large wagon, pulled by quite the most enormous horse. A young boy of about fourteen sat on the wagon's driving seat. On the bed of the wagon, covered by an oiled tarpaulin, was – I presumed – Lady Hardcastle's new piano.

I went back to the kitchen and set Miss Jones to work making tea while the delivery man and his 'lad' began shifting furniture in the drawing room to make way for the new upright piano. Lady Hardcastle joined me. 'I'm so glad it's here. I've been missing having a piano in the house terribly.'

'I know, my lady. It'll be nice to have some music in the house again. But was I dreaming or did he also say something about a blackboard?'

'Ah, yes, that was an idea I had yesterday. After I'd finished talking to the constable I prevailed upon him to let me use his telephone to contact the music shop to complain about the absence of my new piano. The nice man told me it was just being loaded onto a train bound for Bristol and that he'd arrange for it to be delivered today. I explained that I'd been in my new home for over a week without it, despite the fact that I'd placed the order more than a month ago. He apologized profusely and asked if there was anything he could do to make things right. I said that if he managed to get a large blackboard and easel onto the train with the piano, we'd say no more about it.'

'You made him go out and buy you a blackboard?'

'No, silly, they sell them. For music teachers. I bought it, but I made it clear that my goodwill and continued custom were contingent entirely upon the safe arrival today of both piano and blackboard.'

'And so now you have a blackboard.'

'And a piano.'

'Why?'

'It's for making exquisite music. Obviously.'

'No, my lady, the blackboard. Why do you have a blackboard?'

'Oh, yes, of course. Well, you see, I rather got used to using a blackboard for working things out when I was at Girton. Helps me to think, d'you see? So I thought perhaps if I had a blackboard, it might help me to think about this murder business.'

'The murder.'

'Quite so. I thought if I could make notes, draw diagrams, perhaps even pin up little sketches of the people involved, it might help me to make sense of all the information about the murder and maybe find a solution.'

'And so for this one case, you now own a blackboard.'

'And chalk. And a duster. And a box of tacks.'

'Tacks?'

'Thumbtacks. For pinning things to the blackboard.'

'Won't that make holes in it?'

'Oh, Flo, you do worry about the most inconsequential things. Take the tea out to our horny-handed sons of toil and rejoice that we finally have a piano.'

'You have a piano, my lady. I play the banjo, as you very well know. You also have a blackboard.'

'Yes. Yes, I do. Now feed and water the nice men who own the cart that brought it.'

We dined early and sat at the table afterwards sipping some of Lady Hardcastle's excellent cognac – one of her few vices.

'Tell me again exactly what you're going to do with the blackboard,' I said, gesturing towards it with my snifter.

'I have christened it the "crime board",' she said. 'Let me show you.' She stood and collected a sheaf of papers from the sideboard before crossing to the blackboard.

'Good mor-ning, Lady Hard-castle,' I chanted, as I had been taught to on one of my few days at school. My twin sister and I had attended many schools on our travels, but only for a week at a time so we found many of the rituals a little baffling. Being taught on the road by our extended circus family was a much more satisfying experience.

'Do you want to know, dear, or are you just going to chaff me?'

'Can I not do both?'

She sighed. 'So here we have our victim, Frank Pickering.' She pinned a sketch at the centre of the board. 'We know that he was a clerk of some sort at the offices of Seddon, Seddon and Seddon.' She riffled through the stack of papers to find another sketch, which she also pinned to the board.

'What's that, my lady?' I asked.

'Those are the offices of Seddon, Seddon and Seddon, silly,' she said.

'It looks like a school.'

'No, it's a shipping office.'

'It has a clock.'

'Yes, I thought a shipping office might have a clock,' she said testily. 'I shall revise the sketch should we ever happen to see the office.' She drew a chalk line from Mr Pickering to the 'office'. 'And this is Mr Seddon.' She pinned a sketch of a gentleman dressed in a frock coat and top hat next to the building.

'I say, you've dressed him rather smartly,' I said.

'He's an important fellow. Runs a shipping business, don'tcha know.'

'Good likeness, though.'

'Thank you, dear. Now Pickering was also a member of the cricket club.' A picture of a cricket pavilion appeared from the pile. 'And he had argued with Arthur Tressle and William Lovell on the night he died.'

'They look more like Oscar Wilde and W. G. Grace,' I said.

'That's because they *are* Oscar Wilde and W. G. Grace. I've not met either of them yet so I had to give them someone else's face.'

'W. G. Grace I understand, but why Oscar Wilde? Was he known for his cricketing prowess?'

'Not as far as I know,' she said. 'But I can't remember what Jack Hobbs looks like.'

'Who?' I asked.

'New chap. Played for England against Australia. Everyone was talking about him earlier this year.'

'Right you are,' I said.

She continued to pin up sketches and make notes on the board as she talked. 'We know they were all at the Dog and Duck with the rest of the cricket team. "Old" Joe Arnold runs the pub, and Daisy, the butcher's daughter, is his barmaid.'

'William Gladstone and Nellie Melba.'

'I'd visit a pub run by William Gladstone and Nellie Melba, wouldn't you?'

'I dare say I would. You'll be disappointed when you meet the real Joe and Daisy, though.'

'Perhaps. But anyway. We know that Frank Pickering was found hanging from an oak tree in Combe Woods. We suspect that he was already dead when he was put there. There were wheel tracks in the clearing from some sort of cart, and a handcart was taken from the pub around midnight.' She pinned up one of the sketches she had made at the scene as well as a drawing of a handcart of the sort that a market pedlar might use.

'It's all very impressive,' I said, when she had finished her note-making. 'But how does it help us?'

'It shows us the patterns,' she said enthusiastically. 'The connections, the coincidences. It helps us to keep track of what we know.'

'And does it tell us who murdered Frank Pickering?'

She sighed. 'No. Not yet. But if solving murders were easy, any old fool could do it.'

'My favourite old fool is certainly having a go,' I said.

She sat down at the table once more. 'We've got two men who might have a reason to kill Mr Pickering if their jealousy of him were strong enough. Both of them seem to have an opportunity to do so. Mr Tressle seems to have had access to a handcart that would be perfect for transporting the body to fake the suicide, but Mr Lovell could easily have taken it from outside the cricket pavilion where the rowdies left it. We still have no proof that either of them did it, nor any idea how they might have managed to get the body up into the tree. I fear we're getting nowhere, Flo.'

'We know more than Inspector Sunderland already.'

'Perhaps. But let's leave it for now. I feel the spirit of Chopin coming upon me.'

'I love it when that happens,' I said.

'Then come, servant, let us repair to the drawing room and I shall play.'

'I'll tidy these things away and make some cocoa.'

'Very well. Don't be long. The spirits are restless. Dear Frédéric might be elbowed out of the way by Franz Lehár at any moment.'

'Lehár is still alive.'

'He is? That hardly seems fair. Well, such is the sickly power of his sentimental spirit that even life cannot stop him. Hurry, girl, or it'll be *The Merry Widow* for you, and that never ends well.'

'One merry widow in the house is quite enough for me, my lady. I shall be as swift as I can.'

The piano turned out to be a charming instrument and only slightly in need of tuning after its journey. It was nearly midnight by the time we retired.

Thursday morning saw us both engaged in mundane domestic matters, with me continuing to organize our household and Lady Hardcastle catching up with correspondence at her desk in the small study. Things were actually running rather smoothly. Edna, Miss Jones and I had fallen into a nice routine and had more or less settled on a mutually agreeable division of labour.

While I was more than happy to leave the cleaning to someone else, and was utterly delighted not to be responsible for breakfast or lunch, I did miss having complete control of dinner. I felt a little guilty at the thought of restricting young Blodwen Jones to the more mundane duties and from showing off her considerable skills, but when I broached the subject of my taking a little more responsibility for the main meal once in a while, she was delighted.

'I didn't like to ask, miss,' she had said. 'Our Ma can't cook for herself and our Dad . . . well, he's a man, i'n't he? What can he do?'

I chuckled. 'So not always having to think about two main meals a day would actually be a blessing of sorts,' I suggested.

'Well, I'd not have the lovely ingredients that Lady Hardcastle has,' she said. 'Our Ma can't afford much. But it'd make things a lot easier. And if you'd enjoy it . . .' She smiled shyly.

'I'll check that Lady Hardcastle is agreeable,' I said. 'But I think it would work well for all of us.'

At eleven, I took Lady Hardcastle's coffee and cake through to the study along with an envelope which had been hand delivered some time after the rest of the post.

'Thank you, Flo,' she said, as I set down the tray. 'Will you join me? I do enjoy keeping up with everyone, but I could do with a break from endlessly describing our move.'

'I took the precaution of bringing a cup for myself to cover just that eventuality,' I said.

'Then pour, sit, and tell me the news of the day.'

'There's little to report, my lady, aside from the arrival of this rather luxurious envelope.'

'I say, someone's pushed the boat out,' she said, taking the heavy, cream-coloured envelope from me. She opened it and read the engraved card that had been enclosed. 'I am cordially invited,' she said, 'to celebrate the engagement of Miss Clarissa Farley-Stroud and Mr Theophilus Seddon at The Grange on Saturday, the twentieth of June, 1908. Seven o'clock. Carriages at one. I say, how lovely to get a proper invitation for the mantel. Gertie said she'd already sent them. She is a dear. When's the twentieth?'

'This coming Saturday, my lady,' I said.

'Then I must send my acceptance right away. And my warmest and most formal congratulations to the happy couple.'

'Do you know the happy couple at all?'

'I met Clarissa on Saturday at dinner. Quite the most vacuous ninny ever to struggle into a fashionable frock, but sweet with it.

She's been living with a family friend in London while she pursues her dreams of being a society columnist or some such. You know the sort of thing: "Lady Evangeline Dullard of the Hampshire Dullards was seen dining out with the Honourable Tarquin Jackanapes." She's made quite a name for herself by all accounts. Knows all the right people, goes to all the right places. She just giggled altogether too much for my taste.'

I chuckled.

'As for Teddy, you've seen him yourself,' she said.

'I have?'

'You have. He was the sullen youth at the Seddons' lunch table on Tuesday.'

'Ah,' I said. 'I saw him. Tiresomely rude to his aunt over the matter of the butter.'

'Quite. He's as witless as his affianced but without her fizzy personality, possessed as he is of slightly less charm than a blocked drain.'

'I wonder what Miss Clarissa sees in him.' I said.

'Love really does seem to be blind.'

'What does the note say?' I asked, indicating the folded paper that had accompanied the invitation.

'Ah, yes, the note.' She opened it and read. 'Oh, how disappointing.'

'What is it, my lady?'

'Dear old Gertie asks ever so sweetly, and if it's not altogether too much trouble, whether I might see my way clear to letting her hire your services for the evening of the party. She says she's having some minor, temporary staffing difficulties. She's so sweet. Money's a bit tight up at The Grange but she's too proud to say that she can't afford the extra staff she needs. Anyway, she would be so terribly grateful if she could make use of my "most excellent lady's maid" – that's you, dear – as part of the serving staff, reporting to Mr Jenkins the butler, etc., etc. I don't want to turn the old girl down but it was supposed to be your night off.'

'I don't mind, my lady. If you want to help an old family friend, how can I refuse? It would be a chance to be at the party, after all. And I might be able to find out some more gossip to help with the Pickering affair.'

'You're very kind. But still . . .' she said.

'It's not as though I could go to the music hall or anything. Village life is wonderfully peaceful, but the nightlife is the Dog and Duck. I would just have been sitting here reading as always. This way I get to listen to the music, eavesdrop on the conversations, have a sneaky secret dance in the corridors when no one's looking. I'd really rather go.'

'I'll pay you myself, though – I can't let her pay you.'

'No need, my lady. I shall have to make sure I eat more than my fair share of canapés and swig a few glasses of champagne.'

'Don't expect the finest vintage.'

'We shall see. There'll not be cider, either, I know that. Joe was most put out. But it'll be fun. And you seem to have taken to them, so it'll be nice to help your new friends.'

'Old family friends.'

'Indeed, my lady.'

'Very well, I shall let her know. I say, if you do a good job I might be able to make a few bob hiring you out.'

'Like an agency skivvy, my lady.'

'Exactly like that. You wouldn't mind, would you, dear?'

I raised an eyebrow.

She laughed. 'But I expect as much below-stairs gossip as you can glean.'

And so it was agreed. Lady Hardcastle replied at once and the arrangements were made. My own uniform was deemed suitable and I was to report to the kitchens by four o'clock on the day of the party.

7

On Saturday our morning walk took us not towards the fields and woods as usual, but into the village where we called upon Mrs Pantry at the grocer's.

'Ah, Mrs Pantry,' said Lady Hardcastle, as we entered. 'How do you do?'

'How do you do, my lady?' said the shopkeeper. She glowered at the thought of a well-to-do lady entering her shop.

'I wonder, do you have any wire?'

'Wire, my lady?'

'Yes. It needs to be quite thin and quite flexible, but it needs to be able to hold its shape.'

'Thin,' said the shopkeeper suspiciously. 'Flexible.'

'Yes, that's right. And able to hold its shape.'

Mrs Pantry's curiosity warred with her class animosity, with the battle played out clearly across her rumpled features. She was desperate to know more about this odd request, but should she deign to speak to a 'lady'? The curiosity won.

'What d'you want that for?' she said, almost accusingly.

Unfazed, Lady Hardcastle said, 'It's for a moving-picture project I'm working on. I have it in mind to make some puppets and I should like to form their skeletons from wire. Have you seen any of Monsieur Méliès's work?'

'Moving pictures? Whatever next.'

'Whatever next indeed,' said Lady Hardcastle. 'Do you have any wire?'

'I got some milliner's wire. I got it in for Mrs Lane.'

'That sounds ideal.'

'She was makin' an 'at for her daughter's wedding, see.'

'Was she, by Jove. Might I buy some?'

'It's for makin' hats, mind.'

'Quite so. Ten yards?'

'How much? I don't know if I've got that much left.'

'Then I shall take whatever you have.'

'All right,' said Mrs Pantry, grudgingly. 'Can't say I've ever been asked for such a thing.'

Clutching a small parcel containing the milliner's wire, we continued our walk around the green and past the church. Reverend Bland wished us a good day as we passed the church door on our way towards the recently built village hall. Strange musical sounds were emanating from within. The music sounded altogether more modern than one might expect in a rather staid little settlement in the countryside. Curiosity led us to investigate.

The hall had an enclosed porch and we were able to enter the building without having to venture into the hall itself. We peered through the crack in the double doors and listened to the goings-on.

The music – an energetic ragtime song – came to an end.

'Oh, I say,' said a young woman's voice. 'That was simply divine. Mummy will die. I love it.'

A man's voice rose above the ensuing laughter. 'Ah,' said the voice. 'That'll be why we couldn't do our run-through at the house.'

''Ere,' said another male voice. 'She will still pay us, though, won't she?'

There was more laughter. Another woman's voice said, 'Oh do shut up, Skins.'

'It's fine, it's fine,' said the younger woman. 'She's agreed to have you. It's just that I'm not certain she knows exactly what she's agreed to.'

There was a sound of scraping chairs and the clatter of instrument cases being opened. Footsteps approached the door so we made a hasty exit.

We were nonchalantly walking around the outside of the hall by the time a tall, handsome man emerged from the door. He leaned against the wall. A shorter, wiry man joined him.

'Stuffy in there, ain't it?' he said

'You're not kidding, Ed,' said the taller man. 'I do hope this house of hers is better ventilated.'

'Bound to be. They're all cold and draughty them old places, ain't they? We'll be tidy. It'll be an easy job, I reckon.' He caught sight of us as we crossed the road and gave me a wink.

'I should say this evening's entertainment has arrived,' said Lady Hardcastle, once we were out of earshot.

'It would certainly appear that way, my lady. I hope your dancing shoes can cope.'

'Never mind the shoes. It's these poor old pins I worry about.'

'You have the legs of a woman half your age,' I said.

'Yes, but she wants them back so I shall have to make do with these.'

'I haven't danced for years,' I said. 'Not since that ball in Vienna.'

'My word, I'd forgotten that one. You were the Marchioness of Somewhere-or-Other, weren't you?'

'Was it that one? Or was I la Comptesse de Thingummy?'

'You could well have been. It was so hot that summer, wasn't it?'

'It was,' I said. 'Was that the one where we had to sweet talk General von Whatsit?'

'I believe so, yes. Wasn't he on the verge of proposing marriage? To both of us.'

'Naturally,' I said. 'Who could resist? But I do know it was the last time I danced. I was in a posh frock, too.'

'With Lady Sarah's pearls, as I recall. Tonight, though, you shall be in your uniform, handing out canapés and wine. Do you miss it?'

'The danger and fleeing for our lives in the dead of night? It had its attractions, I suppose.'

'Hmm,' she said. 'We shall have to find our fun in other ways.'

Saturday afternoon arrived. I was dressed in my very best uniform, cleaned, pressed and generally dandified as I helped Lady Hardcastle with her own preparations for the evening. She wasn't the sort of lady who was incapable of getting herself ready without help (hair notwithstanding), but it seemed a shame not to do a few maidly things for her before I left.

She had negotiated with Lady Farley-Stroud for her chauffeur, Bert, to come and pick me up and I was just putting the finishing touches to her hair when the doorbell rang.

'That'll be your carriage,' she said. 'Run along. Be good, have fun and, most importantly, gather gossip.'

'I shall do my utmost,' I said, and went to the front door.

Bert had already got back in the car and was waiting with the engine running.

'Hello, Bert,' I said as I got in beside him. 'I hope this isn't too much trouble.'

'None at all, Miss Armstrong,' he said. 'Fact is, I'm glad to be out of the place for ten minutes. It's bedlam up there, it is. Bedlam. Everyone's running about the place, setting up this, tidying that, moving t'other thing. Cook's shouting at the kitchen maid. The butler is shouting at cook, the footman and the parlour maid. The mistress is shouting at Sir Hector. Sir Hector is shouting at the dogs. Miss Clarissa is shouting at Mr Seddon. And I was thinking I'd be next in the firing line if I hadn't had to pop over here to fetch you.'

'Then I'm both grateful for the lift and delighted to have been of some help,' I said as we set off.

'I don't suppose you needs to go over to Chipping Bevington to fetch something for your mistress? Bristol . . .? Gloucester . . .? London . . .?'

I laughed. 'We should get up to The Grange, Bert. Maybe an extra pair of willing hands will lessen everyone's need to shout quite so much. And perhaps they'll all be better behaved with a stranger in their midst.'

'Perhaps, miss, perhaps. But don't let them bully you into doing more than your fair share. There's one or two of my fellow staff members who does as little as they think they can get away with and still complains about how hard done by they are.'

'I shall do my share and nothing more, Bert, I promise.'

'Very wise, miss. They's a bit . . . apprehensive of you, as it goes.'

'They are? Why?'

'Stands to reason, don't it? You come down here from London. Your mistress is a bit . . . she's a bit—'

'Individual?' I suggested.

'Individual, yes,' he said. 'She don't seem to follow the rules much, does she?'

I laughed. 'No, she very much makes up her own rules.'

'Right. So you're from up London—'

'I'm from Aberdare.'

'Are you? Are you indeed? Well, they're worried all the same. Thinks you might be a bit too sophisticated for 'em, they does.'

'But not you?'

'Ah,' he said with a knowing wink. 'I've already met you, see? I knows what to expect.'

I laughed again and he smiled back.

As we entered the gates, I smiled again as I got my first proper look at The Grange.

There was something altogether charming about the higgledy-piggledy manor house. My knowledge of architectural styles is hazy, but my guess was that the present house had begun its life in Tudor times. There were glimpses of ornate brick chimneys at the back, but the main body of the Tudor house had been replaced by an elegantly symmetrical Georgian structure built from the local stone.

What lent it its charm, though, was that at some point in the previous century its owner had chosen to extend the house by building a new wing. Rather than try to match the new wing to the existing building, or even to try to make it 'sympathetic', as I believe the architects say, they had built it in the Gothic Revival style with turrets and towers and pointed, arched windows.

The result, though it was an absolute aesthetic shambles, was a house that looked as though it had been lived in and loved for generations.

We rounded the house and pulled into the stable block, which had been converted to store the motor car.

'If you go through there,' said Bert, indicating a door at the back of the workshop, 'you'll find the way to the servants' passage round the back of the house. Go down the stairs and follow the sound of angry screaming and you'll pretty soon be in the kitchen. I'll be out here . . . er . . . adjusting the carburettor . . . yes, that's it, I'll be adjusting the carburettor if anyone asks.'

'Righto, Bert. Thank you for the lift.'

'My pleasure, miss. Good luck.'

I left him to his skiving and set off in search of the kitchen.

His directions, though vague, were uncannily helpful. The sounds coming from ahead were, indeed, the sounds of pots and pans being clattered about and of Mrs Brown, the cook, screeching invectives at the top of her formidable voice. Someone in the kitchen was not having a happy time of it at all.

I decided that any show of timidity, even polite deference, would most certainly be my undoing and would see me badgered, nagged, hounded, and generally put upon for the remainder of the day. The strict hierarchy generally observed among household servants could be all too easily forgotten if one failed to assert oneself. With that in mind I stood a little straighter, breathed a little more deeply and opened the kitchen door with a confident flourish.

'Good afternoon, everyone,' I said in my most self-assured, take-no-nonsense, lady's maid's voice. 'How are we all today?'

Mrs Brown halted in mid-slam and stood with the pan in her hand, glaring towards the door as though her kitchen were being invaded. Rose, the kitchen maid, carried on with her chopping. She kept her head down and it was apparent that she was crying, but she glanced up and smiled gratefully at me for bringing her a moment's respite from the yelling.

'Oh,' said Mrs Brown, placing the pan on the range, 'it's you, Miss Armstrong. Come to join our merry band?'

'Indeed, yes,' I said breezily. 'I was told Mr Jenkins would need some help upstairs.' I had been told nothing of the sort, but I wasn't going to give Mrs Brown an opportunity to co-opt me into her downtrodden kitchen brigade. 'Is there somewhere I can leave my coat?'

'Rose!' she snapped. 'Show Miss Armstrong to Miss Denton's room, she can leave her coat there. Then come straight back here. No dawdling.'

'Yes, Mrs Brown,' said poor Rose, weakly, wiping her hands on her apron. 'Follow me, miss, I'll show you the way.'

As she led me through the warren of subterranean corridors, I tried to engage her in conversation.

'How long have you been working here?'

She plodded on forlornly. ''Bout two munfs.'

'It's early days yet,' I said. 'Things will get better.'

'Will they?' She was close to tears again. 'I never thought it'd be like this. I can't get anything right.'

'I rather think the problem is with Mrs Brown, not with you. She hasn't impressed me so far. I'm very much thinking of giving her a piece of my mind. All that shouting and banging. It's not on.'

'Oh, please don't make trouble, miss. You don't know what she's like.'

'I've met her sort before, Rose, don't worry. I know how to deal with the likes of her.'

She didn't seem reassured and when we arrived at Miss Denton's room she simply gestured at the door and scuttled off as quickly as she could manage.

I knocked on the door.

'Yes?' said an imperious voice from inside.

I opened the door and poked my head round. Sitting in an overstuffed armchair with her feet on a stool was a small woman with greying hair swept up in an unfashionable style. Her face was set in a scowl. 'Good afternoon,' I said cheerfully. 'I'm Florence Armstrong, Lady Hardcastle's lady's maid. Mrs Brown suggested I might be able to hang my coat in your room.'

'Come in,' she said more brightly, her face softening. 'I'm Maude. Maude Denton. Housekeeper, and Lady Farley-Stroud's lady's maid. Pleasure to meet you.'

'And you, I'm sure.'

'I half want to say no, just to prove that bossy old biddy wrong, but I can't take it out on you, my girl. Of course you can hang your coat in here. Join me for a cup of tea?'

'I should love to, thank you.'

'It's just brewing now. Fetch yourself a cup from the shelf over there, there's a good girl.' She indicated a shelf above the small gas ring. 'I gather you volunteered to come over to help us with the party.'

'That's the plan, yes,' I said, reaching for a cup and saucer.

'What on earth possessed you to do something as silly as that?'

'Well, it was this or sit at home on my own for the evening. This way I might get to listen to the band, at least. And I'm not exactly a volunteer. There was talk about "hiring" me for the evening.'

She laughed. 'Don't hold your breath, m'dear. If any payment is eventually forthcoming, it'll be grudgingly given and probably a penny or two short. Times is hard for the Farley-Strouds.'

'Ah, well,' I said. 'I'm here now. Have you any idea what I'll be doing?'

'Hiding out here with me for a couple of hours is your first duty, m'girl. Then, when the heavy work has been done, we shall swan imperiously about the place doling out canapés and cheap sparkling wine as though they were the food and drink of the Olympian gods.'

'That sounds like a workable plan,' I said. 'I don't suppose you have any biscuits?'

'Funny you should ask,' she said, reaching into a cupboard behind her. 'I happen to have snaffled a plateful from under cook's eternally grumpy nose this very morning. Help yourself.'

It was going to be quite a pleasant day after all.

I was, as predicted, given the task of mingling unobtrusively with a tray of nibbles and indifferent fizz. We were also charged with keeping guests out of the library, which had been given over to the band to use to store instrument cases. It wasn't onerous work.

The musicians we had heard in the village hall were Roland Richman's Ragtime Revue, a band of some repute from London.

They were Clarissa's choice, it seemed. Lady Farley-Stroud's disapproval had been loud and hearty, but she had eventually been persuaded that it was not, despite her firm belief to the contrary, *her* night and that the young people would prefer something a little more lively and up to date. Maude – who had turned out to be excellent company and quite a game old girl – had told me all this earlier in the afternoon. I was so glad she had. That little titbit had made Lady Farley-Stroud's loud exclamations of enjoyment and attempts to tap her feet appreciatively all the more entertaining.

Lady Hardcastle had made her customary unobtrusive entrance somewhere between the early arrivals and the stragglers and it wasn't until nearly nine by the hall clock that we spotted each other. She came over to ask how things were getting along.

'Not so badly, my lady,' I said, proffering my tray. 'Do help yourself to a snack and some champagne-style *vin de table*.'

'I see a career for you as head waiter at the Ritz with a line of patter like that.'

'Thank you, my lady. Have you been here long? Are you having fun?'

'Oh, you know how it is. I've been to better parties, but I've been to far worse. But Clarissa's London friends are quite fun. They seem to have adopted me as some manner of Eccentric Aunt figure so I'm not wanting for respectful admirers.'

'Not a racy big sister, then?'

'Sadly not. I think my Disreputable Aunt years are well and truly upon me. What of you? Have you knocked the staff into shape?'

'There's at least one I wouldn't mind knocking on her *derrière*, but all is generally well, thank you,' I said.

'Splendid, splendid. Oh, look out, here comes Captain Summers.'

'Bad news?'

'Frightful bore. Newly returned from India.'

'Ah, Lady Hardcastle, there you are. I thought I'd lost you,' said a suntanned, luxuriantly moustached man of about my own age.

'What ho, Captain Summers,' said Lady Hardcastle. 'No, not lost, just mingling. Armstrong, this is Captain Roger Summers. Captain Summers, my maid, Armstrong.'

'Oh,' he said with some bewilderment. 'How d'you do?' He turned quickly away from me and back to Lady Hardcastle. I curtseyed slightly, but politely, and melted a step or two backwards.

'Is this what parties are like back in Blighty these days?' he blustered. 'Not sure I've quite got the hang of it yet. And this dashed awful music? American, isn't it? Keep hearing it all over the place.'

'It's quite the thing with the young people,' she said. 'Give it a chance, I'm sure you'll like it.'

'Bah. Give me a military band any day,' he said dismissively. 'And this weather. So dashed cold.'

'Oh, you Raj types and your silly complaints. It's perfectly delightful weather.'

'You were in India, weren't you?' he said. 'Surely you noticed the difference.'

'I was in Calcutta for a year or two, yes.'

'What was your husband doing in Calcutta? Perhaps I knew him.'

'My husband died in China before I got to India.'

Captain Summers was embarrassed. 'I . . . er . . . I'm so sorry. I had no idea . . .' Sadly, though, he didn't quite know when to stop digging. 'But does that mean you were in India on your own? Gracious me.'

'Not alone, no. Armstrong was with me.'

'Well, I never. Alone in India. I've never heard of such a thing.'

'Then this must be a very exciting evening for you,' she said drily.

'What? Oh. Well, I ought to circulate, don't you know. Got to put the old face about a bit. Try to be sociable and all that.'

'Cheerio, Captain,' she said brightly and turned to me. 'Insufferable oaf.'

'He's just a little out of his natural environment,' I said. 'He'll adapt soon enough.'

'We'll make a scientist of you yet, my girl. Yes, he might well adapt. Or become extinct. One can only hope.'

I was still laughing when Mr and Mrs Seddon arrived at Lady Hardcastle's side. Mr Seddon was looking a little the worse for drink, while Mrs Seddon was positively bursting with forced good humour.

'Good evening, Lady Hardcastle,' she gushed. 'How lovely of you to come. We'll all be friends soon. So lovely to have the right sort of people around, isn't it? Oh, and thank you for the lovely note you sent after lunch. Have you recovered from your turn?'

'My t— Oh, yes, I'm much better now, thank you,' said Lady Hardcastle.

'And you're settling in well?'

'We are, thank you, yes. The house is nearly sorted out, my studio is coming together, and we've hired some extra servants. I think we're going to be very happy here.'

'It's marvellous to have you as part of our little gang,' said Mrs Seddon. 'I'm sure we'll see even more of each other once we and the Farley-Strouds are one happy family.'

'I'm sure we shall.'

'I'm so sorry, Lady Hardcastle,' said Mrs Seddon suddenly. 'You will excuse us, won't you? I see the vicar and we need a quick word.'

'Of course, nab him while you can. Toodle-oo.'

They walked off but we could still hear them as they headed towards Reverend Bland. 'Lovely to have the right sort of people around you, isn't it, dear?' slurred Mr Seddon. 'Got to be the right sort of people.'

Mrs Seddon hissed at him to be quiet. 'I'm not in the mood for this now, James,' she said. 'We have other things to concern ourselves with.'

'She's the right sort of people, isn't she, dear?' he continued obliviously. 'Got a title and everything. You know Clarissa won't get a title, don't you, dear? Her brother would, mind you. If she had one . . .'

He was dragged out of earshot before we could hear any more.

'I say,' said Lady Hardcastle.

'They've been bickering all evening. I passed them in a corridor earlier and they were at it. Some couples are like that, aren't they? My aunt and uncle were always at one another's throats, but nothing would part them—'

I stopped talking when I noticed that Percy Seddon and his wife were trailing through the party a little way behind his brother.

'. . . that dashed woman gets on my nerves,' he said.

'Oh, Percy, shush,' said his wife. 'She'll hear you.'

"Bout time someone set her straight. She's a pawnbroker's daughter, not the Duchess of Gloucester. Even after her precious Teddy marries that wet nelly Camilla—'

'Clarissa, dear.'

'Really? What a wet name. Even then she'll only be the mother-in-law of some impecunious minor gentry. You'd think he was marrying into royalty the way she carries on.'

'Really, Percy. Shush.'

'She's forever poking her nose in at the office, too, y'know. In and out like a fiddler's elbow. Talks about the place like she's a partner . . .'

They drifted out of earshot.

Before I could comment, Sir Hector came over with a gaudily dressed stranger. I melted into the background again.

'Emily, m'dear,' said Sir Hector jovially. 'Are you having fun?'

'Enormous fun, Hector, yes. Thank you for organizing such a diverting evening.'

'Bah! Not me, m'dear, it's all down to the memsahib. I couldn't organize m'sock drawer, what?'

She laughed with seemingly genuine delight.

'But where are me manners? Lady Hardcastle, may I present Mr Clifford Haddock. Mr Haddock, this is m'good friend and neighbour, Lady Hardcastle.'

'Charmed, I'm sure,' he said in an unpleasant, nasal voice.

'How do you do?' said Lady Hardcastle, offering a gloved hand, which he kissed ostentatiously. As she withdrew her hand, I could see her mentally counting her fingers to make sure none were missing.

'Haddock's in antiques, don'tcha know,' said Sir Hector. 'Come to appraise some of me knick-knacks. Raise a few bob, what?'

Poor old Sir Hector had a charmingly naive talent for indiscretion, and I could imagine Lady Farley-Stroud giving him her most terrifying Gorgon's stare for openly discussing their straitened circumstances.

'He's got some lovely pieces,' said the oily antiques dealer. He looked Lady Hardcastle up and down. 'And you look like a lovely piece yourself, my dear.'

Lady Hardcastle favoured him with a Gorgon stare of her own. Sir Hector, recognizing the danger contained in such a look, took him quickly by the elbow and began to steer him away.

'I'm glad you're having fun, m'dear,' he said over his shoulder, 'but I think we'd better circulate, what?' He led Haddock in the direction of another small group of people.

'Another charming fellow,' said Lady Hardcastle, as soon as they were out of earshot. 'Where on earth did they dig them all up? And why do they keep picking on me?'

'It's because you're such a lovely piece,' I said. 'You're bound to attract the nicer sort of chap.'

'Is a lady still allowed to flog her servants? I'm sure there used to be a law to that effect.'

'I couldn't say, my lady, but I think that might be frowned upon in this day and age.'

'Pity,' she said.

A roar of laughter made us both turn sharply to see what was going on. The source was a group of young men gathered round the chap I'd seen at lunch at the Seddons'.

'Ah, now there we see the Littleton Cotterell cricket team in their natural habitat,' said Lady Hardcastle.

'Surely their natural habitat would be the cricket pitch,' I said.

'Not at all. The expert observer knows that the antics on the cricket pitch are just a pleasing diversion. The real purpose of the game is to provide an excuse to get to the bar afterwards. Here we see them quaffing and guffawing. Characteristic behaviour.'

'I see. But how do we identify them as cricketers without their distinguishing white plumage?'

'We say to Hector, "I say, Hector, who are those chaps over there?" And he says, "Cricket club, m'dear. Friends of Teddy's."'

'Excellent!' I cried.

'Elementary,' said she. 'The poor groom looks a little embarrassed, though.'

To be honest, I thought Theophilus 'Teddy' Seddon looked more irritated than embarrassed as his friends continued to taunt him. Probably afraid of incurring his mother's wrath, I thought.

'Oh, to be young again,' she said. She took a sip of her drink and grimaced. 'I say, be a love and see if you can't find me something nicer to drink. I bet he's hidden the good stuff somewhere. Have a scout round and see if you can find me a brandy. I'm all for cutting costs, but I shall turn quite green if I have to sip any more of this.'

'Yes, my lady. I shall see what I can lay my hands on.'

I had no real idea where to begin looking for brandy, but I wondered if the decanters full of the 'good stuff' might be stashed in the one room where guests were expressly forbidden to go. I slipped out of the 'ballroom' – the great hall of the Tudor house, complete with minstrel gallery – into the hallway, full of dark wooden panelling and faded tapestries.

I arrived at the library door and reached for the handle. I was startled to feel it pulled from my grasp by someone opening the door from within.

'Oh, I say,' said a strikingly pretty young woman, stepping out and closing the door. 'I'm so terribly sorry. Didn't mean to startle you. Just fetching something from my bag. Didn't expect there to be anyone about.'

It was Sylvia Montgomery, the singer with the ragtime band.

'Please don't worry, madam,' I said, thinking frantically. 'I was just . . . checking that no guests had wandered into the library to interfere with the band's things.'

'It's all safe and well, thank you. We're being well looked after.'

'I'm pleased to hear it, madam. May I say I'm enjoying the music very much. You're very good.'

'Why, thank you, you're very kind. I say, you couldn't do a girl another kindness and tell me where I might find some decent booze, could you? I'm absolutely parched and champagne gives me a headache.'

'Oh,' I said, somewhat disappointed. 'I'd been hoping to find something in there. I'm not actually on the staff here, I work for one of the Farley-Strouds' neighbours.'

'Come to steal their booze, eh? Don't worry, I'll not let on.'

I laughed. 'Yes, my mistress sent me in search of brandy. The sparkling wine isn't agreeing with her.'

'I know how she feels, but I'm afraid you're out of luck here, old thing. I turned the library upside-down but there's not a drop to be had. He's got one of those old-fashioned globe whatnots in there – you know the sort that opens up – but he's taken all the liquor out.'

'How very disappointing,' I said. 'Heigh ho, I shall have to continue my search elsewhere. The household servants are bound to know where I can find something.'

'Bound to.' She made to leave. 'If you manage to track any down – Scotch, brandy, even gin at a pinch – see if you can't smuggle some onto the stage for us. We'll make it worth your while.' And with that she breezed off down the corridor, back towards the ballroom.

I walked in the other direction, downstairs to the servants' domain.

Miss Denton's door was shut, but there was a light coming from beneath it. I knocked. There was a clatter of hasty tidying and then the imperious voice. 'Yes?'

I opened the door and poked my head in. 'What ho, Maude,' I said. 'Don't mean to intrude.'

'Flo!' she said with evident relief. 'You frightened the blessed life out of me. I thought you were old Jenkins come snooping.'

'You're hiding out?' I asked, not terribly impressed by the idea of hiding in the first place one might be expected to be.

'Just a quick break, don'tcha know,' she said, gesturing towards the half-concealed glass on the side table. 'A girl needs to wet her whistle.'

'She does indeed. Is that brandy, by any chance?'

'It is,' she said. 'They hide it in here when they have guests.'

'Well, that's a stroke of luck. I don't suppose you can spare a drop? My mistress is desperate for something to take the taste of the fizz away.'

'I expect we can sort her out, my dear,' she said, slightly slurred. 'They've not quite got round to marking the decanter. Not yet, at least. Fetch a glass from the shelf and we'll transfer it to something more elegant upstairs.'

I did as she asked and left her to her brandy-fuelled shirking, wondering if anyone actually did any work in this household. Perhaps Mrs Brown had a right to be angry.

I set off once more for the ballroom. I was wary lest I should be caught smuggling contraband cognac back to Lady Hardcastle in a servant's glass but I encountered no one. I had to check my step a little as I rounded a corner and heard the library door closing, but whoever it was was on their way into the room and I decided that it was none of my concern. It did remind me that I'd been asked to undertake a little more smuggling on behalf of the musicians, but I really couldn't face going all the way back to Old Ma Lushington and trying to snaffle some Scotch from her secret stash. And when it came right down to it, she was responsible for the booze. As idle as I was beginning to think her, I didn't really want to get her into any trouble by pinching it. The band would have to play sober.

'Armstrong!' proclaimed Lady Hardcastle as I approached. 'You're an absolute gem. A proper little darling wonder. A servant beyond compare.' Evidently, the sparkling wine's unpalatable flavour hadn't actually been inhibiting her consumption of it overmuch. 'What?' she said as I proffered the cheap glass filled with its expensive cognac. 'No brandy balloon? I take it all back. You're a slattern and an idler.'

'It was all there was, my lady. Expediency is all in matters of larceny. Now if you'll just stop hooting, I shall find you some more elegant glassware and you can move onto "the good stuff".'

'Quite right. Quite right. Your reputation is saved.' She swayed slightly and I looked around for a suitable glass. There being none to hand, I tipped the dregs of her wine into a nearby aspidistra pot – to judge from the vinous aroma issuing therefrom, I don't think I was the first – and decanted the cognac into the empty glass.

She was loudly effusive in her appreciation of my attentiveness, and I left her singing my praises to a small group of Miss Clarissa's friends. I once more sought out my tray of drinks and nibbles and set about serving as unobtrusively as possible as I listened to the band. I had found a suitable spot beside a suit of armour just as an instrumental number ended.

'Thank you very much, ladies and gentlemen. We're going to take a short break now, but we'll be back in the jiffiest of jiffies.'

With that, they put down their instruments and stepped down from the low stage one by one. Just my luck.

The trumpeter disappeared, but the others milled about, chatting to each other and accepting the congratulations and admiration of the guests. Roland Richman had been buttonholed by Lady Farley-Stroud. She seemed to be at about the same stage of uninhibited merriment as Lady Hardcastle. From the snippets I could overhear over the chatter, she seemed to be bombarding him with comically ill-informed questions about the music, couched in girlishly flirtatious language, which should have been mortifyingly embarrassing but actually made me warm to her a little. It was good to see that the flame hadn't gone out.

Sylvia Montgomery sidled up to me. 'I say, are you the girl I saw in the corridor just now?'

'I am, madam, yes.'

'Any luck?'

'I'm afraid not, madam. I managed to locate the stash, but it proved more difficult than I had imagined to liberate more than a glassful for my mistress.'

'Not to worry, dear. Wallace "remembered" that he has a little Scotch tucked away in his things. He's gone to fetch it.'

I smiled. 'A generous fellow. He's the trumpeter?'

'He is.'

'He's very good. You're all very good. I'm so glad I came.'

'Then I'm glad you came, too. Thank you. And thank you for trying to see us right. It's much appreciated.'

She turned away and went back to her friends.

The rest of the evening passed all too quickly and I found myself getting busier as the party slowly wound down. I heard little of the band, but they seemed less lively than they had earlier, so I didn't feel I was missing too much.

By midnight I was dismissed with grateful thanks by Jenkins, who assured me that my assistance wouldn't be forgotten and that help was always available to me at The Grange if ever I should need it. I shook his hand and asked if perhaps I might take advantage of his kind offer immediately.

'Obviously Lady Hardcastle isn't staying at The Grange, but we don't yet have our own transport. Might I trouble Bert for a ride back to the house?'

'Of course, of course,' he said with a smile. 'I'll have him prepare the motor car and bring it to the front of the house. He should be ready in ten minutes.'

'Thank you,' I said, and went off in search of Lady Hardcastle.

I found her in the ballroom, sitting on a chair in the corner and surrounded once more by Miss Clarissa, Teddy Seddon and a small crowd of their friends. They had the appearance of a circle of adoring acolytes at the feet of a guru.

I could hear the familiar end of one of her favourite anecdotes about our adventures in China and was gratified to hear that my own part in it had not been diminished by the repeated retellings. I waited until we were safely concealed in the ox cart and heading for the Burmese border before discreetly signalling that I wished to speak to her.

'Well, my lovely darlings,' she said, 'I fear the time has come for dear old Aunt Emily to make her grand exit. My maid – you remember her from the story? She's the chap that broke that ruffian's nose – seems to require my attention. If I know her at all well, she'll have arranged transport home. She's an absolute poppet like that. It's been wonderful to meet you all.' She rose unsteadily to her feet, saying her goodbyes to the excitable youngsters. Clarissa hugged her as though they were now the best of friends.

Lady Hardcastle beamed. 'Thank you, dear, and my congratulations to you both once more. Now then, the rest of you, do have fun, and if you absolutely must get up to wickedness, do please try not to make too much noise. It alarms the old folk.'

With that she left them and walked over to me with exaggerated care. She suddenly remembered that she was still holding a brandy bottle in her hand and turned to give it back to Miss Clarissa.

'Thank you so much for finding this, my dear,' she slurred. 'It's just the medicine Aunt Emily needed.'

I raised an eyebrow, thinking I could have heard a little more of the band if I'd not been off on my own, now seemingly unnecessary, brandy quest. 'Bert is bringing the car round, my lady.'

'You, Flo,' she said, linking arms with me, 'are an absolute poppet. Have I told you that? I don't know what I'd do without you.'

I led her to the front door. We passed Sir Hector and Lady Farley-Stroud on the way and she thanked them for a lovely evening, kissing them both on the cheek. I managed to steer her out of the front door before she went any further – I once saw her kiss her host, a rather diminutive earl, on the top of his bald head to the eye-popping alarm of his wife.

I poured her into the waiting motor car.

8

I knew Lady Hardcastle wouldn't even be awake, much less up and about, until quite late the next morning. I tried to lounge in bed myself but by eight o'clock the indolence was too much for me.

Edna and Miss Jones had taken care of most of the chores so I amused myself with some baking before getting out my sewing box. By half-past nine, there was bread proving beside the range and I was well into the mending. When the doorbell rang, I put down my sewing and went to the door.

'Morning, Miss Armstrong,' said Constable Hancock, as I opened it. 'Is your mistress at home?'

'Good morning to you, too, Constable. She's "at home" in the sense of actually being here, but "at home to callers" I couldn't say. She was at The Grange last evening and is still in her room.'

'I know she was, miss. You too, I understands. That's the reason I'm here, in fact. Would you mind terribly trying to rouse her? I rather needs to speak to her. To you both, in fact.'

'Of course. Is there something the matter?'

'There is, miss, but I'd prefer just to go through it the once if that's not too idle of me.'

'Not at all, Constable. Please come in, won't you? You know where the kitchen is? There's some tea in the pot. Do please help yourself and I'll try to awaken Lady Hardcastle.'

'Much obliged, miss,' he said, plodding obediently into the kitchen.

I ran upstairs and knocked on the bedroom door. There was no reply but I opened it and went in anyway. She was still fast asleep and it took quite a bit of shaking to awaken her.

'Oh, Flo, do leave off, there's a dear. Let poor Emily sleep.'

'No, my lady, you have to get up. The police are here.'

'The police?' she mumbled. 'What, all of them? Whatever do they want? I hope they wiped their feet.' Her eyes closed.

I sighed and shook her again. 'No, my lady, just Constable Hancock. But he needs to speak to us both and I think it has something to do with The Grange.'

'If it's about the missing brandy, tell him I'll buy them a case of the stuff and then invite him to come back tomorrow.'

'I really don't think it's about the brandy, my lady, and I really do think you need to get up. This instant.'

'Have I ever told you how much of a bully you are, Florence Armstrong?' she said, groggily. 'Can't a girl lie in bed with a hang-over once in a while without puritanical maids and officious police-men intruding on her slumbers?'

'You tell me all the time, my lady. Please get up.'

'Very well, very well,' she said, sitting up at last. 'Tell him I'll be down presently. Make tea. And eggs. Scramble eggs for me. With toast.'

'Yes, my lady.'

I left her to get up in her own time and returned to the kitchen where I found Constable Hancock making small talk with Miss Jones.

'Lady Hardcastle will be just a few moments,' I said.

'Very good, miss. Thank you.'

'Miss Jones is making some breakfast for Lady Hardcastle, would you like some eggs?'

'Thank you, miss, yes, please. You're very kind. Is that fresh bread I smells?'

'It is, but it's still proving. I was hoping to have it ready for lunch. I have some left over from yesterday that will be perfect for toast, though. I do love to bake my own bread. It's very relaxing. Do you know anything of baking?'

He laughed the heartiest laugh I'd ever heard him give. 'Me, miss? Baking? You are a caution. Whoever heard of such a thing? No, our Ma always used to make her own bread, mind.'

'Most professional bakers are men, are they not?' I said.

'That they are, miss. But most professional bakers are not policemen. Quite aside from it being a woman's work to bake around the house, I doesn't have time for no baking shenanigans. Baking.' He chuckled again. 'I shall have to tell the sarge about this.'

'Unless he thinks it such a great idea that he has you baking bread for his breakfast.'

His cheery laughter erupted again.

'Gracious, you two seem happy,' croaked Lady Hardcastle from the doorway.

'Good morning, m'lady,' said the constable, standing up straight and looking for somewhere to put his teacup. 'I'm sorry to call so early.'

'Nonsense, Constable, it's already . . .'

'Ten o'clock, my lady,' I said, nodding towards the large clock on the kitchen wall.

'Quite so,' she said. 'Plenty late enough to be calling. So what can I do for you, my dear constable?'

'It seems we only ever meets when there's bad news, m'lady,' he said apologetically. 'There's a to-do up at The Grange.'

'Oh dear,' she said, accepting the glass of water Miss Jones had just poured for her. 'What sort of to-do?'

'Seems one of the musicians died, m'lady.'

'Oh no, how sad. Was he ill? Was it unexpected?'

'I don't suppose as how he expected to be clouted round the back of the head with something heavy, no, m'lady.'

She sipped slowly at her water. 'Gracious me. Is there anything I can do?'

'That's more or less why I'm here, m'lady. Inspector Sunderland has already arrived and asked if I'd come and fetch you both so as how you could give witness statements and such.'

'Of course, of course.' She looked more than a little fragile. 'I don't suppose,' she began with unaccustomed tentativeness, 'you have transport of some sort.'

'I've got my bicycle,' he said, with a wink in my direction.

'Oh,' she groaned.

'Only teasing, m'lady. Sir Hector sent me in his motor car. Bert's waiting outside.'

'Oh, thank goodness. You're a wicked man, Constable Hancock. I think Armstrong is a bad influence on you.'

'Me, my lady?' I said. 'I am a paragon of virtue, I'll have you know.'

Constable Hancock began to chuckle but looked suddenly embarrassed.

'Relax, Constable,' said Lady Hardcastle. 'I think we can safely say by now that you're among friends.'

'Lady Hardcastle,' said Inspector Sunderland, 'thank you for coming. I'm sorry to have to summon you so early on the morning after a party, but you can understand the urgency, I'm sure.'

Lady Hardcastle had taken aspirin as well as sweet tea with her light breakfast. She was already more like her normal self. 'Please think nothing of it, Inspector. I'm only too pleased to help.'

The inspector was tall and slightly angular, with a fluid grace that hinted at athleticism despite his slight build. He might have been a sportsman in his youth – a long-distance runner, perhaps. He had a briar pipe which he kept within reach, or clamped between his teeth, at all times. He never, to my knowledge, actually lit it.

'Thank you, my lady. And thank you, too, Miss Armstrong.'

'My pleasure, Inspector,' I said.

The Farley-Strouds had given the inspector the use of the large Georgian dining room at The Grange for his interviews and we were all seated at the enormous table. The room was airy and bright, with large windows that looked out onto the drive. My attention, though, was caught not by the view from the window but by a picture hanging beside the stone fireplace. The Farley-Strouds seemed to favour rustic scenes and this particular one featured a pair of gun dogs with quite the soppiest looks on their faces. I was smiling at the comical image as the inspector continued.

'I gather you were both here last evening,' he said.

'Yes, Inspector,' I said. 'I arrived at The Grange just before four in the afternoon and spent most of my time below stairs until around seven o'clock when the guests started to arrive. Lady Hardcastle and I left together at around one o'clock.'

'Seven? Isn't that rather early for a ball? I thought these things began around ten.'

'They do, Inspector,' said Lady Hardcastle, 'in fashionable society. But out here in the country they prefer an early start and early to bed. To be fair, it was more of a *soirée* than a ball.'

'I see,' he said. 'And you, Lady Hardcastle? When did you arrive?'

'At around a quarter past eight, I should say.'

'The invitations say "Seven o'clock".'

'They do, Inspector. But, really. Who arrives on time at a party?' She often played the dizzy socialite when she was unsure of people.

She found it kept them a little off guard. Give it a while and she'd be giggling and calling him 'darling'. The usual result of this feigned giddiness was that people were apt to dismiss her as a fool, which, of course, was all part of the game. Once they were taken in by her empty-headed act they tended to give away far more than they had planned. I'd seen it many times before.

'Who indeed, my lady?' he said. He'd met her before and was clearly not taken in.

'Would it be altogether against the rules to let us know exactly what happened? Constable Hancock said that one of the musicians was dead.'

'Indeed it might actually help for you to know,' he said. 'I often find that knowledge of the events can jog the memory. A certain look comes into people's eyes when they have the events spelled out to them and they say, "Oh, so that's why So-and-so said that to What's-her-name." So then, let me see . . . Mr Wallace Holloway, the trumpet player with . . .' he consulted his notebook, 'Roland Richman's Ragtime Revue – whatever happened to a good old sing-song round the piano, that's what I'd like to know? Mr Holloway was found in the library this morning at about six o'clock by Dora Kendrick, the housemaid, when she went in to open the shutters and tidy the room which had been used by the band during the evening before. Thinking him still drunk, she went to rouse him but on approaching his recumbent form, she found him "stiff and cold" with a "deathly pallor" and "lying in a pool of blood", whereupon she screamed the house down and has had to be sedated by Dr Fitzsimmons.'

'Is she all right?' I asked. I'd not seen an awful lot of Dora the day before, but she seemed like a sweet girl.

'She'll be fine,' said Inspector Sunderland. 'Not so fine, though, is Mr Holloway. The "pool of blood" was actually a tiny trickle from a small laceration on the back of the scalp, but it was enough to frighten the girl. Dr Fitzsimmons and I are of the opinion that he was struck on the back of the head with some sort of heavy, blunt object. It split his scalp, causing the bleeding but it also did enough internal damage to his brain to kill him, though not instantly. The doctor suggests that he would have been unconscious and breathing when the assailant left him. Death would have occurred some time later. The doctor estimates that he actually passed at around four o'clock this morning.'

'So it probably wasn't his assailant's intention to kill him?' said Lady Hardcastle thoughtfully. 'Surely a murderer would have made certain his victim was dead.'

'That's certainly more common,' he said, 'but it's not unusual for an attacker to be disturbed before he can finish the job. Or to be simply unused to the business of violence and to neglect to check.'

'I see,' she said. 'But it does mean that we've no idea when the attack itself actually happened.'

'Indeed not, my lady. But we might be able to narrow it down a little. We have statements from witnesses that Mr Holloway was last definitely seen alive at ten o'clock when the band took its break.'

'That's when I last saw him, too,' I said. 'Miss Montgomery – she's the singer – said that he'd gone off to the library to fetch his secret supply of Scotch.'

'Oh?' he said. 'And why would she tell you that, I wonder? Establishing an alibi, perhaps?'

'Possibly, Inspector,' I said. 'But it all seemed perfectly innocent at the time. I'd met her earlier, she'd been searching the library for booze, and she asked me if I could find some for her. She came over during her break to ask me if I'd managed it.'

'I see. Why you? Why not one of the household servants?'

'All servants look alike, Inspector,' I said, indicating my uniform. 'How would she know I didn't work here?'

'Quite so,' he said. 'And you didn't have any luck with your search, I presume?'

I hesitated.

'She found me a little brandy, Inspector,' said Lady Hardcastle. 'But the Farley-Strouds had hidden all the good stuff.'

The inspector frowned. 'Always the way in these big houses,' he said. 'But anyway, that leads me to believe that Mr Holloway was attacked some time between leaving the ballroom at ten and when the band started again at half past. If he'd been able to return, he would have, I reckon.'

'Did no one try to look for him?' I asked.

'Only the band would have known he was missing, miss,' he said. 'And once they'd started playing, there wasn't much they could do about it. They were already a man short. They couldn't very well spare another to go searching for the trumpeter, even if he was bringing the Scotch.'

'I suppose so,' I said. 'I thought they sounded a little less lively after the break.'

'That would be why, miss.'

'Were there signs of a fight in the library, Inspector?' said Lady Hardcastle.

'Aside from the dead body by the bookshelves, you mean? Some. The room was in some disarray, as though it had been ransacked. My guess is that the killer was looking for something.'

'And Mr Holloway caught him at it?'

'Quite possibly. That would certainly account for his being knocked unconscious and left on the deck while the robber fled.'

'It would indeed,' she said.

'That's my working hypothesis at the moment,' he said. 'My next task is to try to establish where everybody was during the course of the evening. I need to know everything you can both remember: where you were, who you saw, when you saw them, and anything else you noticed, no matter how unimportant you might feel it. Can we start with you, please, Lady Hardcastle?'

'Of course. I arrived at about a quarter past eight, as you now know. Sir Hector's chauffeur, Bert, was kind enough to bring me up the hill. I greeted my hosts, who introduced me to Captain Summers – a frightful bore recently returned from India – and then left me to his oafish attentions. I stayed with him for as long as I thought polite and then slipped away while his eye was roving elsewhere. I spoke to Miss Clarissa and her London friends, congratulating the happy couple and whatnot. I had a bit of a wander round, bumped into a couple of the Farley-Strouds' friends that I'd met at dinner the weekend before, and then finally tracked down Armstrong. We chatted briefly, then I was buttonholed once more by Captain Summers whom I managed to outrage.'

'"Outrage", my lady?' said the inspector, looking up from his notebook.

'I revealed that I'd spent some time in India "alone" after my husband had died. He couldn't quite grasp how a lady might do such a thing.'

'Plenty of ladies end up coping on their own in India after their husbands die,' said the inspector.

'But my husband died in China and I made my own way to India with Armstrong. We stayed there for a couple of years.'

'Ah,' he said. 'Out of the ordinary, but hardly outrageous.'

'Not to Captain Summers. He very quickly found someone else to badger. Then the Seddons said hello. He was in his cups and she was trying a little too hard to ingratiate herself. Then Sir Hector brought a rather unpleasant man over. An antiques dealer of some sort.'

Inspector Sunderland flicked back a few pages in his notebook. 'Mr Clifford Haddock,' he said. 'I've already wired Scotland Yard about him. He seems like a very fishy character.'

'Well, quite,' said Lady Hardcastle, raising an eyebrow. 'Then I sent Armstrong off for booze – the fizzy wine was a lovely thought but quite undrinkable – and after that things got a great deal more merry. I ended up holding court with the youngsters and impressing them with my tales of derring-do from Shanghai to Calcutta. Then Armstrong found me and, strongly implying that I was brandified, took me home.'

'You were sloshed, my lady,' I said.

'I was, as you say, all mops and brooms, but it's indelicate of you to point it out to the inspector.'

'It shall go no further,' said the inspector with a smile.

'You're most kind,' she said. 'And that was my evening.'

'Did you notice any unusual comings and goings at around the time Mr Holloway disappeared?'

'No, Inspector, I'm afraid not. It wasn't the liveliest of parties, but it was a party nonetheless. People all over the place. Doors everywhere. Guests coming and going all the time.'

'Yes, that's the problem,' he said, finishing off his notes. 'And you, Miss Armstrong, what did you see?'

I recounted the events of my own evening and was describing my meeting with Sylvia Montgomery.

'Miss Montgomery was coming out of the library as you were on your quest for brandy?' asked the inspector.

'Yes, that's right.'

'So this was during the break?'

'No, I don't think so,' I said. 'I think the band was still playing.'

'There were some instrumental numbers, I believe,' said Lady Hardcastle. 'Perhaps it was during one of those?'

'Perhaps,' he said. 'Do you remember the time of this meeting?'

'I'm sorry, Inspector, I never wear a watch. I have no idea.'

'No matter. Please continue.'

I told him about my meeting with the tipsy Maude Denton. I described my sneaking back to the party with the illicit brandy and how I'd had to hide to avoid being seen by someone who was going into the library.

'Did you see this person?' asked the inspector.

'No, I just heard the door closing. When I peeked round the corner again there was no one in sight so I presumed they'd gone in rather than come out.'

'Could it have been Mr Holloway?'

'The band was still playing when I got back to the ballroom. It was only later that Mr Holloway slipped away and Miss Montgomery came over to ask about the Scotch.'

'Interesting. So that could have been our man,' mused the inspector.

'Or woman,' said Lady Hardcastle quickly.

'True, true. Though a man is more likely to clout someone round the back of the head with something heavy. A woman would like as not try to talk her way out of it.'

'Have you met Armstrong?' she asked with a smile.

'Not given to talking her way out of things?' he said.

'Not usually. She'd not need a heavy object to render someone unconscious, either.'

'No, Inspector,' I said. 'And he'd be able to get up and walk away with a headache when he woke up, too. It shows a considerable lack of skill to kill someone by accident when there are so many effective ways of simply incapacitating him.'

He looked faintly disquieted but carried on. 'And what happened when you returned to the ballroom?'

I told the tale of the rest of my evening, but there was little else of any substance to offer him.

'Did no one go into the library while you were tidying up?' he asked when I had finished.

'No, we were told not to bother with it because the band members were still using it. That's why Dora was in there first thing. It was to be her job to get the room back in order before the band rose and came in to pack up their things.'

'They didn't pack up at the end of the party?'

'No, they finished their performance and left their instruments on the little stage. I didn't see what happened to them after that.'

'They cadged some booze from Miss Clarissa and went off to the rooms that had been set aside for them in the attic,' said Lady Hardcastle.

'Without looking for their friend,' said the inspector. 'They're a strange lot.'

'Oh, I think they wanted to. The one they called Skins was very keen to search for him, but Richman very firmly told him no and he seemed to drop it.'

'Skins . . . Skins . . .' said the inspector, leafing through his notebook again. 'Ah yes, Ivor "Skins" Maloney. The drummer. "Skins"?'

'Drum skins, one imagines,' said Lady Hardcastle. 'It's calfskin, I believe, scraped very thin and stretched very tight.'

'Is it? Is it indeed? Well, I count it a poor day if I don't learn at least one new thing. Today is looking up already. Richman said no, eh? Very interesting.' He sat for a few moments reviewing his notes. 'Well, my lady, Miss Armstrong, thank you for your help. I shall detain you no longer. I shall send word by the young constable if I should need anything further.'

'Of course,' she said. 'Oh, before we go, is there any more news on the Frank Pickering murder case?'

'We have a man in custody,' he said.

'The right man?' she asked.

'Our investigations continue. Justice will be done, rest assured.'

She smiled enigmatically and we left the inspector to his notebook.

Outside in the hall, we were waylaid almost at once by Lady Farley-Stroud. She seemed to be in a state of some distress.

'Ah, Emily, dear, there you are,' she said. 'I'm so glad I caught you.'

'Whatever's the matter, Gertie? You look all out of gathers.'

'Something terrible's happened, dear,' said Lady Farley-Stroud.

'I know. Poor Mr Holloway. We were just speaking to the inspector.'

'Oh, that. Yes. But no, this is something else. I don't know where to turn.'

'You can always turn to me, Gertie, dear. What can I do for you?'

'Come with me, dear,' she said. 'I need to explain things somewhere a little more private.' She began to lead the way towards a room off the hall, which I knew to be Sir Hector's study. Lady Hardcastle followed her for a few steps before turning back to me.

'Come along, Armstrong, don't dawdle,' she said.

I frowned questioningly at her, glancing towards Lady Farley-Stroud to try to direct her attention to the look of disapproval on the older lady's face. She caught the look.

'Ah,' she said. 'Gertie, dear, I know it's not how you do things, but it's very much how I do things. You must have gleaned from my stories at dinner that Armstrong is my right hand. If you need my help, you'll get her help whether you wish it or not. It will save an awful lot of bother if she's involved from the beginning. She'll certainly be involved before the end.'

Lady Farley-Stroud looked very much as though she might be inclined to argue, but her desire for Lady Hardcastle's aid won the internal struggle and with a grudging, 'Oh, very well, then', she bade me follow them both into the study.

I closed the door behind me. Lady Farley-Stroud offered Lady Hardcastle a seat in one of the armchairs by the window but very pointedly ignored me so I took up a position in the corner of the room beside a large bookcase. Lady Farley-Stroud paced agitatedly for a few moments while she collected her thoughts.

'You recall that Hector and I were in India in the sixties?' she began. 'That was where we met your dear mother and father. We had such wonderful times there, Hector and I. It's quite the most beautiful country. Of course, you've spent time there yourself, so you know. I really didn't want to come home, but Hector was posted back to Blighty so like a dutiful wife I packed up all our traps and followed him. And we brought back many lovely things as mementoes, d'you see? Knick-knacks and whatnots to remind us of our time there.'

Lady Hardcastle nodded.

'One of them has been stolen.'

'My dear, how awful,' said Lady Hardcastle. 'Where was it?'

'We had it in our bedroom, on the mantel. It was on a cushion under a pretty little bell jar. Our reminder of happy days and a secure future.'

'You poor thing. It's lucky the police were already here. What did Inspector Sunderland say?'

'We can't tell the police,' said Lady Farley-Stroud in some panic. 'We can never tell the police.'

'Why ever not?'

'It's a rather delicate matter,' began our hostess. 'In sixty-five, Hector performed some small service for the local raja – a thoroughly charming man – who rewarded Hector with a jewel.'

'And it's this jewel that's been stolen? What is it?'

'It's an emerald,' she said. 'About the size of a hen's egg,' she added, almost casually.

'A hen's egg?' exclaimed Lady Hardcastle and I together.

'Just so,' said Lady Farley-Stroud.

'It must have been quite some service that Hector performed,' said Lady Hardcastle. 'A stone like that would be worth thousands.'

'Many, many thousands,' said Lady Farley-Stroud. 'It has quite an interesting story, too, but that's for another day. A few years ago we secured a loan using the gem as security. It took some negotiating, but we managed to persuade our creditors that we should be able to keep the jewel here – it means so much to us both, y'see.'

I could imagine even the hardest-hearted banker eventually bowing to the will of Lady Farley-Stroud.

'They weren't at all happy,' she continued. 'They would much rather have held it to ransom in their own vaults, but eventually they agreed on the strict condition that the safety of the jewel was to be entirely our responsibility. If it were to be stolen or damaged, the loan would be repayable immediately. No security, no loan.'

'Gracious,' said Lady Hardcastle.

'So now you see. We can't let word get out that the emerald has been stolen or the debt would become immediately due. Even were it subsequently recovered we would be in breach of the conditions of the loan.'

'I quite see your predicament,' said Lady Hardcastle. 'But how can we help?'

'I want you to find the thief and return the jewel.'

Lady Hardcastle said nothing.

'Through your mother I've known of you and your exploits for many years, dear,' said Lady Farley-Stroud. 'I'm not such a foolish old woman as people round here would like to believe, and I can put two and two together as well as the next chap. You'd not have nearly so many exciting stories to tell if you'd just been another society lady. You've been engaged in some sort of secret work all these years and I'd wager you know exactly how to get to the bottom of a matter like this. Even if I'm wrong, you're the best-educated person for miles around with the possible exception of Dr Fitz-simmons. Trouble is, I really can't imagine him being able to solve the daily puzzle in the *Bristol News*, much less a jewel theft.'

Lady Hardcastle smiled. 'I'm flattered, Gertie, dear, but I think you might be exaggerating our talents somewhat. Nevertheless, if you're certain that you can't involve the police, then it would be ungracious of us to refuse. What say you, Armstrong? Shall we try to find the emerald?'

'Whither thou goest, my lady,' I said.

'Oh, my dear, thank you,' said Lady Farley-Stroud.

'The problem shall be doing so without arousing suspicion and frightening the thief, should he still be about.' She paused a moment, lost in thought. 'I say, I've an idea. You couldn't have a word with Inspector Sunderland for me, could you?'

9

A short while later, Lady Hardcastle and I were sitting at the dining table with Inspector Sunderland. Lady Farley-Stroud had button-holed him immediately after our own meeting to beg his indulgence.

'Would you mind awfully,' she asked, 'if m'good friend and neighbour were to sit in on your interviews?'

'You'd think me remiss if I didn't at least ask why,' he said.

She thought quickly. 'She's writing a book, d'you see? A detective story. It would be such a boon to see a real investigation at first hand.'

'It's most irregular,' he said. 'Interrogation is a delicate matter. It has to be handled with great care. I'm unsure of the wisdom of letting civilians interfere.'

'Of course, Inspector, of course. But she's bright as a button. Terribly, terribly clever. She'll not interfere.'

He thought for a few moments. 'Very well,' he said. 'To tell the truth, she has impressed me somewhat already. "She's all there and halfway back", as Mrs Sunderland says. Her company may actually be useful. It's your house, Lady Farley-Stroud, so if you vouch for her I shall allow her to sit in. If she hinders my investigations in any way, though, she'll be out on her ear. Agreed?'

'Of course, of course,' she said. 'If she causes you any difficulties I shall give her a stern talking to myself.'

While all this was going on, Lady Hardcastle had made another request of Lady Farley-Stroud. Bert, the chauffeur, and a footman called Dewi (who swore continually and colourfully under his breath in Welsh and didn't think anyone could understand him) had been called upon to bring down a blackboard and easel from the nursery. She had set it up as her crime board in the dining room.

While the inspector sat and looked through his notebook, Lady Hardcastle had been sketching the party guests and we'd both been trying to recall any details of the previous evening that might be helpful.

'To whom else have you spoken, Inspector?' asked Lady Hardcastle, as she finished off a particularly accurate, if unflattering, sketch of Clifford Haddock.

'Just you and one or two of the staff so far,' he said. 'The majority of the guests left shortly after you and most of those who stayed have slept in. Lady Farley-Stroud insisted that I let them sleep, so you were the unlucky ones who got the wake-up call from Constable Hancock.'

'I'm sure it serves me right for something I did in a past life,' she said. 'Are you familiar with the Eastern concept of karma?'

'I've heard of it, yes. An old sergeant of mine when I was new to the force used to talk about it. "Double Entry Bookkeeping for the Soul", he used to call it.'

'Quite the philosopher, your sergeant.'

'He served in the army in India. Married an Indian girl. Fascinating man.'

'Well, perhaps my early awakening was payment in respect of some karmic debt.'

'Not too great a debt, though,' he said. 'There are worse prices to pay than being awakened early with a sore head.'

'Well, quite. And I've been rewarded again with your time and patience. I'm beginning to wonder if I might need to employ a metaphysical accountant. All of which is by way of thanking you for your indulgence, Inspector. I'm certain that you could imagine easier ways of conducting your enquiries than having a lady and her maid sitting with you.'

'Lady Farley-Stroud speaks highly of you, my lady, and my own impressions have been favourable so far. As long as you're here only to observe, I'm sure we'll get along just fine. I'm still not entirely certain why you were so keen to be here, though,' he said. 'Lady Farley-Stroud said something about you writing a book?'

'A detective story, yes,' she said blithely.

'Then I shouldn't complain. It might have an accurate portrayal of the police for once,' he said. 'We'd better get on with it. We shall start working our way through the witnesses one by one. It's painstaking work, but I find thoroughness usually gets results.'

Lady Hardcastle looked at him as though about to mention his lack of thoroughness in the Pickering case, but she thought better of it when he returned her stare.

He flipped through his ever present notebook. 'Miss Armstrong, would you do me a great service and get one of the staff here to fetch Miss Sylvia Montgomery. Let's see what she has to say about her visit to the library.'

Sylvia Montgomery was only slightly less stunning in her day clothes than in her stage outfit. She sat opposite Inspector Sunderland and Lady Hardcastle, regarding them coolly but without apparent hostility as they asked her about the events of the night before.

'. . . and then I slipped out to the library in search of something to drink. I'm not needed during the last couple of numbers in the first set apart from to sway around and look gorgeous, so I usually just nick off at that point. I had a good hunt around, looking in the globe, behind the books, under the chairs, in the window seats. Nothing. Not a drop. So I gave it up as a bad job and that's when I met you.' She looked over towards me. 'I went back into the ballroom and stayed there until we'd finished. We managed to cadge some half-decent Scotch from the birthday girl—'

'It was her engagement party,' the inspector corrected her.

'Was it, indeed? That chinless chap with the wispy moustache?'

'Mr Seddon, yes. Heir to the Seddon shipping business.'

'Really? Good for her. If you can't land a looker, go for the money. Good girl. But anyway, we snaffled her Scotch and went off up to the dingy rooms they'd begrudgingly let us have. We drank until about three and then called it a night.'

'Did none of you wonder what had happened to Mr Holloway?' asked Lady Hardcastle.

'At first, yes. Skins was all for looking for him but Roland insisted he'd probably found a doxy to canoodle with and we should leave him to it.'

'Was he the sort to "canoodle with doxies", miss?' said the inspector.

'He was a trumpeter, Inspector. The prospect of canoodling with doxies at parties was what got him to take up the instrument in the first place.'

'I see. What did you all talk about?'

'When, Inspector?'

'While you were drinking. I presume you didn't all sit there in gloomy silence.'

'Oh, I see. Oh, you know, the usual. How the performance had gone, which numbers worked and which didn't, what engagements were coming up. That sort of thing.'

'Very good, miss, thank you. I think it might help me to see the library in the company of someone who saw it before the crime took place. See how things have changed, if you get my meaning. Would that be too distressing for you, miss?'

She gave him a withering look. He shrugged in response and stood. Together we trooped out of the dining room and headed for the library.

The library was a long, rectangular room with three large windows along one of the long walls and a large stone fireplace set in the centre of the other. Apart from that, every other inch of wall space was fitted with floor-to-ceiling bookshelves.

I loved being in the libraries of big houses. My own love of reading had been born in Britain's public libraries as the circus toured from town to town. But it blossomed into maturity in the house where I had my first job as a scullery maid. I used to sneak into the master's library when the family was away to explore his wonderful collection.

That library in Cardiff and the library at The Grange were very similar. There were four comfortable leather armchairs, one in each corner of the room. The empty drinks globe stood beside one of them and small tables were set beside the other three. I could see the bloodstain on the polished wood of the floor near the fireplace and when I looked more closely I could see that there was also a bloody mark on the corner of the stone hearth.

'It looks like he hit his head on the hearth when he fell, Inspector,' I said.

'Very good, miss, very good indeed,' said the inspector. 'The doctor and I rather think that's what caused the fatal damage to Mr Holloway's brain.'

I felt ever so slightly patronized, but part of me was also rather pleased with the praise.

At the other end of the room was a jumble of instrument cases. A double-bass case lay on its side with its red velvet lining ripped out, making it look like another bleeding corpse. Round cases of pressed cardboard, like oversized hatboxes, were strewn haphazardly about, lids and leather straps lying chaotically among them.

'Is that how you left your things, miss?' said the inspector.

'I should jolly well say not,' said Sylvia, walking towards the jumble of cases. 'Our instruments are our livelihood, Inspector, and we treat them with the utmost respect. Even the cases we keep them in.' She reached out to tidy them, as though the chaos were an affront.

'Please don't touch anything, miss. Our fingerprint expert hasn't been here yet.'

'Oh,' she said, pulling her hand back. 'Sorry.'

Until now I'd been puzzled by her reaction to the whole thing. The band all seemed to get along well and she'd not appeared to be in the least bit upset by the murder of one of her friends. Even the sight of the bloodstained floor had left her unmoved. But somehow this apparently unimportant mistreatment of the instrument cases had affected her, as though it were the worst violation of all. She looked shocked and anguished for the first time.

'Please sit down, miss,' said the inspector, taking her by the arm and leading her to one of the armchairs. 'I did try to warn you this might be distressing.'

'Yes,' she said absently, 'you did. I'm so sorry, Inspector, you must think me a frightful ninny. I suppose it hadn't really sunk in until I saw what they did to our things. It wasn't real somehow. Do you know what I mean?'

'I do, Miss Montgomery,' he said.

'Wait a moment,' she said, suddenly much more alert. 'Where's Wallace's case?'

'I beg your pardon, miss?'

'Wallace's trumpet case. Have you removed it?'

'No, miss, we've not touched a thing at that end of the room. Like I say, we're waiting for the fingerprint man.'

'I thought you detectives did all that sort of thing yourselves,' she said, clearly having trouble maintaining her train of thought.

'Some do, miss. We're trying a new system, though. Specialists, if you get my meaning.'

'Oh, I see.'

'Mr Holloway's case?' he said, trying to get her train of thought back on the rails.

'It's not there.'

'And it was there last night? He didn't leave it in his room, perhaps?'

'No, they unpacked in here. We warmed up here.'

'Warmed up?'

'You know, ran through a few scales and so on. I did my voice exercises.'

'Ah, like sportsmen.'

'Just like that, yes. We need to loosen up, get ourselves prepared. And we did that in here. I distinctly remember Wallace getting his trumpet out of its case and putting it on top of one of Skins's drum cases.'

Inspector Sunderland stepped over to the jumble of cases and examined them all minutely. Seeming to find nothing of importance, he looked around the room for any trace of the trumpet case.

'Hmm, that's most interesting,' he said at length. 'It's definitely not here now. It looks as though we might have found out what it was the thief was after. But why . . .?'

'An empty trumpet case?' said Lady Hardcastle.

'Certainly a trumpet case without a trumpet in it,' he said. 'But I doubt it was "empty" if it was worth clouting someone over the head for. Did you see anything else in there, Miss Montgomery?'

'In the case, Inspector? No. A trumpet, a mouthpiece. He usually had a cleaning cloth and little bottle of valve oil in there. Oh, and one of those stick things they poke into the tubes for cleaning.

There might have been some brass polish. I saw him using all that sort of stuff at one time or another but I never really looked inside. It's not the done thing, you know, poking around in another musician's things. Not the done thing at all.'

'Fair enough, miss. Thank you. Now, I think the best thing for you would be to take some air.'

He rang the bell and, a few moments later, Jenkins appeared.

'Ah, Jenkins,' said the inspector. 'I wonder if I might ask you to find Miss Montgomery here a spot in the garden where she might relax a while in the fresh air. She's had something of a shock. If you were able to find her a little brandy, I'm sure that would be most beneficial.'

Jenkins looked briefly horrorstruck at the thought of having to treat a mere musician – no better than a tradesman in his eyes – as an honoured guest, but a nod of agreement from Lady Hardcastle persuaded him that it was, after all, something he should just get on with.

'Yes, sir, of course,' he said emotionlessly. 'Will there be anything else?'

'No, Jenkins, thank you.'

'Oh, Jenkins,' said Lady Hardcastle. He stopped at once and turned to face her. 'We'll be returning to the dining room presently. Be an absolute darling and have some coffee sent in, would you?'

'Of course, my lady.' He had no complaints about helping a proper lady. 'Luncheon will be served at one, my lady. In the garden, since the inspector', he paused and looked pointedly at Inspector Sunderland, 'has commandeered the dining room. Will you be joining us?'

'I don't think so, Jenkins. Would Mrs Brown make us a plate of sandwiches, perhaps?'

'I'm sure she'd be more than happy to, my lady.'

He closed the door behind him.

'Of all the uppity, stuck-up, hoity-toity . . .' said the inspector.

'Oh, come now, Inspector,' said Lady Hardcastle. 'He's just a little old-fashioned.'

'I ask him to help a girl in distress and he's looking down his nose. You ask him to run around and bring you coffee and sandwiches and he almost trips over his shoes in his haste.'

'It's the accent and the title, dear boy,' she said with a wink. He harrumphed to indicate that she had entirely proved his point. 'Oh, and . . .' she glanced down at her ample chest.

The inspector gave her a look of good-natured exasperation. 'Really?' he said, and left the room.

'You, my lady, are going straight to Hell,' I said as I followed him. She grinned.

We entered the dining room to find a bewildered Captain Summers looking forlornly at the empty sideboard.

'What ho,' he said breezily. 'I seem to be a bit late for breakfast, what?'

'A little, sir,' said the inspector. 'It's very nearly lunchtime. And you are . . .?'

'I might ask you the same question, sir,' said Summers pompously, disdainfully eyeing the inspector's neat but unfashionable suit.

'I do beg your pardon,' said the inspector. 'Inspector Sunderland of the Bristol CID.'

'CID, eh? Detective, eh? What are you detectin'?'

'There's been a murder, Mister—'

'Captain. Captain Summers.' His face had whitened. 'A murder?'

'Yes, sir, last evening at the party. Are you quite well, sir? Do you think you ought to sit down?'

'I . . . er . . . yes. Do you mind, my lady?' He looked over towards Lady Hardcastle. 'I feel a little queer.' He sat on one of the dining chairs, still looking very pale. 'Funny how a chap can spend his life fighting for king and country – queen and country, too, come to that – seeing death and carnage all around, and then be knocked for six by a death in the house. It was in the house, Inspector?'

'It was, sir, yes.'

'Good lord, not in here?'

'No, sir, in the library.'

'I see, I see.' He looked around, still somewhat befuddled. 'Who was it?'

'One of the musicians, sir,' said the inspector. 'Mr Wallace Holloway, the trumpeter with the band.'

'Good lord. Music wallah, eh? They were good. I mean, that's what everyone kept telling me. Not entirely my cup of char, if I'm completely honest with you, but . . . I mean . . . a chap doesn't deserve to die for playing American music.'

'I don't think he was killed by a music critic, sir. We're almost certain it was a robbery.'

'A robbery? Good lord. Good lord. What would a trumpeter have worth stealing?'

'That's precisely what we're currently wondering, sir. Did you see anything last evening? Anything that might help us piece together what happened?'

'"Us"?' he said, looking around at Lady Hardcastle and me.

'I meant the police force, sir. Lady Hardcastle and Miss Armstrong are . . . observing.'

Captain Summers looked blankly at us. 'Observing?'

'Yes, sir.'

'I see. I see. Jolly good.'

'Would you mind telling us about last evening, Captain? Did you see or hear anything unusual, for instance?'

'Not a thing, Inspector, no.'

'Perhaps you could take us through the evening as you remember it?'

'Of course, of course. I'd been staying at The Grange for a couple of days, d'you see. Friend of Sir Hector. So I was one of the first at the party. Bit early for my taste, but I tried not to fuss. So many things have changed here since I've been away.'

'Here, sir? You've been to The Grange before?'

'No, I mean, yes, I have, but I meant Blighty. Gone to the dogs if you ask me. France, too. Stopped in Paris on my way here, see an old friend, what? Shabby place now. But there I was, best bib and tucker—'

'Military dress, sir?'

'What? No, mess jacket still in India. Travelling light, what? Be back there soon. No point hauling all me traps halfway round the world then hauling them all the way back.'

'Quite, sir. Please, continue. What did you do?'

'I was trying to circulate, do the sociable thing, d'you see? Trying to get back into the swing of it all. Society, and all that. Hoping to be married soon, want to start a new life back in Blighty in a year or two. Doesn't hurt to make a few friends.'

'Oh, congratulations, sir,' said the inspector, amiably. 'Who's the lucky lady?'

Captain Summers smiled ruefully. 'There's the rub. Not quite asked her yet. Colonel's daughter and all that. Got to play it a bit carefully, what? Need to woo her. Impress her, d'you see? Can't rush at these things like a bull at a gate.'

'I see, sir, yes. Were you in the ballroom all evening? You didn't nip out for some fresh air?'

'Can't say as I did, no.'

'And did you notice any of the other comings and goings? Did anything strike you as odd?'

'Not really, Inspector. Folk come and go all evening at a shindig like that.'

'Did you see Mr Holloway leave the room?'

'The dead chap?'

'Yes, sir.'

'Can't say as I did.'

'So you wouldn't have noticed, say, if someone followed him out?'

'No, Inspector, not at all. I'm not really much help, I'm afraid, am I?'

'Everything is helpful in an investigation like this, sir,' said the inspector, patiently. 'I can see you've had a shock, though, so I shan't detain you further. Thank you for your time.'

'Free to go, what?'

'Free to go, sir. I should be obliged if you were to stay at The Grange until this is cleared up. I may need to ask you some further questions when I know a little more about the events of the evening. I might be able to jog your memory a little.'

'Certainly, Inspector, certainly.' He stood to leave. 'Lady Hardcastle,' he said with a bow, and walked round the table to the door.

As he closed the door behind him, Inspector Sunderland rolled his eyes. 'What a buffle-headed ass,' he said. 'Nice to see the Empire is in the hands of such bright and brave individuals.'

'He'd had a shock,' said Lady Hardcastle reproachfully.

'A shock, my Aunt Fanny. Man's a soldier. He's seen death before. Said so himself.'

'Maybe so. But as a friend of mine once pointed out, there's a difference between chaps dressed up as the enemy pointing their guns – or spears, or what have you – at you across a battlefield, and some ne'er-do-well sneaking about in the night doing folk to death in an English village.'

'You're right, of course, my lady. I shouldn't be so harsh. But the man's a buffoon.'

'Oh, he's a buffoon of the first water, no question about it. And so terribly old fashioned with it. Quite the relic. But we should perhaps make allowances. England isn't all he remembers it to be. I think he has a rather romantic notion of what "Blighty" should be like, and all this has quite shattered his illusions.'

'I dare say,' said the inspector distractedly, as he made some notes in his notebook.

There was a knock on the door and Jenkins entered with a tray of coffee, sandwiches, and some shortbread biscuits.

'Your luncheon, my lady,' he said, pointedly ignoring the inspector. 'Mrs Brown thought you might appreciate some biscuits, too.'

'She's very thoughtful, Jenkins,' said Lady Hardcastle. 'Please thank her for us.'

'Yes, my lady. Will there be anything else?'

'No, Jenkins, thank you.'

'Very good, my lady,' he said with a slight bow. He left as quietly as he had entered.

Inspector Sunderland seemed to be on the verge of another tirade, but thought better of it and went to pour the coffee instead.

'Please,' I said, stepping forward. 'Allow me.'

'Certainly, miss. If you insist.'

'Thank you, Inspector,' I said, as I poured coffee for the two of them. 'Just doing my duty.'

'Don't show off, Armstrong,' said Lady Hardcastle. 'Pour yourself one, too.'

I curtseyed. 'Thank you, m'lady. You're very generous to a poor servant girl, you are. Very kind and generous. I doesn't deserve it, m'lady, really I doesn't.'

'Are you two a music hall act?' said the inspector.

'No, Inspector, we're just good friends,' said Lady Hardcastle and motioned for me to sit with them at the table.

'Well, that told us nothing we couldn't have guessed for ourselves,' said the inspector, still gazing thoughtfully at his notebook.

'I wouldn't say that, Inspector,' said Lady Hardcastle. 'I think it gave us quite an insight into the man's character.' She rose and made a few quick notes of her own on the crime board.

'Showed us that he's a buffoon, you mean? I suppose it did at that.' He snapped his notebook shut and tucked in to the coffee and sandwiches. 'If you don't mind my asking, what on earth is the blackboard all about?'

'It's my "crime board", Inspector. I read Natural Sciences at Cambridge and it's quite the thing in scientific circles to do one's thinking "out loud" by means of the blackboard. Everyone can see one's reasoning, spot the flaws. I became rather used to thinking on a blackboard so I started using one for my criminal investigations.'

'I didn't think they allowed women at Cambridge,' he said.

'We're allowed to study, Inspector – and Girton is a simply splendid college – they just refuse to grant us degrees.'

'I see. And what do you mean by "criminal investigations"? Have you done this sort of thing before?'

'We started just recently. We're . . . sort of . . . as it were . . . just taking an interest in the Pickering case.'

'You're meddling in the Pickering case?'

'Not meddling, as such,' she said.

'But you're not satisfied with the work of the police force.'

'That's not it at all, Inspector. It was obvious that you were busy and we just thought . . .'

'You thought you could do a better job because you write detective novels and you believe the official police to be a shower of clodhopping oafs.'

She laughed. 'Well, not clodhopping oafs exactly. But you must admit you were a little distracted when you spoke to us. And we know for a fact that you didn't get the full story from Joe Arnold at the Dog and Duck.'

He frowned. 'It's none of your business,' he said, after a moment's contemplation, 'but since you're claiming to be writing murder mysteries of your own, perhaps it would be as well to let you in on a few things by way of making your work more accurate. No, I haven't completed my investigations. No, I'm not at all certain that Bill Lovell is the murderer, though I'm certain he's up to something and sweating him in the cells for a couple of days did him no harm—'

'He's been released, then?'

'He's about to be released, yes. His arrest, though, was extremely useful to me for other reasons. My colleagues and I were dealing with a particularly sensitive case in the city which involved several street urchins being abducted from the streets. We were certain that they were about to be shipped off to Eastern Europe somewhere for who knows what horrible purpose. It was essential that the newspapers didn't get wind of it and blow the gaff on what we were up to. If the villains had been tipped off, all those kiddies would have gone for good. But a nice arrest for murder always keeps the gentlemen of the press amused for a while and we were able to go about our business unmolested.'

'The gang . . .?'

'Are banged up, yes, my lady. And Lovell is at liberty once more.'

'I must say, it's all rather cynical,' she said.

'That's as may be, but it's not quite as inept as you believed, now, is it?'

'I'll grant you that.'

'That's a start. Now then, you say you know that we haven't got the full story from Arnold? How do you know that? Have you spoken to him?'

'Armstrong did, didn't you, dear?'

'I did,' I said.

'What did you learn?' he asked.

I briefly recounted my meeting with Joe and Daisy, complete with my observations about their characters.

He chuckled. 'I'll have to have a word with this Arthur Tressle character,' he said. 'I gather the cricket team were here in force last night.'

'They were,' said Lady Hardcastle. 'Teddy Seddon – the groom-to-be – plays cricket.'

'Seddon . . . Seddon . . .' he said, flicking through his notebook. 'Oh, my word, I hadn't realized they were *those* Seddons.'

'You know of them?'

'I've heard of the firm, yes.'

'They're shipping agents, aren't they?' said Lady Hardcastle. 'Were Seddon, Seddon and Seddon involved in your child abductions? Is that why you know the name?'

He looked at her appraisingly for a few moments. 'I'm not at liberty to comment,' he said.

'I don't wish you to be indiscreet, Inspector,' she said. 'Shall we attack these delicious sandwiches and speak of lighter things for a while?'

And so we ate together, making small talk. We'd all noticed that the house had seen better days, that there was a faint air of shabbiness about it. The inspector asked about the Farley-Strouds' financial position.

'Inspector!' she said. 'You ought to know better than to ask about an Englishman's money.'

'Call it professional curiosity,' he said.

'I see. Well they're not exactly impecunious,' she said, 'but there doesn't seem to be a lot of spare cash around for decoration and modernization.'

We finished the sandwiches and moved on to the biscuits.

'I say,' said the inspector. 'These are rather nice. Mrs Sunderland makes a lovely shortbread, but nothing like this.'

'I'm sure Armstrong could get you the recipe, if you like.'

'Tell me, my lady, if you were a policeman's wife, waiting anxiously for him to come home, never knowing what danger he'd got himself into that day, and you'd made some delicious shortbread for him to have with his cup of tea by the fire, how would you feel if he came home and said, "Here you are, my beloved, I thought you made the finest biscuits in all the land, but I have found a far better recipe. Take these inferior things back to the kitchen and make me some of these others, as prepared by a servant in a manor house I've been visiting"?'

'You build a convincing argument, Inspector,' she said. 'Armstrong, keep that recipe a secret. Do not divulge it to anyone, most especially not the inspector.'

'Right you are, my lady,' I said.

'You two . . .' said the inspector, sipping his coffee. I got the feeling that he was warming to us despite himself. 'Now then, to business. Let us cleanse our investigatory palates by interviewing someone who might actually tell us something. What do you say we talk to someone else from the band? I got the impression that Miss Montgomery wasn't all that close to them. Let's see what one of his fellow musicians has to say.' He consulted his notebook. 'Let's go straight to the top. Roland Richman. He might be able to tell us a little more.'

'He might, he might,' said Lady Hardcastle.

The inspector nodded. 'There's another reason for talking to Mr Richman.' He flipped back a few more pages in his notebook. 'One of the servants says she saw him in the passage outside the library. She can't remember when and didn't think much of it at the time because the musicians were supposed to be there, but it does place him near the scene of the crime.'

'Would you like me to fetch him, sir?' I said.

'That would be grand, miss, thank you.'

10

I had found Roland Richman in the ballroom, tinkling away at the piano. Actually, that's not entirely fair – he had been playing a rather beautiful piece, which had turned out to be one of his own compositions. He followed me somewhat reluctantly to the dining room and, after the usual introductions, Inspector Sunderland plunged directly into the questioning.

'You'll forgive my directness, sir, but I do need to get to the bottom of all this as swiftly as I can. I have a witness who says she saw you . . .' he flipped ostentatiously through his notebook, '. . . "hanging about in the corridor outside the library". She can't remember when, but perhaps you can?'

Mr Richman laughed. 'I suppose it did look like I was just hanging about, yes. I was waiting for someone.'

'Who, sir? And when?'

'I was waiting for Wallace. I don't know the precise time, there are so damn few clocks in this place. But it was during our break.'

'. . . "during the break",' said the inspector, making a careful note. 'And did you meet Mr Holloway?'

'No, he never turned up. And now I know why.'

'Perhaps, sir. Did you look for him at all?'

'No, we were to meet in the corridor. I didn't want to go wandering off in case I missed him.'

'And you didn't think to look in the library? That's where he told you he was going.'

'That's what he told the others, Inspector. I knew where he was going – he was going to the corridor to meet me.'

'I see, sir. Did you see or hear anything else?'

'No, there was the usual hubbub of a party, I saw that servant girl—'

'Rose, sir,' interrupted the inspector.

'Really?' I blurted in surprise. 'Good for her. I'm glad she escaped from the kitchen to see a bit of the party.'

'Lucky girl,' said Mr Richman unenthusiastically. 'There were a few others but I was keen to get my meeting over with and get back to work so I didn't really pay much attention.'

'What was your meeting about, sir?' asked the inspector.

'Band business, I expect. He didn't say. Just said he needed to speak to me in private. Probably after a rise if I know Wallace.'

'How long did you wait for him?'

'Again, Inspector, I have no idea. No clocks.'

'Quite so, sir. But you eventually went back to the party and played your "second set", I believe you call it.'

Mr Richman smiled. 'Our second set, yes. Then off for a night-cap and an early night.'

'Early night, sir?'

'We usually turn in about six in the morning, Inspector. We entertain people at night for the most part.'

'Indeed you do, sir, one forgets that others lead such different lives.'

'Were you and Mr Holloway friends?' asked Lady Hardcastle.

'Friends, my lady?' said Mr Richman. 'We got on well, if that's what you mean. He'd been with the band a few years and we're a small group. It wouldn't work if we didn't get on.'

'Of course,' she said. 'But what I meant was were you close friends, or just colleagues?'

'I'd say we were friends, yes.'

'And did you have anything to do with one another outside your work?' she persisted.

'What do you mean?' said Mr Richman. 'We had a drink now and again, maybe met for a meal or two. But we work quite a lot, Lady Hardcastle, we spent a lot of time together.'

'You had no other interests outside your work, then? No shared business interests?'

'I'm sure I have no idea what you're on about,' he said blankly. 'What manner of business do you imagine we'd have time for?'

Lady Hardcastle smiled. 'Forgive me, Mr Richman, my mind wanders sometimes. I was just trying to find out a little more about Mr Holloway.'

'You saw him outside the village hall with me yesterday,' he said. 'He was a thoroughly decent chap, that's all you really need to know. An excellent musician, a good friend, and a proper gentleman. Not a gentleman as you'd know them, my lady – he came from the same back streets as the rest of us – but he was a proper gentleman. I shall miss him.'

'Of course, Mr Richman. Forgive me for intruding on your grief.'

He nodded sadly.

'I've been asking everyone to remain at the house until this matter is resolved, sir,' said the inspector, wrapping up the interview. 'I trust that won't be an inconvenience.'

Mr Richman took a look round the library. 'The place could do with decorating,' he said. 'But I suppose I could slum it for a while.'

'Thank you for your patience, sir. I'll send for you if I think of anything else I need to ask.'

Mr Richman stood. 'Thank you, Inspector.' He left quietly.

'Do you have something on your mind, my lady?' asked the inspector.

'Just probing, Inspector. I was trying to find out if he and Holloway were up to anything else. Something illicit, perhaps. Did I spoil things for you?'

'Probably not, my lady,' he said. 'It's not the way I should have chosen to play it, but it was illuminating to see him so rattled when you asked him. Perhaps they were up to something after all.' He consulted his notebook. 'Let me see now . . . whom shall we see next? Ah, yes, Mr Clifford Haddock. Let's see what happens when we get him on the hook.'

'It's certainly the plaice for it,' I said.

'Could we just get on with it,' said Lady Hardcastle wearily.

'I . . . er . . . oh, oh, I shall salmon him at once.' I left in a hurry.

I found Mr Haddock with Sir Hector in a corridor towards the rear of the house. He was keenly examining what I thought was a rather revolting clock, which sat atop an ornate Chinese cabinet.

'Ah, now then, Sir Hector,' the dealer was saying, 'this is a lovely piece. To be honest I'd only give you a few bob for the cabinet – reproduction, you see – but this clock is a very handsome piece indeed. Eighteenth-century French. I'm sure I could find you a buyer for this one, yes, indeed.'

Sir Hector noticed my approach and rolled his eyes at the dealer's continuing prattle. He seized the opportunity to interrupt. 'Yes, m'dear? Is there something we can do for you?'

'Sorry to interrupt, Sir Hector,' I said deferentially. 'But Inspector Sunderland would like a word with Mr Haddock.'

'Good lord,' said Haddock. 'My turn for the Spanish Inquisition, eh?'

'In the dining room, please, sir,' I said.

'Well, I'd better not keep the Old Bill waiting, eh?' he said. 'This way?'

'Yes, sir, I'll take you.'

He set off in the direction I had come from and I turned to follow, but Sir Hector grabbed my sleeve.

'Something fishy about that chap,' he said. 'Oh, I say. "Fishy". Well done, Hector. You heard what he was saying about m'whatnots? Completely the wrong way round. The cabinet's the genuine article – picked it up in Shanghai in fifty-eight – and the clock's a cheap imitation made by a chap from Bournemouth. The memsahib can't abide clocks. Would never let me spend real money on one. Either this Haddock chap hasn't got a clue or he's trying to cheat a chap, what?'

'I wouldn't rule out either one at this stage, Sir Hector,' I said.

'Fancy yourself as a bit of a detective, too, eh? The memsahib told me what she's got you two up to.'

'Something like that, sir. That and the fact that he's an oily little tick.'

He laughed a delighted laugh. 'Nail on the head, m'dear. Oily tick indeed. You'd better catch him up before he pilfers anything, what?' He laughed again and waved me on my way.

I hurried along the corridor and caught up with Haddock just as he was passing the dining room door.

'This way, sir,' I said, opening the door for him. He doubled back and entered the room.

'Ah, Mr Haddock, I presume,' said the inspector as I closed the door behind me. 'I'm Inspector Sunderland and this is Lady Hardcastle.'

'Pleased to meet you, I'm sure,' said Haddock. 'And a pleasure to meet you again, Lady Hardcastle. We had all too brief a time together last evening. I should have liked to have got more acquainted. Sir Hector tells me you're a widow. It's a shame for such a beautiful lady to be all alone.'

Lady Hardcastle nodded a greeting but made no further response.

'Take a seat, please, Mr Haddock,' said the inspector.

He did as he was asked.

'Well, then, Inspector,' he said. 'How can I help you?'

'I'm sure you're more than well aware of what happened here last evening,' said the inspector. 'So I shan't bore you by restating the details. As you can no doubt imagine, we're anxious to try to build a picture of the events surrounding Mr Holloway's death. I gather you're a guest of Sir Hector?'

'Yes,' he said, with a smarmy smile. 'He invited me down to appraise some of his *objets d'art*. I believe he's looking to sell a few pieces.'

'And since you were here anyway, you were invited to the engagement party.'

'Yes, that is correct.'

'How did you come to be first introduced to Sir Hector?'

'Through a mutual acquaintance.'

'Who might that be, if you don't mind my asking?'

'Mr Roland Richman. He knows Miss Clarissa. The bride-to-be.'

'So you know Mr Richman?'

'Yes,' said Haddock. 'We bump into each other from time to time in London. I'm quite a devotee of this new American music so we frequent some of the same nightclubs.'

'I see, sir, I see. And were you at the party all evening?'

'I was, Inspector, yes.'

'Mr Holloway was last seen alive when he left the stage during the band's break at around ten o'clock. Did you see him leave the ballroom?'

'Not as such. They finished "The Richman Rag" and then they all got down from that little dais they were playing on. I went to have a word with them all to tell them how well they were playing but he wasn't there. I suppose he must have left the room before I could get to them.'

'I see, sir. Did you notice anyone else missing?'

'It was a crowded party, Inspector. People were coming and going all the time.'

'So everyone has been saying. Did you come and go at all, sir?'

'I . . . er . . . I left the room to . . .' He looked around the room at Lady Hardcastle and me. 'To . . . er . . . you know . . .'

'Use the facilities, sir?'

'Just that, Inspector.'

'During the break?'

'Yes. It seemed as good a time as any. It meant I'd not miss anything.'

'And did you notice anything out of the ordinary while you were wandering about the house?'

'I didn't "wander", Inspector. I went straight to the . . . er . . . you know . . . and came straight back.'

'And you were there the rest of the evening?'

'Yes. Sylvia usually starts the second set with "I Can't Get Enough of You" and that just gets me hooked for the rest of the night.'

'I see, sir. And can you remember seeing or hearing anything out of the ordinary at all?'

'Not at all, Inspector, no. As I say, it was quite a lively party and what with the wonderful music and the beautiful ladies—' He leered at Lady Hardcastle again. 'I was quite distracted.'

Inspector Sunderland finished making his notes. 'Thank you, sir, you've been most helpful. I take it you're staying at The Grange for a few more days?'

'I've been invited till the weekend, yes.'

'Very good, sir. If I need to ask you any further questions, I shall send for you.'

'Right you are, Inspector. So may I go?'

'You may indeed, sir. Thank you again for your time.'

'Think nothing of it,' said Haddock, and left the room, closing the door behind him.

Inspector Sunderland made a few more notes and then looked up. 'What did you make of that, my lady?' he asked.

'Aside from his being an oily tick, you mean?' she said, disdainfully.

'I called him that a few minutes ago,' I said with a grin.

'To his face, miss?' said the inspector.

'No, Inspector, though it shan't be long before I do. I found him with Sir Hector, talking about some furniture outside the library. Sir Hector buttonholed me as Haddock set off for the library. Apparently, Sir Hector isn't impressed with Haddock's knowledge of antiques and wondered if he's a fraud or a swindler.'

'Probably a little of both would be my guess,' said the inspector. 'I'll be wiring Scotland Yard to see if they have anything on him.'

'And that was when I passed my opinion of Haddock.'

'What was Sir Hector's reaction?' he said.

'He laughed, of course.'

'Yes, I suppose he would. Not the sort of thing he expected a respectable lady's maid to be saying, I shouldn't suppose.'

'I usually get a free pass on that sort of thing, Inspector. I find that as long as one is polite and attentive to one's duties, one can get away with quite a lot. Especially with someone as obviously mischievous as Sir Hector. I think he likes a laugh.'

The inspector smiled. 'I should imagine he does, miss, yes.'

Lady Hardcastle had a pensive look about her as she examined the links forming on the crime board. 'One does try hard not to be a snob,' she said, 'but he really is a frightful little man. I'm reassured to know that Sir Hector has seen through him.' She drew a dashed line on the board connecting Haddock to the library. 'By his own admission he was out of the room when the murder might have been committed.'

'He's known to Richman, too,' said the inspector. 'That might lead us somewhere. He was lurking about during that time, as well.'

He took a handsome pocket watch from his waistcoat and glanced at it.

'I imagine this is the sort of place that serves tea at four o'clock,' he said.

'On the dot,' said Lady Hardcastle. 'And if I know Sir Hector, he'll still call it "tiffin".'

The inspector sighed. 'It's another world. And that means that most of the house guests will be occupied.' He consulted his notes. 'Let's see if we can find someone else from the band, then. How about the bass player, Mr Bartholomew Dunn?'

'Why not indeed?' said Lady Hardcastle. 'Do the honours, Flo, would you, dear?'

I got up and went in search of Mr Dunn.

I found Dunn at the foot of the servants' staircase chatting up Dora, the housemaid. A man with his good looks would never have trouble chatting anyone up, I shouldn't wonder. His clothes were very natty – the latest American fashion, I guessed.

Dora was giggling coquettishly when I breezed up.

'Afternoon, chaps,' I said. 'How are we all getting along?'

Dora glared at me. 'We were getting along just fine, thank you.'

'Glad to hear it. Mr Dunn? Inspector Sunderland would like a word with you in the dining room if you can spare him a few moments.'

Dora's look suggested that she had much more entertaining ideas for Dunn's next few moments and that if I were to fall down dead there and then, she'd not waste even one of those precious moments mourning my parting. Dunn, though, was evidently a more pragmatic man who recognized that a summons from the police, even one expressed with such casual politeness, couldn't be ignored.

He tenderly kissed Dora's cheek. He seemed confident that he would be able to reignite her passions as soon as he'd finished with this Inspector Sunderland.

'I'll find you the instant I've finished with him,' he whispered.

Dora looked at me again, a smug grin replacing the angry glare. 'You'd better,' she said, and set off upstairs.

He watched her go and then turned to look at me. 'The dining room, you say? Would you be a poppet and show me the way? I'm new round here.'

'New round here, but pretty experienced everywhere else, from the look of things,' I said. 'Follow me.'

He grinned and I led him through the house to the dining room.

He gave us much the same account of the evening as had Richman and Haddock. He seemed to be quite a sociable sort of a chap, though, and Inspector Sunderland decided to exploit this as he moved onto more personal matters.

'Tell me a little more about the band, Mr Dunn. Paint me a picture of the characters.'

'Blimey, really? Well, there's Rolie, of course, Roland Richman, our beloved leader. He's a pretty decent musician as it happens, and he's got very strong ideas about where he wants the band to go. Ambitious, you know? He's quite a sharp businessman, too, for a musician. We never lack for work and we always seem to get paid. I've been in plenty of bands where neither of those were true. Then there was Ed. Nice chap. Easygoing, if a little easily led. Beautiful tone to his playing, too. Trumpets can be a bit brash in the wrong hands, but he had a delicate touch. He could make it cry if he wanted to. We used to have a clarinet player, but there was a falling out and it turned out we didn't need him anyway – Ed covered that side of things beautifully. We missed him in the second set. I suppose we'll be missing him for always now.' He lapsed into silence.

'You seem very fond of him,' said Lady Hardcastle.

'I'm fond of them all, my love,' he said. 'Skins is quite a lad.'

'Mr Maloney?' asked the inspector.

'The very same. We work together most closely; the "rhythm section" they call bass and drums. He's tight. Technically excellent player – I think he trained with one of the big orchestras. But he has a feel for the music, too. He's a dream to work with. Bright lad. Lots of fun. Always the life and soul. It's always a laugh when Skins is around.'

'And what about Miss Montgomery?' asked the inspector.

'Sylvie? Not so sure about her. She's only been with us a couple of months. I've not quite worked her out yet. She seems friendly enough and she sings like an angel. Or like an angel in a brothel . . . beg pardon, ladies. She has this earthy quality to her voice, like . . . well, you know. Not the sort of pure, trained, precise sound you get from most ladies. She's got a voice like smoked honey served on warm bread by a naked serving wench.'

'Steady on, lad,' said the inspector. 'Ladies present.'

'Pish and fiddlesticks,' said Lady Hardcastle. 'Don't be such a fusspot. I'm just sorry I didn't pay more attention while she was singing. It sounds like quite an experience.'

'It is, my love, it certainly is. But as for her character . . . I'm not so sure. I don't think anyone's managed to get close to her. She's quite . . . hard. I've met lads like it, but never girls. The lads have been toughs, you know? Petty villains.'

'Are you saying you think she's a criminal?' asked Lady Hardcastle.

He seemed genuinely taken aback. 'Blimey, no, nothing like that. I was just trying to give you an idea of how she makes me feel.

She can take care of herself, that one, that's for sure. But criminal? Have you seen her?'

'She is rather beautiful,' she said.

'Exactly. How can someone who looks like that be a criminal? Criminals have a look, don't they? It's science. You can tell.'

'So they say,' said the inspector, finally looking up from his notes. 'Well, sir, that was quite comprehensive. Thank you. Is there anything else you think we ought to know? Anyone else you noticed?'

'Not really.'

'What about Clifford Haddock?'

'Old Fishface? What about him?'

'I believe he's known to the band,' said the inspector.

'He's a pal of Rolie's. Seems to be quite keen on the music, so we see him about quite a lot.'

'He's an antiques dealer, I understand.'

Dunn laughed, a genuine, heartfelt laugh. 'Is that what he's been telling you? Well, he's got some neck, I'll give him that.'

'So he's not, then?' said the inspector, looking up once more from his notes.

'He owns a junk shop on the Old Kent Road. "Antiques dealer", tch. Wait till I tell Skins.'

'His story is that he was invited to The Grange to appraise some of Sir Hector's "knick-knacks".'

'Fishface is more likely to nick his knick-knacks, I'd say. Mind you, he wouldn't know a Chippendale Whatnot from a bowl of peonies so he's unlikely to pinch anything of real value except by blind chance.'

'He was introduced to Sir Hector by your Mr Richman,' said the inspector.

'Then they've got something cooked up between them,' said Dunn. 'But appraising Sir Hector's prized possessions won't be part of it, I can tell you that.'

'Well, Mr Dunn, you've given us a lot to think about. I'm asking everyone who is still at The Grange to remain here for the next few days, but I understand from Mr Richman's reaction that that won't be too much of an inconvenience.'

'Indeed no, Inspector.' He gave me a conspiratorial wink. 'I've got a little something to be getting on with right now, in fact.'

'Then please don't let us keep you,' said the inspector. 'Thank you for your time. We'll find you if we need you again.'

And with a cheery wave, Dunn all but bounded out of the room.

'I wonder what he's so eager to be getting on with,' said the inspector when he had gone.

'Her name's Dora,' I said. 'I think he's hoping to comfort her after her shock this morning.'

'Poor thing,' said Lady Hardcastle with a grin. 'I imagine that experiencing something like that would require a lot of comforting.'

'I think I interrupted them before any proper comforting could begin,' I said. 'But from the look of her, I'd say she was more than ready for a serious comforting.'

'Which would account for his haste,' she said. 'Sometimes comforting cannot wait.'

The inspector seemed amused. 'You two have a way about you that I find most refreshing in this rarified world of ballrooms and tiffin. I'm beginning to think it might not be so bad having you about after all.'

'Thank you, Inspector,' said Lady Hardcastle graciously. 'I'm greatly enjoying your company, too.' She consulted her wristwatch. 'I say, it's getting on, isn't it? I really ought to be going or I might get stuck here for dinner. You don't mind if I toddle off, do you, Inspector? You know where I am, after all.'

'By all means, my lady. You may come and go as you please. I presume you're intending to join me tomorrow?'

'If it wouldn't be too much trouble,' she said.

'None at all,' he said. 'You have both proved to be surprisingly apt pupils. I need to attend to a few matters in the city tomorrow morning so I shan't be here until around lunchtime. Perhaps you might use the morning to allow today's events to percolate through your mind? I should be most interested in any thoughts you might have upon the matter.'

'Of course, Inspector. And what are your own thoughts?'

'At the moment, my mind is entirely open. Richman and Haddock are up to something, I'm sure of that. I'm less certain of Miss Montgomery now that we've spoken to Dunn, too – I shall make some more enquiries about her. I'll need to speak to this Skins character at some point. I still have to make up my mind about the cricket team.'

'Oh dear.'

'It sounds like a lot, my lady, but it's nothing to worry about,' he said. 'It's always like this at the beginning of a case.'

'That's a relief,' she said, standing up. 'Come, servant, let us away.'

'Yes, my lady,' I said with a curtsey, then with a friendly bob in the inspector's direction, I followed her out into the passage.

We walked through the hall and out of the front door. Lady Hardcastle had wondered briefly about saying goodbye to her hosts, but since we'd made no progress at all on Lady Farley-Stroud's investigation, she thought it might be just as awkward to seek them out as to slip away without a word.

As it turned out, her deliberations were redundant. As we started on our scrunchy way across the gravel in front of the house we were intercepted by Sir Hector, who had been out walking the dogs.

'What ho, Emily, m'dear. Leaving us already? Won'tcha stay for dinner? Cook's already making such a fuss about having to feed the band and a few unexpected stragglers that another mouth won't hurt. Be honest with you, it would rather amuse me to see if I could make her turn a new shade of purple. She's an angry woman, what? Very angry.'

'It's a lovely invitation, Hector,' she said, 'and ordinarily I'd love to take you up on it, not least for the effect it might have on Mrs Brown. But I fear we have matters to attend to back at the house. Another time, perhaps?'

'I shall insist upon it, m'dear,' he said jovially.

'And we shall see you tomorrow, anyway.'

'Yes, the memsahib told me what you're up to. Appreciate your efforts, m'dear. Really can't afford to lose the Eye, can't afford it at all. Be eternally grateful to you if you could get it back.'

'We shall do what we can, Hector, dear. Every effort.'

'Can't say fairer than that,' he said. 'But listen to me prattlin' on, m'dear. Mustn't hold you up, what?'

'Thank you, Hector, we ought to be on our way. And I'm sure we shall bump into you again tomorrow.'

'Lookin' forward to it, m'dear. Toodle-oo for now.' And with a cheery wave, he was off across the gravel towards the door.

'I wonder how the emerald came to be known as "the Eye",' said Lady Hardcastle as we walked along the grass beside the long, winding drive, enjoying the late afternoon sunshine. 'I must remember to ask Gertie. But what's for dinner?'

I reminded her that Miss Jones had got us some pork chops and that there were still some new potatoes in the larder. As we walked out of the gate and down the hill, she remembered that there was a bottle in the recent delivery from her newly appointed Bristol vintners that would complement such a meal very nicely.

'Howzat, you chump!'

Our walk home took us past the village green where it appeared that cricket practice was well under way.

'How do you know it's not a match?' asked Lady Hardcastle when I commented on it.

'Because there are only nine men on the pitch and three of them are still in their work boots,' I said. 'And I recognize them all from the party so they must all be from the village team.'

'We'll make a detective of you yet.'

The batsman had clearly grown bored of hitting well-placed balls to give his friends some fielding practice. The next ball pitched perfectly for him and he laid into it, sending it sailing towards us as we walked along the boundary. Without thinking, I reached up my left hand and plucked the ball from the air as it passed over my head.

The players jeered their teammate. I might have simply tossed the ball to the young man who was running towards us if the fateful words 'by a little girl' hadn't been carried to us by the evening breeze.

'"Little girl", indeed,' I said indignantly.

'Well, you are quite tiny, dear,' said Lady Hardcastle, laughing at my irritation.

'I'll show them what little girls can do.' With that, I launched the ball back towards the wicket. It bounced just once before flying directly into the wicketkeeper's gloves.

'Nicely done,' said Lady Hardcastle. 'That'll teach 'em.'

I earned a smattering of polite applause from the players, one of whom shouted, 'Thanks, miss!'

The young man who had been on his way to collect the ball was still heading in our direction.

'I say, who's this coming towards us?'

'I should say that was Bill Lovell.'

'What on earth makes you say that?' she said.

'You see our cook Blodwen over on the other side of the green? The attractive, dark-haired girl with her is Daisy the barmaid. Their conversation became much more animated once he set off towards us and there was a good deal of pointing. I should say that means it's Daisy's chap. She wouldn't make so much fuss if it were just one of the other lads.'

'I say, you really are getting rather good at this, aren't you?' she said. As the young man approached she said, 'Mr Lovell, is it?'

He seemed surprised to be recognized. 'It is. Lady Hardcastle?'

'In the flesh. I believe we saw each other at the Farley-Strouds' party but we weren't introduced. How do you do?'

'How do you do, m'lady?' he said. 'Forgive my blundering over here, but I believe I have you to thank for my release from the cells.'

'I should love to be able to claim the credit, Mr Lovell, but I'm afraid I played no part in that.'

'Oh,' he said with slight embarrassment. 'Daisy – Miss Spratt – said you was investigating the murder. She and her pal Blodwen are convinced you're the brainiest lady they've ever heard of. They're sure it was all your doin'. I do beg your pardon.'

'Not at all, not at all. I wish I had helped but it was all Inspector Sunderland's doing.'

'But you are looking into it?'

'We are, yes. We've got ourselves a little sidetracked by all the goings-on up at The Grange, but we found poor Mr Pickering and I'm really rather eager to find out who was responsible. I'm certain the police will get their man, but it can't hurt to make a few discreet enquiries in the meantime.'

'You don't reckon it was the same man, do you?' he said.

'Armstrong and I did consider that,' she said. 'Though we can't see any way that the two men are linked. Can you?'

'Other than the fact that the cricket team was at the pub the night Frank died, and we was all at The Grange the night that musician chap died, no.'

'Are you saying that you suspect one of your teammates, Mr Lovell?'

'I shouldn't like to cast no aspersions on no one,' he said. 'I was falsely accused myself and I shouldn't like it to happen to no one else.'

'And yet . . .?'

'I should say nothing more, m'lady,' he said. 'But I should like to thank you once again for anything you might be doing to help bring justice for Frank. He was a good lad.'

He turned and trotted across the pitch to his teammates. As he did so, a familiar young man broke away from the group in the middle of the pitch.

'We're frightfully popular this evening,' said Lady Hardcastle as Teddy Seddon jogged to meet us.

'Good evening, Lady Hardcastle,' he panted as he arrived.

'Good evening, Mr Seddon,' she replied. 'Was that you we saw bowling a moment ago? It looked most surprising. You seem to bowl just like my late husband did, but the ball went the opposite way.'

He smiled. 'Not many ladies pay much attention to cricket,' he said. 'It's called a googly. The South Africans used it against us in the Test Series last year. I thought I'd give it a try.'

'What a splendid name. I confess, I never paid much attention to the game. I did, however, pay rapt attention to my husband.'

'Ah, of course,' he said, almost as though he was relieved that his preconceptions had been confirmed.

'Did you enjoy the party?' she asked. 'Did I miss too much fun after I left?'

'It was very enjoyable, thank you. And no, you didn't miss much unless you would have enjoyed our ill-advised game of croquet by candlelight.'

'Oh, I say,' she said delightedly. 'What larks.'

'There was certainly more larking than playing,' he said. 'Awful news about that poor musician chap. Clarissa is in a terrible state.'

'Yes, shocking news.'

'She says she saw you about The Grange today. Is that where you've just come from?'

'Why, yes, it is,' she said. 'We're just on our way home.'

'There's an inspector there, she said.'

'Yes, that's right. I'm sure he'll have it all sorted out in no time. There's nothing for her to worry about. We can keep an eye on her for you, though, if that would put your mind at ease.'

'You're very kind,' he said. 'Though I must say I should prefer it if the beast who did it were awaiting his appointment with the hangman.'

'Inspector Sunderland is an able officer. He'll bring the murderer to book.'

'I hope so,' he said. 'Leaving a chap for dead like that. At a girl's engagement party. It's not on. Not on at all.'

An impatient shout from the middle of the pitch reminded young Mr Seddon that his presence was required elsewhere. He bade us good evening and loped back to his practice.

Less than an hour later we were tucking into our meal, which also included peas, which Mr Jenkins had kindly given us from the Farley-Strouds' kitchen garden. We were also sipping at the newly delivered wine, which did, as promised, complement the simple food perfectly.

Between mouthfuls, Lady Hardcastle gestured at the crime board with her knife.

'The thot plickens,' she said.

'It does at that,' I agreed.

'It doesn't help with the Pickering case, though,' she said. 'But I think we ought to let the inspector get on with that one.'

'We've not heard much to help find the missing jewel, either.'

'Maybe, maybe not,' she said thoughtfully. 'The inspector seems to be focused very much on the friendship between Richman and Haddock. We know that Haddock is a great deal less reputable than one might hope of a guest at a society engagement. I'd not be in the least bit surprised to find that he's got something to do with the jewellery theft.'

'He does sound like a right rum 'un,' I said.

'He does, but I can't quite see how he fits into the murder, so I'm not sure that the inspector will pay him much more attention. If he's here to case the gaff or lift a few of the Farley-Strouds' more portable knick-knacks, he's not going to be fishing through the band's instrument cases. And even if he were, and was caught mid-rummage, why the scuffle? Holloway knew him. There might have been stern words but no one would have been smacked on the back of the head and left for dead.'

'It might have been an accident,' I suggested.

'It might, but there's still no real reason for him to be in there; the gem was in Gertie and Hector's bedroom.'

'Would he have known that? Something like that is more likely to be on display in a drawing room or library, somewhere it might be admired by guests.'

'Good point,' she said.

'Why do we not think the culprit has already done a bunk?'

'I've been thinking about that one,' she said, now gesticulating with a small potato on the end of her fork. 'All the guests were friends and family. I'm rather of the opinion that we can safely rule out the assorted aunts and uncles. One should never overlook staff, but they've all been there a while as far as I can make out and they all seem rather loyal. Clarissa's London friends might be suspects, so we'll keep an eye on them. Teddy's friends on the cricket team seem like a rowdy lot, but they're all local lads. I can't imagine any of them knowing what to do with a huge emerald, even if they did manage to pinch it. Still, we shouldn't discount them. But my money's still on the band. There's something about that Richman that I don't trust. Not at all. I wouldn't put it past him to pinch the sparkle and pass it on to his pal the fence.'

'"Sparkle", my lady? "Fence"? Half a day on the job and you're already picking up the underworld argot.'

'One never knows when one might need to blend in with the crib-crackers, filchers and buzlocks.'

'And, of course, it's only your vocabulary that might make it difficult to blend in.'

'Of course. I am a social chameleon. I can blend in anywhere.'

'Do you remember we saw a chameleon in that menagerie in Brussels? I only saw it turn black. I think their powers of blending in, like your own, might be a trifle exaggerated.'

'Pfft,' she said. 'I can mix with commoners and kings. Did I tell you I met the king?'

'I was there, my lady.'

'So you were, so you were. But enough of thieves and bludgeoners, what say we clear our minds completely and indulge in some of the finer things in life. I seem to be in the mood for some ragtime. Fetch your banjo. We shall drink cognac and syncopate the night away.'

11

I was missing my kitchen a little so I had prevailed upon young Blodwen Jones to allow me some space to make one of my favourites, a ham pie. It was pleasant work and she and I chatted amiably as we both went about our business, trying hard not to get in each other's way.

'You're the talk of the village, you are,' she said as she chopped an onion for the dish she was preparing for our evening meal.

'Me?' I said.

'You and the mistress both. They says you're investigating two murders now.'

I smiled. 'Oh, yes, we're doing that.'

'And Daisy says she heard it from her dad who heard it from Rose in the kitchen at The Grange who heard it from Maude Denton, that you knows how to kill a man with your bare hands.'

And now I frowned. 'Ah, yes, I'm afraid that's also true. Not that I've had to do such a thing for quite a few years now, of course. But one learns a few tricks in the course of a busy life.'

She goggled. 'How'd you learn to do somethin' like that?'

'In the late-nineties, Lady Hardcastle and I were . . . "stranded", I suppose you might say, in China.'

'Crikey! What was you doin' there?'

'Lady Hardcastle's husband, Sir Roderick, was posted there. Foreign Office.'

'Well, I never!' she said. 'This is the furthest I've ever been from home, right here. China, eh.'

'It was all rather a pleasant adventure until Sir Roderick was murdered and we had to flee for our lives.'

'No!' she said. 'You never!'

'On my honour,' I said. 'It took us more than a year to get to Burma. We made do as best we could but we had some help along the way from a young Shaolin monk. He was the one who taught me some of his fighting skills.'

She goggled again. 'Here, I don't suppose you could teach me some of them tricks. Might come in handy down the pub on a Saturday night. Specially during the cricket season. Them lads—'

'Boisterous lot, are they?'

'I should say so. Course you knows all about what happened two weeks back, don't you? You spoke to Daisy about it, didn't you?'

'I did, yes. You and Daisy are close, aren't you?'

'My best pal, I should say. Her dad's the local butcher, you know.'

I puzzled briefly over how butchery and friendship might be connected, but I decided not to pursue it. Instead I said, 'She seemed very upset that her Bill had been arrested.'

'Course she was. Bill Lovell's a lovely bloke. Wouldn't hurt a fly.'

'So I gather,' I said. 'But you can see why Inspector Sunderland might have suspected him. He did threaten Mr Pickering, after all.'

'But we all says that, don't we? We all says, "I'm gonna bloomin' well kill you", but we none of us does it, do we?'

'You have a point, certainly.'

'And anyway, it couldn't have been Bill 'cause he has a whatcha-macallit . . . sounds like the bloke with the forty thieves . . .'

'An alibi?' I suggested.

'That's it. He went straight round Daisy's house and was shoutin' up at her window. He was there ages, Daisy's ma says. Daisy come back from work and he tried to speak to her, but her ma tells him to sling his hook. But he never, he stands out there like a lost puppy or somethin'. Daisy reckons her ma was all set to chuck a pail of water over him to make him go away. She reckons it was half past midnight by the time he gave up and went home.'

'It's good that he can prove where he was, but it might not be enough for the police – we've no idea exactly when Mr Pickering died.'

She looked briefly forlorn, but then brightened suddenly. 'But you can prove it, can't you? You can solve it, you and Lady Hardcastle.'

'Well, I—'

'Course you can. I keeps tellin' Daisy how clever you are.'

'Please don't let poor Daisy pin all her hopes on us. We'll do our best, but—'

She looked so forlorn. 'Please try. For me and Daisy.'

What could I say? I squeezed her arm and we carried on with our cooking.

Edna interrupted our early lunch in the garden to tell us that Constable Hancock was at the door. I hurried in to find him still standing on the doorstep.

'Why, Constable Hancock,' I said with a smile, 'what a pleasant surprise. I trust we find you well?'

'Passing well, miss,' he replied, touching the brim of his helmet with his right index finger. 'I wonder if I might have a word with Lady Hardcastle.'

She had arrived silently at my shoulder. 'You may have whole sentences, my dear constable,' she said, as I opened the door wider to allow him in. 'Do come inside and tell us your news.'

He took off his helmet and placed it on the hall table.

'Tea, Constable?' she said, genially. 'We were just finishing lunch. Perhaps you'd care to join us in the garden?'

'That would be most agreeable, m'lady,' he said, and Lady Hardcastle led him out to the garden while I nipped to the kitchen to ask Miss Jones to prepare a pot of tea for us all.

By the time I arrived back in the garden, the constable had made himself comfortable.

'I just wanted to keep you up to date with the developments in the Pickering case,' he said. 'Seeing as how you've been involved, like.'

'That's very thoughtful of you, Constable, thank you,' said Lady Hardcastle. 'Has anything new turned up?'

'Well, the coroner's court reconvened this morning, m'lady. The police surgeon's evidence showed that Mr Pickering had been strangled first with something broad and soft, perhaps a scarf, and that the body had only then been hung up by the rope we found. Based on Dr Fitzsimmons's measurements – whatever they might be – they put the time of death at around midnight. I'm still not quite certain how they knows that.'

'Body temperature and the ambient temperature at the scene,' Lady Hardcastle interrupted. 'The body cools at a known rate once a person is dead so it's possible to estimate how long ago that was. Then there's rigor mortis, of course, but that doesn't set in for about twelve hours. Since we found him the following morning, that wouldn't have helped.'

Constable Hancock seemed impressed. 'Tch, the things you know, m'lady. Anyway, they weighed all that up and brought a verdict of wilful murder and impressed upon Inspector Sunderland to redouble his efforts to track down the perpetrator.'

'Poor Inspector Sunderland,' said Lady Hardcastle. 'As if he doesn't have enough on his plate. Did he give any indication of what he might be doing next?'

The constable looked puzzled. 'I should say you're better placed to find that out than I, m'lady. He'd not confide that sort of information in the likes of me. I knows as how there's some down there at Bristol still trying to build a case against Bill Lovell, though. I heard that from a pal of mine at the police headquarters in Bristol.'

'Oh,' I said. 'That will never do.'

Again the constable's face betrayed his astonishment. 'Will it not, miss?' he said. 'And why's that?'

'I was just speaking to our cook, Blodwen Jones. It appears that Bill Lovell has an alibi.' I recounted the conversation I'd had with Miss Jones.

'Well, I dare say the CID boys knows what they're doin',' said Constable Hancock earnestly. 'Clever chaps down at HQ. But I s'pose I ought to let them know about lovesick Lovell.' He stood. 'I'd best be on my way. Thank you for the tea, m'lady.'

'Not at all, Constable. Thank you so much for keeping us informed – it really is above and beyond. Armstrong will show you out.'

Lady Hardcastle was no longer in the garden by the time I shut the door, but I quickly tracked her down to the dining room, examining her crime board.

'You're not going to leave this one alone, my lady, are you?'

'No, dear, I'm not. It must be possible to work it all out.'

'But Inspector Sunderland can do that.'

'Yes, I'm sure he can. I suspect that the inquest was among the "few matters" that he had to attend to in the city this morning. But he's going to be busy with the murder at The Grange for a while, isn't he? And while he's doing that, the trail goes colder and colder. I'm sure we can help things along a bit.'

'How, my lady?' I said, sitting on one of the dining chairs and staring at the crime board.

'We can draw up the schedule of events, for a start. No, that's no good, that's a hopelessly inadequate term. We need something snappier . . . I know: "time line". We need to draw a time line just as we would on a graph and plot the events. I'm sure it would help.'

I had no real idea whether it would help or not, but as she worked, drawing her line on the blackboard and marking the movements and events we knew of, it did start to make sense.

'Right then,' she said. 'Let's see what we have now. We know that Frank Pickering, Bill Lovell and Arthur Tressle were all at the Dog and Duck on the night of the murder.'

'Along with the rest of the cricket team, my lady.'

'Indeed. We know little of their actions, though. What we do know is that Pickering had rows with Lovell and Tressle in turn. Lovell said he'd see him hanged and Tressle said he'd never let him "do it", whatever "doing it" might entail.'

'Old Joe was certain it was about Pickering taking over control of the cricket club,' I said.

'We shall assume he's right for the time being. Pickering left the pub just before eleven, followed soon after by Lovell. Tressle stayed until about a quarter past, and then he, too, left.'

'He was the last one out,' I said.

'Just so,' she said. 'And with him gone, Joe sent Daisy home and locked up.'

'Then Daisy walked home where she found Lovell waiting to talk to her,' I said. 'He'd been there for a while so he probably went straight there from the pub. He stayed in the street until half past midnight, according to Blodwen.'

Lady Hardcastle wrote quickly. 'Meanwhile, Arthur Tressle's whereabouts are unknown until he's discovered in the cricket pavilion the next morning sporting a hangover and in possession of a stolen handcart.'

'It seems that someone ought to speak to Arthur Tressle. At the very least he's a key witness.'

'He very much is. We ought to get down to the police station. If Constable Hancock is going to telephone the inspector with the new information about Lovell's alibi, he can tell him he ought to speak to Arthur Tressle, too.'

It took us a few minutes to ready ourselves for the short walk into the village.

We arrived at the little cottage that served as our local police station just as Constable Hancock was about to set off on his bicycle.

'Good day again, ladies,' he said. 'Is there anything I can do for you?'

'Have you spoken to Inspector Sunderland yet?' asked Lady Hardcastle.

'I left a message with the desk sergeant at the Bridewell,' he replied. 'Seems he was unavailable. May I ask why?'

'We had a little cogitate,' she said, 'and we think he ought to speak to Arthur Tressle. He's an important witness.'

'I dare say the inspector will fathom that for hisself,' said the constable. 'We don't just appoint any old duffer to the CID, you know.'

'Indeed, no. Perhaps we could save him a job, though, and speak to Mr Tressle ourselves. Where in the village does he live?'

Hancock chuckled. 'He don't live in the village, m'lady. He lives down in Bristol.'

'Bristol?' she exclaimed. 'Doesn't anyone involved in all this actually live here? I thought he played for the local cricket team.'

'That he does, m'lady. He grew up round here, went to the village school over Woodworthy, but soon as he got hisself a job he moved down to the city. Been down there near ten years. He comes up here for cricket matches. Loyal to his old club, see. It was unusual for him to be in the village on a week night but they had their special club meeting or whatever it was.'

'Do you have his address?' she asked.

'I'm not sure that would be at all proper, my lady. If you'll take my advice, you should go back home and wait for the official police to do their job. I'll pass on your message and if Inspector Sunderland needs any further information, I'm sure he'll contact you.'

'You're quite right, Constable, of course. I can be such a fussy old biddy at times, please forgive me my interference.'

'Think nothing of it, m'lady,' he said, swinging his leg over his bicycle saddle. 'It's reassuring to know that the public takes such a keen interest in our work. I must be off, though. Good day to you.'

'And good day to you, too, Constable,' she said. We watched him leave and then she turned to me and said, 'Let's see if we can't wheedle Tressle's address out of Sergeant Dobson', before leading the way inside the police station.

'Good afternoon, m'lady,' said the sergeant, looking up from his paperwork. 'And to you also, Miss Armstrong.'

'Good afternoon, Sergeant,' said Lady Hardcastle. 'How are you this fine day?'

'Passing well, my lady. What can I do for you?'

'I was wondering if you could help me,' she said. 'I've had a letter from Arthur Tressle, you see. He's heard that I've been meddling in a few things and he's asked if I might go and visit him. The trouble is, in his haste he rather scrawled his address and I can't quite make it out. Do you have a record of it anywhere?'

The sergeant grinned. 'I've seen the notes he writes for the cricket club, m'lady. Fellow ought to be a doctor, the state of his handwriting sometimes. I'll have a look – we should have it somewhere.'

He disappeared into a back room while I frowned at Lady Hardcastle.

'What?' she said innocently. 'I thought you'd be pleased that I hadn't lost the old skills.'

Before I could say anything, the sergeant returned with a scrap of paper torn from a notebook.

'Here you are, m'lady,' he said with a smile. 'It's a bit of a jaunt, mind. Other side of the city.'

'Thank you so very much,' said Lady Hardcastle. 'You've saved me from a horrible embarrassment. I shall leave you to your work. Good day to you.'

'Good day, m'lady,' he said, returning to his ledger. 'And to you, Miss Armstrong.'

We stepped out into the June sunshine.

'I've absolutely no idea where this is,' said Lady Hardcastle, showing me the scrap of paper. 'We can take a train into town but I've no idea how we'd proceed from there. What we need is . . . oh, I say, what a dunderhead. Come, tiny servant, I have it.'

'Have what, my lady?' I said. 'Where are we going?'

'To The Grange,' she said, triumphantly. 'We'll get Gertie to lend us her car. And Bert, of course.'

Lady Farley-Stroud had been only too delighted to oblige Lady Hardcastle, saying that it was the least she could do after all we were doing for her. Within just a few minutes Bert was waiting for us on the drive with the engine running.

Bert knew Bristol well and we soon reached the terraced street on the outskirts of the city. There were children playing in the street as we drew up outside the address Hancock had given us and they came rushing over, noisily exclaiming over the gleaming motor car and bombarding poor Bert with a cacophony of questions about it. Fortunately for us, this meant that the lady and her maid in the back were of no interest at all and we slipped quietly up to the front door of the small house.

The door was answered by a small woman of late middle age wearing a housecoat and headscarf.

'Yes?' she said suspiciously. 'What do you want?'

'Is Mr Tressle at home?' asked Lady Hardcastle.

'What if he is?'

'I'd like to speak with him if I may.'

'I don't allow my lodgers no lady visitors. This is a respectable house.' She made to close the door.

Lady Hardcastle took a card from her silver case and handed it to the landlady. 'Please give him my card and tell him I'd like to speak to him. Tell him it's about the Littleton Cotterell Cricket Club.'

The fearsome woman took the card and glanced at it. Her manner changed instantly. 'Oh. Oh, come in your ladyship,' she gushed. 'Cricket club, you say? Please wait in the best parlour and I shall tell Mr Tressle you're here. Can I get you something? Tea, perhaps? Or something a little stronger?' She grinned a gap-toothed grin.

'Thank you, no. You're very kind but I've only recently had some tea. Just fetch Mr Tressle for me, if you please.'

A few moments later, a neatly dressed young man with thinning hair appeared at the door. He squinted through grimy spectacles at the calling card he'd been given.

'Lady Hardcastle?' he said, looking myopically at each of us.

'That's me,' said Lady Hardcastle. 'This is my maid, Armstrong.'

'Pleased to meet you both, I'm sure. Mrs Grout said you'd come about the cricket club. You haven't come about the cricket club, have you?'

'No, Mr Tressle, I haven't. Shall we sit down?'

They each sat on one of the two overstuffed armchairs while I stood beside Lady Hardcastle.

'Is it about . . . you know . . . Frank Pickering?' he asked.

'Yes, it is. You know that Bill Lovell was arrested for his murder?' she said.

'He was released, wasn't he?'

'He was. But you knew he didn't do it, didn't you?'

'I didn't think he could have, no. He doesn't have it in him to kill no one.'

'I've seen enough to know that we all have it in us to kill someone,' she said. 'Some people need more of a push than others, that's all.'

'I dare say.'

'You were the last one to leave the pub the night Pickering was murdered,' she said. 'What did you see?'

'Not so much as you might hope,' he said.

'Can you tell us what happened? All we know is that you and Pickering had a fight in the Dog and Duck. It was about him taking over the cricket club by all accounts. You were heard saying that you'd not let him do it.'

'Who told you we argued about the cricket club? Daisy?'

'I spoke to her,' I said. 'Both she and Joe Arnold were adamant that you'd had a fight.'

'Oh, I didn't say we'd not had a fight,' he chuckled mirthlessly. 'Just not about the club, that's all.'

'About Daisy?' said Lady Hardcastle.

'Her? Certainly not.'

'Then what on earth was the fight about, Mr Tressle?' asked Lady Hardcastle.

'It was a confidential business matter,' he said.

'Business? What business did you and Mr Pickering have?'

He looked slightly disbelieving for a second. 'We worked together, Lady Hardcastle. I'm a clerk at Seddon, Seddon and Seddon.'

'Why,' said Lady Hardcastle with some exasperation, 'did no one think to tell me that before? Armstrong? Did you know?'

'No, my lady,' I said.

'Please tell me,' she said when she had collected herself, 'exactly what happened that evening.'

'We had our meeting at the Dog and Duck and we all got a little drunk,' he began.

'What was the meeting about?' she asked.

'Arrangements for the club's annual supper dance,' he said.

'Give me strength,' she said. 'I'd been given the impression it was some sort of coup.'

He laughed. 'No, nothing like that. With our business concluded, we settled down for a few more convivial drinks. That's when Bill Lovell has a go at Frank.'

'Yes, we heard about that. What next?'

'Then Frank and I has our . . . our private discussion—'

'Your argument.'

'Things did get a little bit heated, yes. Then Frank leaves, and we stays to have one more before home time. We leaves the pub in good time but a couple of the lads gets into some tomfoolery on the green—'

'They stole Mr Arnold's handcart,' interrupted Lady Hardcastle.

'They did, yes. We ended up larking about at the cricket pavilion and by the time I looked at my watch I was too late to get to Chipping Bevington for the last train home, so I kipped down on the dressing room floor. I've done it before and I don't doubt I'll have to do it again.'

'And you didn't see Frank at all?'

'Not after he left the pub, no.'

'What was your argument about, Mr Tressle?' she asked. 'I really must know. If it has anything to do with what happened to him—'

'Look, I can tell you if you think it will help, but when I say it's a confidential business matter, I mean it. It would ruin lives if it got out.'

'We're being bound to plenty of vows of silence at the moment, Mr Tressle. I'm sure we can manage one more. Only as long as it doesn't hinder the official investigation, mind you. If it's germane, then the truth will have to come out. Until that time comes, I give you my word that I shall keep it in the utmost confidence if I possibly can.'

He sighed. 'Very well. Frank was the senior clerk at Seddons and he'd taken it upon himself to review some of our bookkeeping practices. He had it in mind that we could increase profits if we kept better track of our receipts and payments. In his own time he'd been going through the ledgers – stacks of them. Weeks it had taken him.

'And then one day he starts looking anxious and distracted. Really in a state about something. So I asks him what's the matter and he says he can't tell me. It gets worse for a few days until he finally says he needs to talk to someone and would I meet him in a pub down by the Centre after work.

'So I meets him there and we're drinking our beers and he suddenly says, "We're in trouble, Art." And I says, "What do you mean, trouble? What kind of trouble?" And he says, "It's Seddons. I've found something in the books. Someone's embezzling. Hundreds. They've covered their tracks, or they think they have, but nothing adds up. The firm's almost bankrupt, Art." And I says, "Blimey." Well, what else could I say, really? So I says, "Blimey, have you spoken to Mr Seddon about it?" And he says, "No, do you think I ought?" And I says, "Well, you've got to, a'n't you? You've got to say something if we're about to go under." And he just sits there looking like he's been poleaxed. Then he says, "You're right, Art. I'll go round his house tonight. Drink up and I can get the next train." And then off he goes.'

'I take it things didn't go well,' I said. 'I spoke to Mr Langdon recently and he mentioned an acrimonious evening visit.'

'Mr Seddon's butler? Nice bloke. No, it didn't go well. Next day me and Frank found somewhere private to talk and I asked him what had happened. He says, "I told Mr Seddon what I'd found and he just looked at me blank like he didn't know what I was talkin' about. Then he tells me not to repeat my slanders or he'd have me in court 'fore I could whistle. How dare I come to his home in the middle of the evening and start questioning how he runs his business, he says. I said I was only trying to help and he says he can do without my sort of help, thank you very much. Then he tells me to get out. So I got out."'

'Slamming the door as he went, according to Langdon,' I said.

'I shouldn't be surprised if he did. So then I says, "Well, what's next, Frank?" And he says, "I've got to go to the police, a'n't I?" And I says, "But if it all gets out, the firm will be ruined and we'll all be out on our ears." And he says, "And what if it gets out and they find out I knew and didn't say anything. I i'n't going to gaol to cover up for no embezzlers."'

'He didn't go to the police, though. At least not as far as I'm aware,' said Lady Hardcastle.

'I begged him to sleep on it,' said Tressle. 'And to his credit he left it a few days, but when we met up at the Dog and Duck that night he says he's made up his mind and he's going to the police next day. That was the row. I lost my rag, I can't deny it. I knew if it all came out I'd lose my job, and who's going to employ a clerk from a firm that collapsed through embezzlement? I told him not to do it.'

'And threatened him,' said Lady Hardcastle.

'If everyone who ever threatened to kill someone actually went through with it, you'd be pretty lonely, I reckon. Most of the people you'd ever known would have been murdered and the rest hanged for killing them. But then he grabs me by the shoulders and leans in and says all quiet like, "I know who did it. I worked it out. I'm going to give them one last chance to come clean then I'm going to the law and neither you nor they can stop me. Support me, Art," he says. "Back me up. You're my oldest friend there. We've got to do the right thing." Then some of Old Joe's mates step in and pull us apart. So Frank sits down, then that dizzy ninny Daisy comes over to say something to him. He looks at his watch like he's got an appointment and that's the last I saw of him.'

Lady Hardcastle was pensive on the drive back to The Grange. Eventually she spoke.

'It's not Tressle,' she said.

'No, my lady,' I said. 'His story is very convincing.'

'I tend to agree. Convincing, but not frightfully helpful.'

'It gives Teddy Seddon a strong motive,' I suggested. 'He would certainly want to protect his inheritance. He's a member of the cricket club, too. It does seem to revolve around them.'

'Was he at the pub that night?'

'Ah, no, I've not heard his name mentioned,' I said disappointedly. 'Given how keen everyone is to talk about the engagement, I should have thought they'd mention him if he were. Unless everyone's protecting him.'

'To what end?'

'Well, the wedding does seem to be the most exciting thing to have happened in the village for some while. What if they all know it was him and have decided to close ranks and protect him?'

'I love a conspiracy as much as the next girl,' she said. 'But I think we can put that one near the bottom of the list for now.'

'You're right, my lady. Still, it would be helpful to know where Teddy Seddon was that evening.'

'Agreed,' she said. She resumed her scrutiny of the passing countryside.

12

'Ahoy!' called Lady Hardcastle through the open front door of The Grange.

'"Ahoy"?' I said. 'Really?'

'What else should one say, dear?' she said.

'Might one ring the bell?'

'Well, I suppose if one is terribly boring one might ring the bell, but I thought my way would be more fun.'

It had been an unexpectedly strenuous walk to The Grange. It was a journey of around two miles, a distance we should scarcely have noticed had most of those three-and-a-half thousand yards not been uphill. Still, on a bright June afternoon, with the bees buzzing, the birds chirping and the sun still shining on the evil and the good, it wasn't so much of a hardship.

We were saved from having to ring by the arrival of Sir Hector and his unruly spaniels.

'What ho, Emily,' he said from behind us. 'Go on in, why don'tcha? Inspector Doo-dah is in the dining room already.'

'Oh, good afternoon, Hector, dear,' she said. 'Thank you. How's Gertie today?'

'Bearing up, you know. Quite a bit more hopeful now that you're involved.'

'We shall endeavour not to let you both down.'

'Quite so, quite so,' he said. 'Well, must be getting on, these girls need their exercise. Do ring downstairs for coffee, won't you. Late lunch today if you fancy it. Make yourselves comfortable, what?'

'Thank you, Hector. Enjoy your walk, dear.'

We entered through the hall and then into the dining room. Inspector Sunderland was standing at the crime board, apparently comparing the notes there with the notes in his ever present notebook.

'Ah, good afternoon, Lady Hardcastle,' he said, genially. 'Good afternoon, Miss Armstrong.'

'And good afternoon to you, Inspector,' said Lady Hardcastle.

'It's a pleasure to have you back with me, I must say.'

'It is? Well, thank you. I'm a little surprised to hear it, but it's pleasing nonetheless. I confess I was still harbouring concerns that we might be an unwanted imposition.'

He chuckled. 'Not one for beating about the bush, are you, my lady? You have my good lady wife to thank. I told her of my frustration at having you sitting with me yesterday and she told me in no uncertain terms that I should take great care not to behave like . . .' – he consulted his notebook theatrically – '. . . "an insufferable oaf".'

Lady Hardcastle and I both laughed.

'I shall do my utmost to remain as un-oafish as possible,' he said with a small bow.

'You're very charming, Inspector,' said Lady Hardcastle. 'Did your dear wife say anything else?'

'A good many things, my lady, a good many things. But the long and the short of it is that you're doing neither me nor my investigation any harm by your presence and that I should be "glad of a little feminine insight". She has strong views on the importance of women in the world.'

'She sounds like just the sort of woman the world needs more of, Inspector.'

'I count myself as very fortunate to know her,' he said with a fond smile.

'As for "feminine insight", I fear that might be something of a myth. I've certainly not heard of any studies on the subject. We can bring you news of the Pickering murder, though.'

She told him Tressle's story.

'That's most helpful, my lady. I might have to have words with the sergeant about releasing personal information about witnesses to members of the public, mind you.'

'Oh, he was just trying to help a lady with a little difficulty she was having,' said Lady Hardcastle.

'Hmm,' said the inspector. 'It's a shame you didn't think to ask him about Teddy Seddon while you were there.'

'It only occurred to me in the motor car on the way back here,' she said. 'I still had it in the back of my mind that Tressle might be the murderer when we went into town. It wasn't until I was able to think it through on the way back that Armstrong made the Teddy connection.'

'No matter,' he said. 'It gives us another avenue to explore. I shall get my own sergeant to make some enquiries. If he were out this way he would probably have been brought by motor car. I'll get one of the lads to lean on the Seddons' chauffeur, see what he has to say for himself.'

'Thank you, Inspector.'

'What for, my lady?'

'For taking us seriously.'

'I should be a fool not to, I think,' he said.

'You're very kind.'

'Not at all, my lady. Perhaps if you don't think it an impertinence we might take some time to try to get to know each other as we go about today's business. I confess to being more than professionally curious about you both.'

'Then we must do our best to satisfy at least some of that curiosity. But first things first: have you been offered coffee? Tea?'

'No, not a drop. Jenkins showed me in here with his customary cold courtesy and then left me to it.'

'That will never do. Flo, dear, be a pet and ring the bell. Let's see if we can get some coffee and cake.'

I did as I was asked and while we waited for Jenkins to arrive, we sat together at the table.

'Well, now, Inspector,' said Lady Hardcastle. 'What is it that you wish to know?'

'Let me see,' he said, chewing pensively on his ever present, unlit pipe. 'You were born in . . . London?'

'I was indeed,' she said, 'some . . . let me see . . . forty years ago.'

'There's no need to go into personal detail, my lady,' he said quickly. 'I shouldn't wish to embarrass you.'

'Nonsense, Inspector. We make altogether too much fuss about ladies' ages.'

'Your father was influential but not titled – you have your husband's title.'

'Daddy was something high up in the Treasury. So far, so good,' she said.

'Swiss finishing school.'

She laughed. 'I should bally well say not. I was tutored by a succession of increasingly frustrated governesses. My older brother went up to Cambridge and I made such a fuss about wanting to go too that my parents eventually relented. I managed to win a place at Girton where I read Natural Sciences.'

'Cambridge?' he said with approval. 'Very impressive. What else? You wear a wedding ring and you have a wife's title, but you never speak of your husband. A widow?'

'Yes, Roddy died nine years ago.'

'I'm sorry. But your life has been an eventful one. You're adept at getting information from people. I can't decide whether that's a talent or something you've learned through experience.'

'Shall we say a little of both?'

'Interesting,' he said. 'You've travelled. You mentioned that you'd spent time in India. And you weren't just a Raj wife, either. You paid attention to the local ways. You know at least something of Eastern religions, for instance.'

'Well done, Inspector,' she said. 'Yes, I married my university sweetheart and we had lots of adventures together all over the world. Then I employed young Flo here as my maid and the three of us had some more adventures. Roddy was murdered in Shanghai. We fled. We came home. We had yet more adventures in London. We settled in Littleton Cotterell.'

'These "adventures",' said the inspector. 'How is it that a civil servant's daughter came to be having murderous adventures in Shanghai?'

'All in good time, Inspector. You surely don't expect me to give you the fourpenny version all at once. You must allow me to tease it out.'

'Very well, my lady. And what of you, Miss Armstrong? Where are you from?'

We were interrupted by the arrival of the butler and after Lady Hardcastle had asked for a pot of coffee and a few slices of cake, the inspector turned his inquisitive gaze once more upon me.

'Do go on,' he said.

'Ah,' I said. 'Well . . . now . . . you see . . . that's a rather more complicated question.'

'We have a few moments,' he said. 'I want to talk to the drummer this afternoon but I don't suppose he's going anywhere.'

'Well, now, I was born in Cardiff, but I grew up all over the country.'

'Don't tell me,' he said with wry smile, 'your father was a circus performer.'

I looked at him with my eyebrows raised.

'He wasn't,' he said. 'Was he?'

'The Great Coltello. He was a knife thrower. So I grew up in the circus but then when my grandma fell ill, they moved back to Aberdare where my mam was from.'

'He was Italian?'

'No, he was Joe Armstrong from Carlisle. *Il coltello* is Italian for "knife".'

The inspector continued to look dubious. 'It would certainly explain your relaxed attitude to the social niceties,' he said. 'And how did you—'

There was a knock at the door and Jenkins entered with the coffee tray.

'A reprieve from the interrogation,' said the inspector. 'Actually, I think it's time we had a word with Mr Maloney. I'll pour your coffee if you go and find him for me.'

I found Skins sitting on the low wall outside the door that opened from the ballroom. He had his back to the house and was looking out across the grounds and down into the valley of the River Severn. I coughed politely.

'Mr Maloney?' I said.

He turned and smiled. 'Call me Skins, pet, everyone does. What's your name?'

'I'm Armstrong, sir,' I said.

'And that's what your mother calls you, is it?'

'As long as she calls me in time for supper, sir, I don't mind. Inspector Sunderland would like to speak to you.'

'No problem, darlin', you lead the way.' He stood up and I was surprised to see that he was not much taller than me. Whip thin, too. 'But seriously, what do they call you?'

I went back into the ballroom through the open back door and he dutifully followed as I led him through the house towards the dining room.

'Seriously, Mr Skins, they call me Armstrong.'

He chuckled. '"Mr Skins". You are a caution.'

'So I've been told, sir. My name is Florence. My mother calls me Flossie, my friends call me Flo, and you . . . I shall make up my mind about you presently.'

'You can't say fairer than that, Miss Armstrong. I eagerly await the results of your deliberations. But please don't call me "sir" – I ain't nobody's superior. 'Cept when it comes to the drums, then I'm the absolute cake. Second to no man, and all shall bow before me.'

I smiled and we walked on.

'Nice gaff this,' he said, admiring the oak panelling in the passageway. 'Must be nice working here.'

'They tell me it is, sir, but I'm afraid I don't work here.'

'Oh, right,' he said. 'So how come you're dressed up in all the clobber, and running errands for this inspector geezer? The detectives round here have maids or something?'

'Something like that, sir,' I said and opened the dining room door. 'Lady Hardcastle, Inspector Sunderland, this is Mr Maloney.'

I gestured for him to enter and he walked in grinning.

'Call me Skins, guv,' he said, reaching out to shake the inspector's hand. 'Everybody does.' He waved a salute across the table. 'Lady H.,' he said, and sat down before anyone could say anything. I took up my unobtrusive place in the corner.

'Thank you for agreeing to speak to me, Mr Maloney,' said the inspector, pulling out his own chair and sitting down. 'My sympathies on the death of your friend. Were you close to Mr Holloway?'

'Close enough, Inspector,' said Skins. 'We'd been working together for maybe . . . I don't know . . . maybe three years. Travelling and that. You get close to a bloke when you work together like that, don't you?'

'You do, sir, yes. And what about the rest of the band, are you close to them?'

'Again, guv, close enough. Me and Barty get on best, I'd say, and Rolie's all right for a manager, I s'pose. So, yeah, not bad.'

'What about Miss Montgomery?' asked the inspector.

'Odd bird, that one. Sings like a nightingale, mind you.'

'Odd, sir?'

'Oh, you know. Bit stand-offish. Like she's always got something else on her mind. Other fish to fry. Know what I mean?'

'Actually, sir, I think I do, yes. Now then, this engagement-party engagement, sir. It's your normal line of work?'

'Our bread and butter, guv, yes.'

'So it must have been reassuring to know it was coming up.'

'Do what, guv?'

'Good to know there was a nice little earner on the horizon, takes the pressure off paying the bills, eh?'

'It would have been grand, guv, yes. 'Cept this one was sprung on us.'

'Oh?'

'Yeah. Train ticket and "Pack your bags, we're on the six o'clock train tomorrow morning and if you miss it, you're sacked." Not really time to look forward to it.'

'I see, sir. Was that usual?'

'With Rolie, everything's usual. He's a bit of a fly one, our Rolie. Like Sylvie; always got an iron or two in the fire what we don't know about. Usually we know about bookings weeks, even months, in advance, plan them together, like. But every once in a while . . .'

'What happens every once in a while, Mr Maloney?'

'Every once in a while, Inspector, he takes a whim and we scarper off dead quick like.'

'Scarper, sir? Is it like that? Running away?'

'Or running towards. I never know for sure.'

'But you have your suspicions?'

'You can't help but have suspicions, guv.'

'And what were your suspicions this time?'

'Nothing I could make sense of, that's for sure, but I've heard what happened in the library and I've been wondering about a few things.'

'I've been closeted away in here for the most part, sir, so I've not heard the gossip. What have you heard about Mr Holloway?'

'Coshed and left for dead, they told me,' said Skins.

'Indeed, sir, yes. At first we thought it was a robbery.'

'A robbery? Wally?'

'Is that unlikely, sir?' asked the inspector.

'We're musicians, Inspector, only one step out of the gutter – not even that to hear some people talk about us. We ain't got nothing worth nicking.'

'Meaning you no offence, sir, but that was my thought at first. I presumed he'd stumbled upon a burglary and had been walloped for his troubles. But then we discovered that his trumpet case is missing, and that got me thinking,' said the inspector.

'Thinking someone was there to nick his trumpet case, you mean? An empty trumpet case?'

'Again, sir, you leap straight to the heart of it. Was it empty?'

'Was it empty? Hmmm.' Skins sat a moment in thought. 'Here's the thing, Inspector, right? See, I don't like talking out of turn, and I ain't the sort to go dropping no one in it, but there's a chance – I mean, just a chance, right? – that there was something in that case. That's what I mean about my suspicions.'

'What sort of a something, sir?' said the inspector, leaning forwards slightly.

'That's the thing, see, I ain't at all certain. I just heard some things, that's all.'

'What sort of things?'

'Well, see, our Roland, he's a bit of a sly one, like I say. Always got a fiddle going, some scheme or other. So, anyway, last month we was playing these dates in Paris – there's some lovely clubs there, they love a bit of the old ragtime, the Frogs – and one night we was in this little dive in Montmartre. And we're sitting there in the break, you know, me, Barty, Rolie, Wally and Sylvie, all together, like, but round two tables. So we're sipping some rough red wine or other, and this bloke comes over and whispers in Rolie's ear. Then he and Wally gets up and goes to sit at another table and they're chatting away, all secretive like.'

'Could you hear what they were saying?' asked Lady Hardcastle.

Skins turned towards her. 'That's just it, my lady. I could and I couldn't.'

'What do you mean?' she said.

'Well, I could hear snatches of it, like, but I couldn't suss out what they was on about. So this bloke what come over, he's saying, "I know how to get it, and I've got a buyer for it, but I'd never get it past the British Customs." And Rolie says, "Don't worry about that, we can take care of that, can't we, Wally?" all chuckly and smug, like. And Wally, he chuckles back.'

'So you think they were smuggling something?' said the inspector.

'Well, that's what it sounds like, don't it?'

'It does. And if Holloway was involved, that means it could have been in his trumpet case. But why get Holloway involved at all? If Richman was the schemer, why share the proceeds?'

'He doesn't have an instrument case, does he?' said Skins. 'He plays piano, so he don't carry nothing but his music. Our bags sometimes gets checked, but never our instrument cases. Never figured that one out, but that's the way it happens. Rolie must've needed someone with a case he could hide something in.'

'It would have to be something small,' said Lady Hardcastle. 'But that doesn't narrow it down much. It could be anything.'

'Quite so, my lady,' said the inspector. 'Did you get any hint as to what it might be, Mr Maloney?'

'No, nothing. There was more mumbling and then we was back on for the second set.'

'Did you get a good look at this chap that came up to speak to them? Had you ever seen him before?'

'No, like I said, it was a bit of a dive. Dark, with little puddles of light from candles in old wine bottles, you know the sort of thing. Oh, actually, come to think of it, you most probably don't. But anyway, they ain't the sort of places where you can get a good butcher's at someone if he fancies keeping out of sight.'

'What about his accent?' asked Lady Hardcastle. 'Could you tell where he was from?'

'He spoke English. The few words I heard seemed normal, like, like he was comfortable with the language, but a couple of words didn't seem to come natural, like it wasn't his *own* language. Know what I mean? He sounded posh, like, but foreign with it.'

'But no idea what sort of foreign?' asked the inspector.

'Do I look like a language professor, guv?'

'No, sir, but you have a musician's ear. You hear tones and rhythms that the rest of us might miss. It's second nature to you. And you travel. You must have heard many dozens of accents.'

Skins sat a while in contemplation. 'All right, then. So I don't reckon he was English. Nor French – you can tell them, even the ones what's really good at English. He was like . . . I tell you what, there was some sounds like the Lascar sailors up the East End.'

'Indian?'

'Yeah, but not rough like them, more like he was an educated man.'

'Was there anyone else there, Mr Skins?' I said.

'Anyone else?'

'You know, anyone that the Indian gentleman might have spoken to? Anyone else suspicious? Anything that might give us a clue as to what was going on?'

'Oh, I see. No, darling, it was a regular Paris nightclub. Mix of people. Some rough, some smart. Everyone from street toughs to music aficionados to military types and posh ladies and gents out for a bit of adventure.'

'Oh,' I said, disappointedly. 'So no one stood out?'

'Not really, pet, no. Just your average Saturday night crowd in Paris.'

I nodded.

'Thank you, Mr Maloney, this is all most helpful,' said the inspector, as he made yet more notes. 'I appreciate that it's inconvenient, but could I prevail upon you not to leave The Grange for a few more days? I might need to talk to you again.'

'Inconvenient, guv?' said Skins, with a grin. 'Free lodgings, free meals, and fresh air? You're kidding, right?'

'Well, when you put it like that, sir, I suppose you could treat it as a holiday.'

'Too right, guv. Anything else I can do for you?'

'Not for now, sir. Thank you very much for your time.'

'My pleasure, guv.' He stood to leave. 'Lady H., Miss Armstrong.' He bowed. 'Don't forget, I'm still waiting to hear what I can call you.'

I smiled and bowed in return and he left the room.

'What can he call you?' asked Lady Hardcastle after Skins had closed the door.

'I've not decided yet, my lady.'

'Is it a difficult decision?'

'No, my lady, but one can't take such things lightly. There's power in a name.'

'There is, there is,' she said. 'Well, Inspector, what do you make of all that?'

'If he's not spinning us a yarn, it seems Mr Holloway and Mr Richman were up to no good. There seems to have been someone else involved who was . . .' – he consulted his notes – '. . . "posh but foreign" who might have been Indian and might have been paying them to smuggle something small into the country. Or it could be a load of old nonsense. But I should say it's worth talking to Mr Richman again as soon as we can; at the very least he might give the lie to Mr Maloney's tall tales.'

'Would you like me to fetch him, Inspector?' I said, but before he could answer there was a knock at the door.

It was Jenkins.

'Begging your pardon, Inspector, but a telegram has arrived for you.' He presented the telegram on a silver tray.

'Thank you, Jenkins,' said the inspector.

'May I clear the coffee tray, sir?'

'Yes,' said the inspector distractedly, as he read the telegram. 'Please do.'

'Very good, sir,' said Jenkins, and went unobtrusively about his business. 'A late luncheon will be served in half an hour on the terrace, sir, my lady. Shall you be joining us?'

'Would you think me very rude,' said the inspector, looking up from the telegram, 'if I asked for a plate of sandwiches in here? I really do have a lot of paperwork to get through. Notes and suchlike.'

'Of course not, sir. I shall have something sent here for you presently.'

'Thank you, Jenkins.'

'And you, my lady?' said Jenkins.

'Actually, Jenkins, dear, I have one or two errands to run in the village,' said Lady Hardcastle. 'So if the inspector is busy, I shall be slipping out for a while. I can get out of your way for a while, Inspector.'

'Please don't leave on my account, my lady,' he said. 'But if you need to be elsewhere, please do. Shall we reconvene at three?'

'That will be splendid. So, no, Jenkins. Thank you for the kind offer, but I shall be away for an hour or two myself.'

'Very good, my lady. Perhaps coffee when you all return to work?'

'You, Jenkins, are the very model of a modern . . . ummm . . . something or other,' said Lady Hardcastle. 'Whatever would we do without you? That would be splendid. Thank you.'

Jenkins left, beaming.

'What's in the telegram, Inspector? Anything juicy?' she said, as Jenkins closed the door.

'Quite possibly, my lady. Quite possibly very juicy indeed.'

'And . . .? Is that all we get?'

'For now, my lady. I think this afternoon's interviews should prove very nearly conclusive.

'I say,' she said. 'How exciting. But for now, we must away. Servant, neither shilly, nor shally. Let us leave the good officer of the law to his deliberations and hie us to the village.'

And with that, we were gone.

We left the house through the front door and set off for a walk into the village in the warm summer sunshine. The grounds were clean and tidy, but not luxurious, with the same air of faded opulence that clung to the house itself. The whole place was charming, comfortable and welcoming.

The Farley-Strouds couldn't afford to maintain The Grange as once they had, and they should probably have sold up and bought a nice little flat in Bristol or Gloucester. But that would have meant giving up the life they knew and loved, not to mention putting at least a dozen servants out of work, so instead they made do. I decided that I very much liked the competent and capable Lady Farley-Stroud and her charmingly baffled husband. The village was very much enriched by their presence.

'I say, is that a redpoll over there?' said Lady Hardcastle as we walked along the grass beside the drive.

'A what, my lady?'

'That tiny bird. Is it a redpoll, do you think?'

'I couldn't say. But that's definitely Lady Farley-Stroud over there.'

She was dressed in her customary tweeds. The giant sun hat, stout gloves, and a pair of secateurs in her hand indicated that she had been gardening.

'What ho, Gertie,' called Lady Hardcastle. 'The garden is looking lovely.'

'Not entirely my doing,' said Lady Farley-Stroud proudly. 'Gardeners do all the heavy work, but I do take an interest.'

'It shows, dear,' said Lady Hardcastle.

The older lady beamed. 'How goes your investigation?'

'We heard something just now which might help, actually. I have a sneaking suspicion that your jewel is still around here somewhere.'

'Really? Why, that's excellent news. Who has it? When shall you be able to lay your hands on it?'

'We're not quite there yet, dear, but we're definitely closing in. It was frightfully hard not to tell the inspector all about it. Some of the answers he got would have made much more sense if he knew about the emerald, but we had to keep it to ourselves.'

'Thank you, m'dear, I do appreciate it. You'll be able to tell him all about it when you finally track it down. I don't expect he'll be too upset.'

'I do hope not. Yesterday you said there was a story behind the gem. I should love to hear it sometime.'

'Are you in a rush now?' asked Lady Farley-Stroud. 'Come for a walk in the gardens and I'll tell you all about it.'

'Why not. You don't mind, Flo?'

'Not at all, my lady,' I said, and we fell in step with Lady Farley-Stroud as she led us back towards the house and the formal garden at the rear.

'The story,' said Lady Farley-Stroud as we walked, 'begins in Nepal. Did you ever venture north, m'dear? Beautiful country, Nepal. Hector and I spent some time up there. Beautiful. Fascinating, too. It's a very ancient country. Complex history. Very religious. Lots of idols about the place. In the last century, one of the villages presented one of these idols to the new king. As a coronation gift, d'you see? Beautiful thing by all accounts. Cast in gold. Jewels all over it. And the most impressive of all the jewels was an emerald. It sat right in the middle of the idol's forehead. His all-seeing eye. Deepest green. Size of a hen's egg.'

'And that's your gem?' said Lady Hardcastle.

Lady Farley-Stroud laughed. 'Patience, m'dear. All in good time. So they placed the idol in a temple to the north of the capital – Kathmandu, d'you see? – and the people would come from miles around to see it. Once a sacred object, but now just this thing of great beauty. They revered it almost as much as when it had been a symbol of their religion.'

'You paint a vivid picture, dear.'

'I wish I had your gift with words, m'dear. I just stumble through. At first the idol was guarded day and night by the Royal

Guard. Men on it round the clock, d'you see? But no one was going to steal it – the people loved it too much. So after a while they stood the guard down and it sat there on its pedestal, looking out as people came to gawp.'

'Let me guess,' said Lady Hardcastle. 'It was stolen?'

'It was stolen,' said Lady Farley-Stroud. 'Public outcry. Young and old, rich and poor, everyone was horrified. Joined the hunt for the thief. They looked for a month. Several false accusations. But then they caught a gang of Indian thieves at the border. Attempting to smuggle the statue into Bengal. They hanged the gang on the spot. Returned the statue to Kathmandu. It would have ended there, but while it had been missing there'd been some damage. Several of the jewels had been prised loose, including the Emerald Eye. They got most of them back, and replaced the rest with similar stones, but the Eye was never found.'

'So your gem is the Eye?' suggested Lady Hardcastle.

'You're like the girl who skips straight to the last page of the book,' said the older woman. 'Let it unfold, m'dear, let it unfold. So the Eye was missing and the king's agents searched everywhere. They picked up new trails here and there, but every time they got close, it slipped from their grasp. Eventually it came into the possession of Hector's friend, the raja. The raja was an honourable man, though. Very honourable. So he immediately sent word to the king of Nepal that his grandfather's emerald had been found. The king was delighted, but by then he had decided that it was not destined that the Eye should be his and so he gave it to the raja as a birthday gift.'

'I say,' said Lady Hardcastle. 'It really does have a remarkable story, doesn't it?'

'It does, m'dear. And so very famous throughout northern India. And that's why it's so distressing to have lost it. Losing the security for the loan is bad enough, but the Eye is almost . . . how shall I say it . . . almost mystical. I can't bear to think we might have lost it for ever.'

'Not for ever, dear,' said Lady Hardcastle, patting her friend fondly on the arm. 'I'm certain that we're closing in on it. We'll get it back for you.'

'Thank you, Emily. I feel simply awful that I'm making such a fuss about an old stone when a man lost his life in our library, but I just can't help it.'

'Don't worry about that, either. Inspector Sunderland seems like a fine detective. He'll see justice done in no time.'

'I do hope you're right,' said Lady Farley-Stroud. She stood for a while, lost in her thoughts but then suddenly pulled herself together with a little start. 'Sorry, m'dear, you must take no notice. It's all been rather a strain, that's all. And poor Clarissa. It's all quite overshadowed her big news. At least it wasn't the wedding, I suppose.'

To her evident surprise, Lady Hardcastle reached out and hugged her.

'Oh,' she said. 'I say. Thank you, Emily, dear. I . . . I . . . I'd better be getting on, I suppose.' She turned away, sniffing slightly and we took that as our cue to slip discreetly away and resume our walk into the village.

We walked in silence for a while, each lost in our own thoughts about the two cases. The obvious question had occurred to us both.

'It's more than just a little bit probable that the murder and the theft are linked, isn't it, my lady?' I said as we emerged from the end of the lane and saw the village green ahead of us.

'The odds seem to favour it, certainly,' she replied. 'A single serious crime is unlikely, even in these perilous times, but two un-related crimes in the same place . . . jolly near impossible, I'd say.'

'So we ought to tell the inspector about the Eye, don't you think?'

'Eventually, but not yet. I'd be extremely surprised if the murder and the theft had nothing to do with each other, but let's see where his mystery telegram takes him this afternoon. And, before that, I need to send a wire of my own. I want to know a little bit more about that awful army fellow, the buffer from India . . .'

'Captain Summers, my lady?'

'That's the chap. There's something about him that's not quite right.'

'Other than that he's an old-fashioned fool?'

'Old-fashioned, yes. But no one could be that stupid and keep hold of a commission in the modern army. He was so vague about what happened at the party, too.'

'That's no reason to suspect him of anything other than being a bit of a . . . what was it the inspector called him . . . a buffle-head.'

'Let's consider it our contribution to his investigation, then. He's almost certainly winkled out the jewel thieves for us, so why don't we take a look into Summers's background and perhaps eliminate him from suspicion. It would be one suspect fewer to look at, after all.'

I could tell when I was being soft-soaped, and I knew that there was more to her intended investigation than simply a desire to "eliminate him from suspicion". But I also knew her well enough to know that it was worth trusting her intuition, so I decided not to argue.

'Let's stop off at the post office on our way to the pub. I shall wire Harry – he's bound to know someone he can ask to get more on Summers.'

'Right you are, my lady,' I said.

13

With our errands run and a sandwich eaten in the Dog and Duck, we were back in the dining room at The Grange with Inspector Sunderland. To judge from the wreckage of his own lunch on the silver tray on the table, he'd been very well looked after. I wondered if we were going to have trouble keeping him awake after such a handsome meal, but he seemed as alert as ever.

'So, ladies, to business,' he said. 'I'm sorry if I seemed distracted before lunch but I'd had some interesting news and I was keen to get one or two things confirmed before we resumed this afternoon. Sir Hector was good enough to let me use his telephone. I've had confirmation from Scotland Yard and, through them, from our contacts in the *Sûreté* in Paris. It seems that Mr Roland Richman is indeed a known smuggler. He's been picked up a couple of times at Dover with bottles of cognac in his duffel, but never anything more. The French lads were sure he was responsible for moving some diamonds that had come down from Amsterdam last year but nothing was proven.'

'That does seem to square with what Skins told us,' I said.

'It does, miss, yes. But there's more. It seems that acting on information from Customs officers in Marseilles, the *Sûreté* has just picked up one Praveer Sengupta, an English-educated Indian gentleman from Bengal. They have strong evidence against him on a number of smuggling charges.'

'Well, well,' I said. 'So he's "posh but foreign". This is all very encouraging.'

'Very encouraging indeed, miss.'

'What's our next move?' I asked. 'Do we rattle Richman's cage? Thumbscrews and Chinese water torture till he squeals?'

'We know a little about smuggling in the West Country. We're famous for it. As a matter of fact, I'm close to cracking a local outfit – much more efficient than these jokers. I think we'll get more from him if we just sit him down and ask him a few more questions. All calm and polite, like.'

'If you insist,' I said. 'But I know a few ways of hurting him that'll leave no marks if you want.'

He gave me a puzzled frown. 'I'll bear that in mind, miss. But if you could just fetch him without causing him any damage, that'll do for now.'

'Righto, sir,' I said brightly. I turned to Lady Hardcastle. 'He's not nearly as much fun as I thought, you know.'

Once again, Roland Richman was sitting in the dining room at The Grange, but he didn't look nearly so comfortable and self-assured as he had last time.

'Well, then,' he said, almost nervously. 'To what do I owe the pleasure of this second meeting? Has something happened? Do you know who did it?'

'Not quite yet, sir,' said the inspector. 'But a couple of things have come to light which need some clarification.'

'If I can help, Inspector, you know I shall.'

'Thank you, Mr Richman. I wonder what you can tell us about Mr . . .' – he consulted his notebook – 'Mr Praveer Sengupta.'

'Praveer Sengupta,' said Richman thoughtfully. 'Name rings a bell. Indian gentleman, I take it? Have we performed for him? I vaguely recall playing an engagement at a do in Cheltenham with some ex-Raj types. Was that it?'

'Not quite, sir, no. This particular gentleman has just been arrested in Paris. Have you ever been to Paris?'

'More than once, Inspector. But I don't recall—'

'You see, I've been in communication with my opposite number in the *Sûreté* in Paris. I've been told that you met Mr Sengupta in a bar in Montmartre last month.'

I'd been wondering how he was going to reveal what we knew without dropping Skins in it. And without actually lying, too. Clever chap, that Inspector Sunderland.

Richman, meanwhile, didn't seem nearly so delighted.

'Ah,' he said, at last.

'"Ah", indeed. Shall we start again? What business did you conduct with Mr Sengupta?'

'It was some . . . ah . . . some courier work,' said Richman.

'Delivering messages around Paris? Was the music not paying so well?'

'Not as such, Inspector, no. It was more, ah . . .'

'To put you out of your misery just a tiny bit,' said the inspector, 'perhaps I should tell you that I've also been in contact with my colleagues at Scotland Yard. They, in turn, have close contact with His Majesty's Customs to whom you are well known on account of your occasional smuggling exploits. Once again, sir, your dealings with Mr Sengupta?'

'Oh, very well,' said Richman impatiently. 'Sengupta paid me to move a little something.'

'You brought this "little something" into England with you?'

'What? No, he wanted us to take it out to him.'

'And what form did this little something take?' asked Lady Hardcastle.

'Oh, you know, just a little . . . contraband. We don't have it yet so I'm not certain you have any grounds to be asking. As far as I'm aware, "contemplating breaking the law" isn't actually a crime in itself.'

'Don't try to be clever, Mr Richman,' said the inspector.

'I don't have to try, Inspector.'

Both Inspector Sunderland and Lady Hardcastle gave him withering looks.

'You told us before about having arranged a meeting with Mr Holloway. Was it connected with this smuggling?'

'No. But honestly, Inspector, even if it were, I'd be unlikely to say so, now, wouldn't I? Is there anything else I can help you with?'

The inspector thought for a moment. 'Not for now, sir, no. But consider your card marked, Mr Richman. I shall be watching you.'

'I shall get on with some serious quaking in my boots just as soon as I've got my quaking boots on.'

'You do that, sir.'

Smirking, Richman got up and left.

'Sometimes I wish we were still allowed to use more medieval methods,' said the inspector.

'Put him on the rack, you mean?' said Lady Hardcastle.

'That sort of thing, yes.'

'I'm sure Flo's offer still stands if you want him roughed up a bit.'

He chuckled and turned to me. 'Meaning you no offence, miss, but I doubt a little thing like you could do any real harm.'

'I wouldn't be so cocksure, Inspector,' said Lady Hardcastle. 'We spent quite a while in China in the nineties and she picked up a few little tricks. I've seen her take down men twice his size.'

I smiled sweetly.

'Hmm,' he said. 'Still, we have at least confirmed that Richman and Haddock are up to no good. Or at least that they intended to be. I can't yet see how it's connected to the murder of Wallace Holloway, but I'll work it out.'

'Of course you shall. What's your next move?'

'I think we ought to get Fishface back in and see if we can get anything more substantial out of him,' he said. 'Miss Armstrong, would you do the honours, please?'

'Certainly, Inspector. One grilled haddock, coming up.'

I found Mr Haddock on the terrace, playing backgammon with Captain Summers. There were drinks on the table and they seemed to be enjoying themselves.

'Aha,' said Captain Summers, catching sight of me. 'The detective's lady's maid. Don't know what the world's coming to.'

Haddock leered at me. 'What can we do for you, my dear?'

'Inspector Sunderland would like to talk to you, Mr Haddock,' I said.

'What a shame,' he said. 'I was rather hoping you'd come to join us.'

I said nothing and waited for him to rise and follow me.

'Well, Summers, my lad,' he said at length. 'Time and inspectors of police wait for no man. We shall finish our game presently, but for now I have to accompany this delightful girl to the dining room.'

He rose unsteadily to his feet and followed me in through a back door which led through to the ballroom. As we neared the door he caught up with me and put his hand on my behind.

'I'm sure we have time to get a little better acquainted before I see the inspector,' he said. 'What a pretty little thing you *arrgggghhh*.'

There were only two punches and a kick, and quite gentle ones at that. Perhaps it was the throw that did the damage. As I helped him to his feet I said, 'I'm so sorry, Mr Haddock, it's this ballroom floor. Very slippery. I must have lost my balance a little. Are you quite all right?'

He glared at me.

Still grasping his hand I leaned in close and spoke very softly in his ear. 'Please don't touch me again, sir. The floors are quite slippery throughout the house now I come to think about it. Who knows how disastrously I might lose my balance the next time.'

He said nothing for the rest of the short walk to the dining room.

'Ah, Mr Haddock,' said the inspector as we entered. 'Sorry to have to drag you in here once again, but there are still one or two matters to clear up. Oh, I say, you look a bit bedraggled, sir, are you quite all right?'

'Slipped in the ballroom,' he said, glaring at me.

Lady Hardcastle caught the glare and gave me a questioning look of her own. I grinned and she smiled.

'Treacherous things, ballroom floors,' said the inspector, though I think he caught the silent exchange between me and Lady Hard-castle and had his own idea of what might have happened. 'But to business. Would you mind telling us again why you came to The Grange?'

'I came at Sir Hector's invitation to appraise some of his *objets d'art.*'

'And nothing else?'

'I'm sure I don't know what you mean, Inspector.'

'If I were to mention the names Roland Richman and Praveer Sengupta and the illegal movement of goods, would you have a clearer idea of what I might mean?'

'No, Inspector,' he said belligerently. 'Not a clue.'

I took a half-step towards him and he flinched.

'Keep that vicious little harpy away from me.'

'I'd love to,' said the inspector, 'but she doesn't work for me. I've tried to keep her under control, but you know what it's like with women these days. Law unto themselves, they are.'

'Just keep her away from me and I'll tell you what you want to know.'

'Good lad. She's quite reasonable. I'm sure she'll not harm you. At least not while there's anyone watching. So tell us again about your visit to The Grange.'

'It's true that I was invited down here by Sir Hector,' he said. 'But on the day of the party I got a telegram from Richman saying that he was going to be playing and that we should complete our business down here.'

'Your business being . . .?' said the inspector.

'I thought you said you knew,' said Haddock, slyly.

'Indulge me,' said the inspector. 'Let's make sure our stories are congruous, shall we?'

'Of course, Inspector. Why don't you tell me what you already know and I'll fill in anything you're missing.'

The inspector sighed. 'Let's go over your statement concerning events on the evening of the party, then, shall we? You arranged to meet Richman in the interval.'

'I didn't say that.'

'You arranged to meet in the interval, but you didn't show up. Had you already killed Holloway by then? Were you hiding out in case Richman saw Holloway's body and worked out it was you?'

'I . . . what . . .? No! I got delayed, that was all. I went to the . . . er . . . you know. I told you before. When I got back to the library Richman wasn't there.'

'So you just left it at that?'

'No . . . I . . . er . . .'

'You, er, what, sir?'

He sighed. 'I went into the library.'

'And what did you see?'

'Chaos, Inspector. Chaos. The band's things had been torn apart.'

'Did you see Mr Holloway?'

'No. No, I stayed long enough to see what had happened and got out. I wasn't going to hang around and have people think it was me.'

'I see,' said the inspector. 'Did you see anything else?'

He paused. 'I think I heard the far door clicking shut as I came in, but I can't be certain.'

'And it never occurred to you to mention this when we questioned you before?'

'Oh, come on, Inspector. It wouldn't have taken you long to find out my reputation. And then how would it look? I reckoned it would all blow over and I'd be long gone before you figured out who I am and then there'd be no awkward questions and no unpleasantness.'

'I see. Well, if what you say is true, then aside from being a lying little toe-rag, I've got nothing to hold you on. But don't leave The Grange until I say you can. On your way, Haddock.'

'Charming,' said Haddock.

'Don't push your luck, *sir*,' said the inspector.

I shifted my weight slightly and he was out of the door like a startled rat.

Inspector Sunderland sat in one of the dining room chairs, chewing contemplatively on his pipe.

'We're missing something vital,' he said. 'We have a dead body in the library and some smuggling musicians, but I'm jiggered if I can tie the two together. Or even if I need to try. I don't mind telling you, ladies, I'm stumped.'

There was a knock at the door and once again the respectful face of Jenkins peered round. Lady Hardcastle waved him in.

'Come on in, Jenkins,' she said. 'What can we do for you?'

'It's more a matter of what I may do for you, my lady,' he said, proffering his silver tray. 'Another telegram has arrived.'

'Good show!' she said and took the telegram from him.

'Will there be a reply, my lady?'

She read the message, which seemed rather a long one, and a minute passed before she said, 'No, Jenkins, there's no reply. This is everything I needed.'

'Very good, my lady,' he said. 'Tea will be served promptly at four as always. Sir Hector has been enjoying taking tiffin on the terrace. Will you be joining him?'

'Once more I rather fear not, Jenkins. But I wonder if you might do us a service and make discreet efforts to ensure that all the house guests are present. Including the musicians. Would that be acceptable?'

'I shall do my utmost, my lady.'

'Thank you, Jenkins, your help is greatly appreciated, as always.'

'Thank you, my lady. Will that be all?'

'More than enough, thank you.'

'Thank you, my lady,' he said with a bow, and left.

'What's in the telegram, my lady?' asked the inspector.

'Another piece of the puzzle,' she said. 'My brother Harry works in Whitehall. I wired him to see if he knew anyone who might be able to shed any light on one of our witnesses.'

'Oh yes?' he said, sitting up straighter. 'And who might that be?'

'Captain Summers.'

He laughed. 'That fool? What on earth could you learn about him from a brother in Whitehall that you couldn't learn from two minutes in his company? He makes our dog look like Aristotle by comparison.'

'Oh, you have a dog?'

'It's my wife's dog, really. A West Highland terrier. Lovely girl, but a bit small for my preference. I favour a larger dog, myself. But she and my wife adore each other, so what's a fellow to do?'

'Charming,' she said. 'But as for Captain Summers, something he said when we spoke to him. He's back from India and he's desperate to impress a girl – the colonel's daughter, I think he said.'

Inspector Sunderland consulted his notebook. 'Yes,' he said. 'He's hoping to marry in a couple of years but he hasn't asked her yet.'

'Quite so. Now, I'm going to tell you something, and you must promise not to be too cross.'

His eyes narrowed.

'I'm afraid I must also ask you not to report it officially unless you absolutely have to,' she continued.

'It sounds like the sort of thing you ought to tell me with or without such assurances,' he said. 'I'm sure you must realize that obstructing the police in the course of our enquiries is a serious matter.'

'Of course, Inspector, but hear me out and then decide for yourself whether my requests are unreasonable.'

'Very well,' he said.

'I'm not really writing a detective story,' she began. 'I've no talent for that sort of thing. I think that might be more Armstrong's line, to tell the truth.'

'That much I'd gleaned for myself, my lady,' he said. 'You've not spoken about your book, nor asked me any questions about police procedure.'

'The old skills are rusty. One must take care to maintain one's cover story. That was sloppy of me. The truth is that I was asked by Lady Farley-Stroud to investigate a theft of something rather precious. For reasons I shall explain, she didn't want any official involvement. In order that I might find out more about the events of Saturday evening without giving any indication that I was sleuthing, we concocted a story which might get me into your interviews.'

'I see,' he said. 'And what was this "rather precious" something?'
She told him about the Emerald Eye and its history.

'The Eye was famous throughout Bengal where Summers is sta-
tioned, so he's certain to have heard about it. Now, he mentioned
stopping off in Paris on his way here. What if he was in a certain
nightclub with his pal, and overheard Holloway and Richman
talking to this Sengupta chap about an emerald? Could it be the
Emerald Eye? That would impress the colonel's daughter, surely. So
when he's at an engagement party in the house of a family who had
been in India and he recognizes Richman and Holloway, might he
put two and two together and think they're after the emerald? And
what if he goes into the library to see if they've got it? He's interrupted by Holloway while he's ransacking the instrument cases, he
clonks him on the head and then makes off with the jewel leaving
poor Holloway for dead.'

The inspector laughed. 'That's quite the most fanciful story I've
heard for many a year. And what became of the trumpet case?'

'He hid it somewhere.'

'Why?'

'Because . . . oh, I don't know. But this wire from Harry certainly
confirms that Summers is a bounder.'

'We might have to have words about your interference later,
but in truth I appreciate your efforts and your candour – no matter
that it's a little late. But I'm duty bound to say that if we were to
arrest everyone who could satisfactorily be described as "a bounder",
half the government front bench would be sewing mailbags and the
banks in the City of London would be closed for lack of staff.'

'I appreciate that, Inspector,' she said calmly. 'But as you said
to Mr Haddock, "Indulge me". What harm would it do if we were
to search Summers's room while he was at tea?'

'Well, we don't have a search warrant for a start.'

'Nonsense, it's not his house. Hector and Gertie won't mind.'

'Good point,' he said. 'We may as well, then. But if you'll re-turn the favour and indulge me, I think we might search Richman's and Haddock's rooms as well.'

'Very well, Inspector,' she said. 'The band are billeted in the attic, but I don't know where Haddock is staying. We shall have to explore.'

'It shall be an adventure for us then, my lady. Miss Armstrong, will you keep cave for us, please? I'd rather not have to explain myself to any of them if there's nothing there and they catches us poking about.'

'Of course, sir,' I said. 'I shall lurk at the bottom of the stairs and head them off if they look like coming up.'

'Just the job,' he said.

'If I can't deflect them by guile, I'll just knock them unconscious.'

They came back downstairs some minutes later with Inspector Sunderland in the lead and Lady Hardcastle a couple of steps above him, holding the largest emerald I've ever seen and pointing at it with her other hand. Her grin was silly and triumphant, and van-ished immediately when the inspector turned round to see what I was smiling at. It returned as soon as he turned back and I couldn't help but give a little chuckle.

'You found it, then,' I said.

'Wrapped in a sock and stuffed inside one of his dress shoes,' said Lady Hardcastle.

The inspector, though clearly pleased, was trying to main-tain a more professional air. 'If I go and fetch him, Summers will realize that the jig is up and might very well bolt. It shouldn't be a problem but it would be untidy. Miss Armstrong, would you be so kind as to step out onto the terrace and invite the captain to come and have a quiet word with me in the dining room, please.'

'Of course, Inspector,' I said. 'I shall have him with you in a trice.'

I left them to settle into the dining room and hurried out to the terrace where I found Captain Summers sitting next to Clarissa Farley-Stroud. The poor girl was trying her very best to look interested as the empty-headed captain finished off some dreary tale of life in the Raj. I saw a look of relief pass across her face as I leant in and whispered in the captain's ear that Inspector Sunderland wished to see him.

With apologies to the table, he rose and followed me back into the house, along the corridor and into the dining room, where we found Lady Hardcastle and the inspector seated in their usual places at the large dining table. The inspector looked up from his notebook as we entered and casually gestured towards a chair with his pipe, inviting the captain to sit.

'What ho, Inspector,' he said blithely. 'What can I do for you this afternoon? Having any luck with the murder?'

'As a matter of fact,' said the inspector, 'I think we've made some significant progress today, yes.' He held out his hand to Lady Hardcastle, who produced the Eye from under the table. She placed it in his open palm. Summers turned white. 'I wonder if you would be good enough to explain why this rather large emerald should have been hidden in one of your shoes, sir.'

'You've been through my things?' said the captain with an impressive imitation of righteous indignation. 'How dare you, sir! I shall—'

'Please don't embarrass us both with empty threats, Captain Summers,' interrupted the inspector. 'This emerald, a one might say "legendary" jewel known as the Emerald Eye, is the rightful possession of Sir Hector and Lady Farley-Stroud. It was taken from their bedroom some time on Saturday evening during a party held here in the house to celebrate the engagement of their daughter. You know about the party because you were there. You know about the jewel because you stole it. It's my belief that the jewel thief is also responsible for the death of Mr Wallace Holloway and that's the only part of the case that I'm unable to resolve. It will go better for you at the trial if you come clean now and explain exactly what happened.'

Captain Summers sat for a moment in stunned contemplation. 'But I . . .' he began before lapsing once more into confused silence.

'What happened, Summers—'

'*Captain* Summers,' interrupted the captain, still pompously defending his right to be addressed by his rank in spite of his predicament.

'Not for long, Summers,' said the inspector. 'His Majesty's army is keen on murder and theft only in the name of colonial expansion.'

Summers snorted derisively. 'I'm surprised they allow your sort in the police force.'

'My sort?'

'You're one of those socialists, aren't you? Workers' rights and tear down the Empire. I hear that blackguard Keir Hardie wants self-rule for India now. Fools and traitors, the lot of you.'

'We seem somehow to have drifted from the matter in hand,' said the inspector, nodding towards the emerald. 'This matter, in fact, right here in my hand. You stole the emerald from the Farley-Strouds' bedroom, and then what happened? We know that Holloway and Richman were after it, too. Did Holloway challenge you? There was a scuffle? You struck him on the head and ran off?'

The captain was slowly calming down and was starting to think more clearly. 'I can't deny that I had the emerald. I think you've got a bally cheek going through a chap's possessions, but the gem was there and there's nothing I can do about that. And I can't deny that I stole it, but I didn't steal it from the Farley-Strouds' room – frankly I'm insulted that you think I could be so vulgar as to ransack my hosts' room. I took the gem from its hiding place in Holloway's trumpet case but I most certainly did not kill Holloway.'

'Let us for a moment assume that you're telling the truth,' said the inspector. 'What were you doing in the library in the first place? Did you go in to rifle through the band's instrument cases on the off chance that there might be something in there worth pinching?'

The captain sighed. 'I knew it was going to be there. Or at least I strongly suspected and fervently hoped it would be there. I stopped off in Paris on my way here as I told you. Visiting a pal. I overheard some musicians talking to an Indian fellow. They were talking about pinching a jewel from a house in England and smuggling it back out of the country in a trumpet case. When I saw those same musicians here at the party, I thought it might be worth a look to see if they had the stone.'

'It was an opportunist theft, then?' said the inspector.

'Is it stealing if one takes from a thief, Inspector? I didn't steal it from the Farley-Strouds; I just happened to be the one who ended up with the spoils when the music stopped.'

'We'll leave the philosophy to the judge, I think,' said the inspector. 'If you thought the jewel might be in the trumpet case, why did you make such a mess of the other cases?'

'To throw them off the scent a bit. I thought I might be able to make it look more like a random theft than a chap going straight for the gem. Might slow them down. I wasn't thinking too clearly to be honest. It just seemed like a clever thing to do at the time.'

'I see. And what did you do with the trumpet case?'

The captain looked confused. 'I left it there on the floor in the library with the other cases when I hurried out.'

'You hurried out?'

'Yes, I heard the door handle at the other end of the room and thought the band might be coming back, so I hopped it out of the other door.'

'I see. It's just that the trumpet case wasn't there in the morning,' said the inspector.

'Well, I left it in the library. I've been straight with you over this. I didn't steal the gem from the bedroom, I didn't move the trumpet case and I most certainly didn't harm a soul. I can't deny that I had the gem and you must take whatever action you see fit, but I'm innocent of any other offences.'

'We shall let the magistrate decide on that. Captain Roger Summers, I arrest you in the name of the king for the crimes of theft and murder. Anything you say may be taken down in writing and may be used against you at your trial.'

'But . . . I . . .'

'Miss Armstrong, will you be good enough to telephone the station in Littleton Cotterell, please? Present my compliments and ask one of them to come up to The Grange to escort a prisoner back to their cell. We'll arrange for him to be taken to the Bridewell later.'

I went to do as he asked, leaving a deflated Captain Summers staring forlornly at his boots.

It took us quite a while to get away from The Grange. We had hoped to slip away when Constable Hancock arrived to get Captain Summers away. Lady Farley-Stroud, though, had other ideas. She had been so effusively grateful when Lady Hardcastle told her that her emerald had been found that we were trapped for at least another half an hour.

On the way home I added my own congratulations.

'Oh, don't be silly. I made a few leaps in the dark and got one right answer quite by chance, but we haven't solved anything.'

'Perhaps not, my lady, but it was thanks to the power of your deductions that the inspector was persuaded to search Summers's room.'

'Abductions, dear.'

'What?' I said.

'It's abductive reasoning, not deductive. Working from observation to theory is abduction, not deduction.'

'But I thought—'

'Yes, you and so many other people. We know who to blame, of course, and I've written to him more than once care of his publisher, but he takes no notice.'

'Well, I was impressed anyway.'

'Thank you, Flo, you're a poppet. But we still don't know whether Summers is telling the truth. And if he is, then we still have a thief and a murderer to catch.'

'"We", my lady?'

'Oh, surely Inspector Sunderland will let us stay on now that we've proved to be so helpful. It's the least he can do.'

I laughed and we walked home where a delicious meal was awaiting us, courtesy of Miss Jones. All I had to do was cook some vegetables and pour the wine.

14

The early-to-bed life of the country meant that we were both also early to rise, and while that might very well have seen a consequent increase in our levels of health, wealth and wisdom, it did rather mean that we were kicking our heels waiting until it was time to go up to The Grange.

I had left Lady Hardcastle dealing with some urgent correspondence and was just pressing one of her dresses when she appeared at the kitchen door.

'I say, Flo,' she said. 'What with your efforts at the party and your general charm and easygoing nature, do you think your stock is reasonably high below stairs at The Grange at the moment?'

'How do you mean, my lady?'

'Well, if you were to pop up there right now, slip in through the servants' entrance and say you'd been sent on ahead to meet the inspector and me, would they smile and greet you, or would they turn you away?'

'Oh, I see,' I said. 'I imagine I'd get a warmish welcome. Possibly even the offer of a cup of tea and a bun. There's a camaraderie among the serving classes that the likes of you shall never know.'

'It is very much my loss, I feel. If you declined their kind offer and said you'd been asked to wait in the dining room, would they think it odd or out of place?'

'I shouldn't think so, my lady, no.'

'I hoped as much.'

'Is that what you'd like me to do, my lady?'

'No, silly, I'd like you to go snooping. Inspector Sunderland is so stuffy about it – I don't know why he doesn't just turn the place over. But they're used to seeing you about the place and you'd have an excuse to be wandering about above stairs if you were challenged, so I'd like you to have a good old explore. See what you can see. Find what you can find.'

'Oh, what fun,' I said, suddenly rather taken with the idea of some proper detecting. 'May I take your deerstalker and Meerschaum? Perhaps the large magnifying glass?'

She raised an eyebrow. 'Just be as nosy as possible. Look under rugs and into plant pots. Open a few cupboards.'

'What shall I be looking for, my lady?'

'The trumpet case, of course.'

'Righto, then, my lady. I shall discreetly snoop, then meet you and the inspector in the dining room at ten o'clock as though nothing has happened.'

'That's the spirit. Good girl.'

And with that, I hurried off to get my hat and gloves and set off at a brisk pace up the hill to The Grange.

Despite the overcast day, it was nevertheless still a delightful walk. The hedgerows were alive with twittering birds that I was still unable to identify but I was on firmer ground with the mammals. I spotted three rabbits and a squirrel before The Grange hove into view.

I found the gates already open and made my way as quietly as possible round to the servants' entrance at the side of the house. From inside I heard the first signs of life. Mrs Brown was already berating poor Rose and I could just make out the sound of Mr Jenkins's voice as he tried to calm things down.

I poked my head round the kitchen door.

'Morning, all,' I said breezily. 'The door was open, do you mind if I come in?'

Mr Jenkins looked mightily relieved. 'Of course, Miss Armstrong, do come in. To what do we owe the pleasure? Can we offer you some tea?'

Mrs Brown looked as though having to make me a cup of tea would be just about the last straw, so it was fortunate that I had other things to be getting on with.

'Thank you, no, Mr Jenkins, I'm under orders,' I said. 'But perhaps a little later? My mistress is due to arrive in a while to continue the investigation with Inspector Sunderland, but she sent me on ahead to make a few things ready in the dining room. Do you mind awfully? I shall try not to get in the way.'

'Of course, Miss Armstrong. It's never an inconvenience to have you about the place,' he said with a smile. 'The mistress is delighted with your efforts, you know. She's been singing your praises non-stop since you left yesterday. Is there anything we can do to help? The room has been swept and dusted, but I gave strict instructions that the blackboard should not be touched. I trust that was the right thing.'

'Absolutely perfect, Mr Jenkins, thank you. I think I shall be fine, but I shall come and find someone if I require anything further.'

'Please just ring, Miss Armstrong,' he said with a smile. 'There's no need for you to come all the way down here.'

Mrs Brown glared at us both. My mind was working overtime trying to think of ways of irritating her further, but I had other fish to fry. There would be time later for me to think of a way to take the bullying Mrs Brown down a peg or two.

'Thank you, Mr Jenkins, you're most kind,' I said.

'Think nothing of it, my dear,' he said. 'You know your way by now, I'm sure. Please feel free to do whatever you need to do.'

Once above stairs, though, I didn't go directly to the dining room – if we wanted to search that, we'd have all day. Instead, I walked down the corridor to the entrance hall, and then down the opposite corridor to the library. The library was where it had all started and I was certain that it was the place for me to start, too.

There were two doors into the library, one at each end of the room. Most of the traffic in and out so far had been through the door nearest the hall, but the musicians' cases were at the other end. It seemed to me that anyone leaving in a hurry after a struggle would come out of the far door. Being further from the entrance hall and wandering guests, it was by far the more sensible choice.

I decided to try to put myself into the mind of the killer, to see what he saw, to retrace his steps and perhaps find what he might have tried to conceal. I went into the library through the nearer door and took a look around.

The cases were still where we had found them yesterday, but now covered in a thin dusting of fingerprint powder. I stood among them, imagining myself in the role of the unknown killer. Was I looking for something? Or was I looking for somewhere to hide something? In the present, the real me had no idea.

Then what might have happened? Perhaps I had picked up the trumpet case. The door behind me opened. I had turned. It was the trumpet player himself. He challenged me. He thought I was looting the cases. I tried to explain myself. We struggled and I hit him . . . with the trumpet case.

He fell. He was out cold. I could hear the door handle again, so I fled out through the nearest door and into the corridor just as someone came into the room behind me. Had they seen me? I had to get rid of the trumpet case. Perhaps I'd had time to conceal something in it, or perhaps what I was looking for was still in it.

Either way, I had to put it somewhere I could find it again so I could search it properly and retrieve the mystery item. Somewhere it wouldn't be seen. Somewhere easy to reach. I had to hurry.

Back in the present I stood in the corridor. I was not, as I had imagined I might be, simply further along the passageway that led from the entrance hall. This was a completely different corridor, the one where I had found Haddock talking to Sir Hector the day before. The door closed behind me and I turned to see that it was a concealed door, designed to blend in with the panelling. No wonder I hadn't realized that it opened into a different passageway. Unless you were looking for it, you might not even notice that there was a door here at all.

I looked at the ornate Chinese cabinet opposite the door, the one Haddock had misidentified as a reproduction. I'd seen that cabinet several times before and it had never struck me as particularly interesting until Sir Hector had told me a little of its history. But now, in my imaginary panic, it stood out as my potential salvation.

A vase of dried flowers stood on top of the cabinet, next to the revolting clock that Haddock had been so excited about. There was a tantalizing gap between the clawed feet beneath, but it was the brass handle on the intricately inlaid doors that caught my attention. I reached out and opened one of the doors. There, inside, was the missing trumpet case.

I rushed into the dining room, almost bowling the inspector over in my haste.

'Inspector,' I blurted. 'I'm so sorry. I—'

'Calm down, young lady,' he said, kindly. 'What's troubling you?'

As succinctly as I could I told the story of my morning's adventures.

'Well, bless my soul,' he said. 'I shall have to have words with the local uniformed boys. How on earth did they miss that? I'd been assured that everything had been thoroughly searched.'

'It's an anonymous little cupboard, sir,' I said. 'I only noticed it because it's directly opposite the door. It's in a little alcove, so it's easy to ignore it otherwise.'

'That's as may be, miss, but it's a policeman's duty to notice everything. No matter. What did you do with the trumpet case?'

'I left it there. I was already feeling a little stupid for touching the door handle so I didn't want to get my fingerprints on the case as well.'

'Quick thinking,' he said, encouragingly. 'We'll make a detective of you yet. Now then, would you mind waiting here in case your mistress turns up. I'll go and take a look at this trumpet case for myself.'

'Of course, sir. Is that tea fresh?'

'Dora brought it in a few moments ago,' he said. 'She seemed a little put out that you weren't here as a matter of fact. Looked like she had something on her mind. I told her you were running an errand for me.'

'Thank you. I expect she wanted to gloat about being so thoroughly comforted by Mr Dunn the other day.'

He chuckled. 'I don't doubt it,' he said. 'Why don't you help yourself to some tea and I'll be back in a few moments.'

And with that, he left the room.

I poured myself a cup of tea and sat quietly, basking in the glory of my achievement.

At length I heard voices in the corridor. As I rose to find out what was going on, the door opened and Lady Hardcastle came in.

'Thank you, Jenkins,' she said with her head still turned towards the corridor. 'You're a sweetheart. I don't suppose you could magic up a pot of coffee? And perhaps some of Mrs Brown's delicious biscuits?'

There was a muffled 'Certainly, my lady' from the corridor and then the sound of Jenkins's unhurried footsteps on the wooden floor. Lady Hardcastle closed the door.

'Hello, dear,' she said, putting her bag on the table. 'No Inspector Sunderland? How did your snooping go?'

Once more I described my search, and the unexpectedly easy discovery of the missing case.

'Oh, I say, how exciting,' she said.

'I should say so. In the words of Sergeant Dobson I was "all of a pother".'

'I'm not surprised. Actual detecting. Well done, you. We have even more to tell the inspector when he turns up.'

'Oh, sorry, my lady, I neglected to say that he's already here. I told him about the case and he's gone to look for himself.'

'Splendid,' she said, and sat down to await his return.

We didn't have to wait long. We'd only just begun to chatter excitedly, speculating on what the significance of the discovery might be, when the inspector came in, carrying the trumpet case.

'Aha,' he said. 'Good morning, Lady Hardcastle. I trust you're well.'

'Splendidly well, thank you, Inspector,' she said. 'And rather proud of dear Flo, too. What a find!'

'Quite a breakthrough, my lady, yes. Well done, Miss Armstrong. This should help things along nicely.'

'How exciting,' I said. 'But don't we have to wait for . . . what did you call him? The "fingerprint man"?'

'We'll send it to Bristol later, but for now, as long as we're careful, we shouldn't do too much harm. As you see, I made certain to put my own gloves on before I handled it. There's unlikely to be anything in it – we already have the trumpet itself and the stolen emerald, after all – but it's worth having a look.'

Very carefully, the inspector flipped open the two catches and slowly lifted the lid. The lining was of red velvet, slightly padded to protect the instrument in transit. There was a lidded compartment along the side nearest the handle and the inspector opened it by lifting a small leather tab. The compartment did indeed contain a small glass bottle of some oily substance and a rag, as well as the "stick thing" that Miss Montgomery had described. The inspector lifted these few items out and it was obvious that the red velvet base of the compartment was slightly askew. A false bottom. Inspector Sunderland pried it loose.

'And there,' he said, 'is where they hid the emerald for transport back to Paris.'

'How very thrilling,' said Lady Hardcastle. 'A secret compartment.'

'May I have a look at the case, Inspector?' I said.

'By all means,' he said.

I took my own gloves from my handbag and put them on. On impulse, I flipped down the cover of the storage compartment and closed the case, latching the lid shut. I picked it up and hefted it. A passable weapon in a scuffle. The edges were reinforced with leather, with a double layer on each corner. I imagined myself swinging the case to strike someone and pictured one of those corners making contact with his head. I looked closer at the corner farthest from me.

'Look here, Inspector,' I said. 'Blood. I should say this is the murder weapon.'

He looked where I indicated. 'I should say you're right, miss,' he said. 'Chalk up one more win for the amateurs. Even I'd missed that.'

Lady Hardcastle beamed at me.

'How does it help us, though?' I said.

'There may well be fingerprints if you and I haven't smudged them all, miss,' said the inspector. 'And every piece of evidence helps us build the picture.'

'I suppose so,' I said dubiously.

'Oh, and then there's this.' He produced a telegram from his jacket pocket. 'I've been waiting for a wire from Scotland Yard in answer to a few enquiries and this arrived at the station in Bristol this morning.' He handed me the telegram.

I read in silence for a few moments and then handed the telegram back to the inspector. 'I say,' was all I said.

'Well?' said Lady Hardcastle, impatiently. 'What does it say?

'It says, my lady,' said the inspector, 'that Sylvia Montgomery is better known to Scotland Yard as Olive Sewell, a notorious sneak thief with a particular fondness for diamonds, and that Clifford Haddock, junk-shop owner and oily tick, is currently under investigation for fencing stolen goods, most particularly a diamond necklace owned by the Countess of Teignmouth. The necklace in question was last seen before a party at which Roland Richman's Ragtime Revue provided the musical entertainment. Superintendent Witham is even now on an express train to Bristol and asks that we detain our songbird until he can make his way to The Grange to ask her a few questions of his own.'

'Gracious,' I said.

'Indeed,' said the inspector. 'Sergeant Dobson is already on his way up here to keep an eye on her, but we need to get her in here for another little chat before he arrives. But I'm afraid you shan't be here, Miss Armstrong.'

'Oh,' I said disappointedly. 'Shall I not?'

'Indeed you shall not, miss. While Lady Hardcastle and I apply the thumbscrews in here – you did remember to bring the thumbscrews, my lady?'

'Sadly no, Inspector. Thumbscrews and coshes are entirely Flo's province.'

'No matter, we shall improvise. But while we do that, Miss Armstrong, you shall be putting your new-found searching skills to good use in Miss Sewell's room. We should have searched it yesterday but we all got a bit carried away once we'd located the emerald.'

I brightened at once. 'Oh, goodie,' I said. 'I shall turn the place over good and proper, guv, you see if I don't.'

'That's the spirit,' he said. 'I doubt there'll be anything suspicious there, but it's worth a look while we have her safely in here out of the way.'

'My maid, the bloodhound,' said Lady Hardcastle.

'You flatter me, my lady,' I said. 'You couldn't have given it a few moments' more thought and come up with a more attractive dog?'

'Pish and fiddlesticks,' she said. 'You know full well what I meant by it.'

'Pfft,' I said eloquently.

'I think I'd better ring for that Jenkins character to go and find Miss Sewell,' said the inspector, but as he reached for the bell, there was a knock at the door and Jenkins appeared with the coffee.

'My dear Jenkins,' said Lady Hardcastle. 'What a propitious arrival. Set the coffee down over there, if you please, and then might I ask another favour of you?'

'Of course, my lady,' he said. 'Whatever you need.'

'Would you dispatch one of your minions to Miss Montgomery's room, please. Present our compliments and ask if she would be good enough to join the inspector and me in the dining room.'

'Certainly, my lady. I shall send Dora, if that suits – a run up and down stairs might do her some good. She's being insufferably cheeky and mischievous these past couple of mornings, I don't know what's got into her.

There was the briefest of pauses. Lady Hardcastle composed herself before she said, 'That will be splendid, Jenkins. Thank you so much.'

He bowed respectfully, showing no sign of being discomfited by the reaction his innocent comment had provoked, and left the room.

'You'd better get going, dear,' said Lady Hardcastle. 'Lurk somewhere for a few minutes to give them time to get down here, and then slip up to the attic rooms and do your snooping.'

I left the dining room and headed for the library, reasoning that there would be no one there.

I hid out in the library where Sir Hector had built an impressive book collection. I noticed a copy of *Emma*, the book I'd been caught reading by my first employer all those years ago. He had been the one who had encouraged my continuing education which had, in turn, led to my move to London and my eventual employment by Lady Hardcastle. There were some much more recent novels, too. I made a note to ask Lady Hardcastle to ask Sir Hector if he wouldn't mind my reading some of them. I should have liked to linger but, disappointingly, duty called.

I managed to get all the way to the top of the servants' staircase without meeting anyone, but that wasn't really a surprise at that time of day. During the working day, all the servants would be hard at work (surreptitious comforting notwithstanding) but the musicians were self-proclaimed late risers and might still be in their rooms.

There was a brass cardholder on each doorframe, holding a small white card bearing the occupants' names written in a scrupulously neat hand. The rooms nearest the stairs belonged to the household servants, so I kept going down the passageway to the smaller rooms at the end. Roland Richman had his own room, as had the late Mr Holloway. Skins and Dunn shared a room, which meant that the last one must be Miss Sewell's.

I opened the door and entered quickly, not wanting to linger outside lest I be spotted. I closed the door.

There was a bed: slept in and unmade. There was a washstand: jug empty, bowl full, face towel scrunched up on the floor. There was a small wardrobe: door open, clothes strewn on the floor. Miss Sewell had the voice of an angel, but she lived like a pig.

I stood with my back to the door, trying my imagining trick again. I imagined I'd stolen something from the house in addition to the emerald, something just for me. I had just a few moments to stash it and get back to the party before I was missed.

I looked around. There were stockings on the floor, a dress over the back of the chair. A suitcase stood open in the corner. Time was running out, what was I going to do with this stuff? My eyes fell on the make-up case standing on a small chair. It was the only thing in the room that was in any way tidy and ordered.

I opened the case and lifted out the top tray of neatly arranged powders, lipsticks and creams. The compartment at the bottom was slightly less well ordered, but it contained a few items of interest: a pair of diamond earrings that I'd seen Lady Farley-Stroud wearing a few weeks earlier, a double string of pearls, and, at the very bottom, a beautiful diamond pendant, which matched the earrings perfectly. I replaced the top tray and closed the case.

When I returned to the dining room, the interview was in full flow.

'. . . and I'm telling you that I've never heard of this Olive Sewell character.'

'A case of mistaken identity, then, miss?'

'I should say so, yes.'

'I see,' said the inspector, acknowledging my arrival with a nod. 'Perhaps Miss Armstrong has found something that might shed a little light on the matter.' He noticed what was in my hands. 'Another sort of "case" entirely, it seems. Is this yours, Miss Montgomery?'

'It looks exactly like mine, certainly,' she said.

'You won't mind if I take a look inside?'

She sighed. 'Be my guest, Inspector. Be my guest.'

He opened the make-up case and looked inside, taking in the neatly arranged items in the top section. Then he lifted the tray and removed it.

'Well, well, well,' he said. 'And what do you suppose we have here?'

She sighed again. 'If there's not a pair of diamond earrings, a pendant, and a string of pearls, then your bloodhound has got stickier fingers than I have,' she said, glaring at me.

I confess I was getting a little weary of the bloodhound references by this point, so I glared back.

'So it's not a plant, then? Not some sort of police fit-up?' asked the inspector, holding up the jewellery.

'Well, I could deny it, but I'm sure you consider your little Welsh maid here above reproach, so what would be the point? It's a fair cop. You've got me bang to rights, guv, and no mistake.'

'I have indeed, and I'm arresting you in the name of the king for theft. Anything you say may be taken down in writing and may be used against you at your trial.'

She looked unconcerned.

'I heard you found the emerald,' she said. 'I suppose I'm going to cop for that, too.'

'It seems unlikely that there would be more than one jewel thief on the premises at any one time, don't you think?'

'Well, that Summers bloke either pinched it from the old dear's bedroom or from the trumpet case, so he's got to be in the running.'

'True, true. But you're being remarkably flippant for someone who might also be accused of murder, Miss Sewell. You were seen leaving the scene of a particularly cowardly killing and here you are in possession of a few items of rather expensive jewellery. I'd say you ought to be taking things a little more seriously.'

'*Mrs* Sewell, if you insist on using that name,' she said, coldly. 'I lifted a few of the lady of the house's less revolting items of jewellery, Inspector. It would be a waste of all our time to deny that now. But I didn't kill anyone. You already know I was seen in the library while Wallace was still on stage.'

'So tell us exactly what happened.'

Another sigh. 'Well, Inspector, I'm reasonably sure I told you before that I left the stage during the instrumental numbers and went off in search of some decent booze. I started in the library but there wasn't a drop to be had, so I left there and decided to explore the rest of the house. That was when Bethan Bloodhound here saw me.'

That earned her another glare.

'There was no one else in the library?' asked Lady Hardcastle.

'No one,' replied Sylvia. Olive.

'You noticed nothing out of the ordinary in there?'

'Nothing. I've told you all this before. Just a big library with the band's instrument cases at one end and absolutely no booze anywhere. I mean, really. Not a drop.'

'I know,' said Lady Hardcastle. 'Whoever heard of such a thing?'

'It's not like they couldn't afford it,' said Montgomery/Sewell.

'Well, actually—' Lady Hardcastle began.

The inspector ostentatiously cleared his throat.

'Sorry, Inspector,' said Lady Hardcastle. 'Do, please, continue.'

'Thank you, my lady, you're most kind,' he said. 'Mrs Sewell?'

'What?'

'You left the library, and—'

'Oh, yes. Pretty much everyone was still in the ballroom so I took the opportunity to have a bit of a poke round upstairs. And . . . well . . . you know . . . one thing led to another—'

'And Lady Farley-Stroud's best jewels accidentally fell into your pocket as you walked past them?' said the inspector.

'In a nutshell.'

'Except that it wasn't quite the spur-of-the-moment thing you're making it out to be, was it? You were here specifically to lift the emerald because Richman had arranged to smuggle it back to Paris. The other baubles were just a bit of freelance work to boost your own income from the job.'

She sighed. 'I suppose so,' she said.

'I must say I do admire your brazenness in staying here so long. A lesser gang would have scarpered in the night after the robbery. Or last night once you knew the gem was lost. But here you are, calm as you like.'

'It's all about impressions, Inspector,' she said, coolly. 'If we'd done a moonlight, you'd have known something was up right away, but if we hang about there's a chance you might not figure it all out. We'd be free to go without a stain on our characters and with no threats hanging over us.'

'It's just a pity you couldn't have done it all without leaving a stain on the library floor.'

'I swear I had nothing to do with Wallace. I've already said.'

'We shall see,' said the inspector, finishing making his notes and closing his little notebook.

'Wait a moment,' said Lady Hardcastle. 'What threats? Who might threaten you?'

Montgomery/Sewell gave her a most scornful look. 'Oh, you know. Rival firms. It doesn't do to be caught operating on someone else's turf. One has to observe the proper etiquette.'

There was a knock at the door and the redoubtable Sergeant Dobson peered in.

'You sent for me, sir?'

'Ah, Sergeant, yes. Mrs Sewell here will be off to the cells soon, but she's expecting a visit from Superintendent Witham of Scotland Yard first. Please keep her secure until he arrives.'

'Right you are, sir,' said the sergeant. 'Handcuffs, sir?'

'No, Sergeant, that shouldn't be necessary. Just take her shoes and don't let her out of your sight.'

'Very good, sir. I can take her down the cell in the village if you likes, sir.'

'The superintendent is coming here. Find a quiet room somewhere and make yourselves comfortable until he arrives. We can arrange less comfortable accommodation later.'

'Righto, sir. Come along, madam, if you please.'

Mrs Sewell rose from the table and followed the sergeant.

'Just to be sure, Inspector,' she said from the doorway. 'I didn't kill Wallace and I'd like five minutes alone in a room with whoever did. He was a good man, and a damn fine trumpeter.'

She closed the door behind her.

'Another dead end,' said Lady Hardcastle, staring dejectedly at the crime board.

'Possibly, my lady,' said the inspector. 'Although it's also possible to look at it in a more positive light. Every dead end rules out another line of enquiry so that eventually there'll be only one left. I really don't fancy her for the murder, though. She's a talented sneak thief who prides herself on leaving no traces. The sort where the victims don't even realize they've been robbed until days, weeks, sometimes even months later. I've heard of cases where it's been up to a year before someone notices that a special item of jewellery has gone missing. She's not the sort to go clonking chaps round the back of the head. Too calm and cool, that one.'

'And where do we go from here?

'Well, I shall probably arrest Richman and Haddock for being accessories before the fact, and then return to Bristol to consider my next move. But I think we ought to take a closer look at those young chaps from the cricket club first.'

'Will you stay for lunch? I'm sure Gertie won't mind feeding us all.'

'If you can swing it, that would be most welcome, my lady.'

'I shall leave it to Flo. Apparently she shares a bond of comradeship with the lower orders which the likes of you and I, Inspector, shall never know.'

'I'm flattered to be counted as the likes of you, my lady, but I think I'm more like the likes of them, if truth be told.'

'Pish and fiddlesticks,' she said. 'You're a gentleman through and through.'

15

I had a quiet word with Mr Jenkins. He in turn managed to persuade Mrs Brown to prepare a light lunch for us: a deliciously summery cold collation with a fresh salad from the kitchen garden.

'You'll have to forgive my curiosity,' said the inspector. 'I'm afraid policemen tend to become very inquisitive about all things. But do you always eat together?'

'Whenever we can,' said Lady Hardcastle.

'I must say that I find it very strange, and yet oddly refreshing. It feels both wrong and right at the same time.'

'As long as we're not making you too uncomfortable, Inspector.'

'Far from it,' he said with a smile. 'Though I would wager I'm in the minority there.'

'To some extent. But I sense a change in the air. The Labour movement is gaining supporters, after all. I'm not at all certain I should like to be overthrown by the proletariat in the way that Herr Marx suggested, but a little mutual respect between all classes would work wonders.'

'I'll drink to that.'

We tucked into our meal.

'It must be frightfully out of the ordinary for you to be out here so much, Inspector,' said Lady Hardcastle.

'How do you mean, my lady?'

'Well, two murders in less than a week? It's all a bit much for a small village like this I should have thought.'

'Well, now, my lady, that's the funny thing. How are you on the subject of statistics and probability?'

'I get by,' she said, breezily. 'I read Natural Sciences, but I like to keep up with new developments in mathematics, too, and I like to think I can hold my own if the subject should turn to statistics.'

'I rather thought you might. You see there's a funny thing about this part of Gloucestershire. There's those as would say that London would definitely be England's murder capital. Others are sure it's Birmingham, or Manchester, or Liverpool. Some even suggest my own home city of Bristol. There's a cluster of villages in Oxfordshire that regularly vies for the title, but have a guess where it really is.'

'I should suppose, given the devilish twinkle in your eye,' she said, 'that it's here.'

'It is, as you suggest, my lady, right here. There are more murders per head of population in this part of Gloucestershire than anywhere else in the country. A person is more than twice as likely to be murdered here than anywhere else. It's the reason we in the Bristol Constabulary are so often called off our own patch to help out – we have to share the load with the Gloucestershire boys or they'd be swamped.'

'Good heavens.'

'Most people go their whole lives without knowing of a single murder, and yet you've already seen two in a week.'

'I'd known more than my fair share before I even arrived. Perhaps it's me.'

'Yes, of course, my lady, there was your husband. I'm terribly sorry, I didn't mean to be insensitive.'

She waved a friendly dismissal. 'Please don't worry, Inspector. It was a long time ago now.'

He nodded and continued. 'But no, it's not you, it's what they call a statistical anomaly and it's centred on Chipping Bevington.'

'I see.'

'And so I'm often out this way. I'm sure we shall see a lot of each other as the years go by.'

'I'll drink to that,' she said, raising her glass. 'Oh, I say. I've just made a toast to the continuation of murder and mayhem. I'm so terribly sorry.'

'No amount of toasting will change the facts, my lady. Don't worry. But you can do something for me, if you will.'

'Anything, Inspector. Name it.'

'The next time you feel compelled to get involved in a case – to start meddling and interfering and generally making a nuisance of yourself – please don't spin any yarns about writing detective stories. Please promise simply to call me, wire me, or even send a trusty carrier pigeon my way and I'll be glad of any help you can offer.'

'Righto, Inspector,' she said. 'I promise.'

'That's agreed, then. And for my part I promise not to send burly constables to your home when you'd probably rather be resting in bed nursing a hangover.'

'It was a rather nasty one.'

'I hoped it might be.'

I was beginning to warm to this Inspector Sunderland.

'Do you really think any of the emerald folk killed Holloway?' I asked once the meal was ended.

'Not the band, certainly,' said the inspector. 'As far as I can make out, they're all very fond of each other. If one of them had killed Holloway, accidentally or not, that person would be a great deal more distressed than any of them appears to be. They're all saddened by the loss of their friend, but no one is showing any of the signs one might expect from someone who had killed that friend. Summers, on the other hand . . . He's a peculiar one, that's for sure. We have only his word for it that his only offence was to take the emerald.'

'If only we could work out the exact sequence of events,' said Lady Hardcastle. 'That would help, surely.'

'It would be of immeasurable assistance,' he said. 'But almost everyone has mentioned the dearth of clocks here at The Grange. I've been quite unable to pin anyone down to an actual time for anything.'

'It's Lady Farley-Stroud's doing,' I said. 'Sir Hector said she has a phobia of clocks.'

'Chronomentrophobia,' said Lady Hardcastle. 'It's quite rare.'

Inspector Sunderland and I just looked at her.

'What?' she said.

I shook my head. 'And with all the music and dancing, no one has much of a memory for anything at all,' I added.

'Of course!' said Lady Hardcastle. 'What an absolute cod's head I've been. Excuse me for a moment, won't you. I shan't be long.' And with that, she upped and went, leaving the inspector and me looking at each other with amused bewilderment.

'What do you think she's up to?' asked the inspector.

'Blowed if I know,' I said. 'She's a woman driven by whim and caprice. But usually also by perspicacity and insight, so I generally tend to let her get on with it.'

'All in all, miss, I'd say from my brief experience of her that that's probably wise. Have you worked for her long?'

'About fourteen years now,' I said.

'And is it a life that suits you?'

'Very much so, Inspector, yes.'

'My sister is in service,' he said. 'But I'm not sure if I could do it. I like being my own man.'

'Sadly, I'm not in a position to be my own "man",' I said. 'But you still have to answer to your superiors; you still have to do someone else's bidding from day to day.'

'True enough, miss. Though I do have a certain amount of freedom to conduct myself as I please in the execution of my duties. A certain amount of autonomy, you might say.'

'As do I, Inspector. More, perhaps, than most servants. Ours is a . . . I hesitate to say "unique" working relationship, but it's certainly unusual. We have shared adventures over the years which most could scarcely imagine. It broke down some of the traditional barriers between an employer and a servant.'

'I've noticed the way you speak to each other,' he said with a chuckle. 'It's rather refreshing, to tell the truth.'

'It causes quite a few raised eyebrows and more than a little disapproving tutting, but we carry on regardless.'

'Well, you seem happy in your work and there's not many as can say that in this day and age,' he said. 'When this case is wrapped up I should like to treat you both to a drink or two and hear the stories of your adventures.'

'That would be delightful, Inspector, thank you. Perhaps Mrs Sunderland would like to come, too?'

'Actually, miss, I rather think she would. I think she'd like you.'

'Then I shall put you in the mistress's appointments book and we shall sup together as friends one evening.'

'I shall look forward to it.'

We chattered on for some little while. The inspector was just beginning to tell me a little about his own family when Lady Hardcastle returned, clutching a slightly crumpled sheet of paper.

'I expect you're wondering,' she said with evident glee, 'why I've asked you all here.'

We looked at her mutely.

'Oh, come along,' she said. 'I've always wanted to say that. Isn't that what they say in the detective stories?'

'Usually when the mystery is solved, my lady,' I said.

'Oh. Well, I don't suppose we shall be around at that moment, so this moment shall have to do.'

'You have fresh information?' asked the inspector.

'I do indeed,' she said, brandishing the paper. 'We've been lamenting the absence of clocks and the fact that we have no idea about the timing of events, haven't we? It suddenly struck me just now that there was one person in particular that we hadn't yet spoken to. I wondered if that person might have been paying a great deal more attention to who was at her party and where they were during the evening. I spoke to young Clarissa. It seems that she does indeed have a very clear recollection of the events of the evening.'

'She seemed a bit vague when I spoke to her on Sunday morning,' said the inspector. 'I couldn't see that she had anything particularly helpful to add.'

'Oh, she's one of those fortunate creatures whose heads will never be troubled by the arrival of anything so inconvenient as a structured, logical, or even original thought. Nevertheless, she's a charmingly social girl. She loves a party and she is absolutely devoted to her friends whose happiness is of paramount importance to her. She knows exactly how things played out, and it doesn't look well for Captain Summers. Would you give me a hand to turn this blackboard round,' she said, indicating her temporary crime board.

The inspector stood and manfully turned the easel round, revealing a blank surface upon which Lady Hardcastle immediately began sketching a plan of the ground floor of The Grange. When she was done, she pinned the piece of rumpled paper in the top corner of the board and turned back to us with a smile.

'There we are,' she said. 'That's the ground floor of the house, and that piece of paper was recovered from the stage. It's a running order, or "set list" as I believe the musicians call it. Clarissa had kept it as a souvenir of the evening.'

'Ah, I see what you're getting at,' said the inspector. 'What a clever idea.'

I wasn't yet certain what the idea was, but I chose to keep my befuddlement to myself.

'Now Clarissa, mindful of her mother's phobia, doesn't wear a wristwatch. It also happens that she thinks them rather vulgar,' said Lady Hardcastle, looking at her own watch. 'But she has a marvellous memory for tunes, and between us we managed to piece the events together using the songs to mark the passing of time.'

Aha, I thought, actually that was rather clever.

Lady Hardcastle continued. 'Now, the early part of the evening proceeded much as it might at any other party. People arrived, drinks were served, guests mingled, circulated, chatted, and congratulated the happy couple. And the band played. They were all on stage together until they reached this song,' she said, tapping the set list. 'This is "Standing Room Only" and is an instrumental number, which meant that the singer Sylvia Montgomery – I'm sorry, Olive Sewell – wasn't required. She left the stage and, by her own testimony, went off to the library.' She drew a little circle in the library with the letters OS in it. 'Sewell spent a few minutes in the library and then left, whereupon she met Flo in the corridor.'

I nodded.

'They parted company and Sewell returned to the ballroom.' She rubbed out the OS circle in the library and redrew it in the ballroom. 'Flo continued with her errand in the servants' section of the house, and when she returned, she thought she caught a glimpse of someone else going into the library. She couldn't be certain, though, and had no idea who it might have been. She couldn't even be sure if there had been someone there at all. During the next song . . .' – she tapped the set list again – '. . . "The Richman Rag", Clarissa noticed Captain Summers leave the ballroom. We don't know where he went, but from his own account of events we know that he ransacked the instrument cases at some point during the evening. He claims that Holloway wasn't there when he did, so it seems probable that he went to the library. He might well have been the person that Flo saw going in there.'

'It goes some way to corroborating his story, certainly,' said Inspector Sunderland.

'When "The Richman Rag" ends, the band take their well-earned break, and Wallace Holloway goes off to the library, ostensibly to retrieve a bottle of Scotch that he had hidden among his things, but actually to check that the emerald was safely stowed in his trumpet case.'

'And when he got there, he discovered either Summers or an empty case.'

'Exactly so,' she said. 'At about this time, Clifford Haddock left the ballroom, followed a short while later by Richman, presumably to confer and check that their felonious endeavours were proceeding as planned. Haddock went straight to the bathroom, believing he had time before the planned rendezvous. He was delayed, leaving Richman waiting for him outside the library. Richman thought that something had gone wrong and abandoned the meeting.'

She drew a series of lines on the plan, indicating Haddock going upstairs in search of the bathroom, Richman waiting outside the library, Richman returning to the ballroom and Haddock coming back downstairs.

'At this point,' she continued, 'Haddock found that Richman wasn't where he expected him to be, so he decided to check whether he had gone into the library. He went in, just as someone came out through the other door.'

She drew a new line showing the missing guest leaving the room.

'The chaos Haddock saw in the library shocked him. The instrument cases stored there by the band had been ransacked and there were signs of a struggle. He left the library and then he, too, returned to the ballroom. His arrival was, again, noticed by Clarissa during the first song of the second set, "An Angel Fell". The band was without Holloway at this point but while some people noticed a slight change in the sound, few noticed the absence of the trumpeter.'

'It looks very black against Summers,' said the inspector, thoughtfully.

'It does rather, doesn't it? By his own account, he fled when he heard someone else coming in, and from the sequence you've constructed there, it seems probable that it was Holloway. So it's just as likely that instead of fleeing as he says, he was caught mid-rummage by Holloway. They struggled. He clouted Holloway with the trumpet case then legged it into the hall where he hid the murder weapon in the cabinet.'

'Perhaps the fingerprints will tell us,' I suggested.

'They might at that,' said the inspector. 'I'll make certain the trumpet case goes into town with Olive Sewell. I ought to make a few notes about this timing idea of yours, too, my lady. This really is most excellent work.'

He began writing in his ever present notebook and Lady Hardcastle was just about to ring for some coffee when there was a knock at the door and Dewi the footman came in.

'Begging your pardon, sir, but there was a telephone call for you,' he said. 'Gentleman couldn't stay on the line so he asked me to say . . .' He screwed up his face in concentration, trying to remember the exact words. 'Tell the inspector that Superintention Wickham has been delayed at Swindon by a fallen tree on the line and has had to return to London. Hold Sewell locally until someone from the Met can pick her up.'

'Thank you . . . Doughy, is it?' said the inspector.

'Close enough, sir,' said the young man, followed by some rather harsh words under his breath in his native Welsh.

'Watch your tongue, lad,' I said in the same language. 'You never know who might be listening.'

He blushed crimson. 'Sorry, miss.'

'Right,' said the inspector. 'Can you please find Sergeant Dobson and ask him to bring Miss Montgomery to me.'

'Yes, sir. Right away, sir.'

He hurried out.

'What was all that about?' asked the inspector.

'He cast doubt on your parentage, suggested what he imagined your mother did for a living, and then expressed his contempt for the English in general.'

'The cheeky little beggar,' he said, slightly hurt. 'My mother was a schoolteacher.'

'It's just his little act of rebellion, Inspector. Like a safety valve on a steam engine.'

'I understand that, miss. But, I mean. Really.'

A few minutes later there was yet another knock at the door and a very flustered Sergeant Dobson peered in.

'Ah, Dobson, good man,' said the inspector. 'There's been a slight change of plan and I'm going to need you to take Miss Montgomery to the police station after all.'

'Ah, now, see, I've got some bad news on that score, sir.'

'What sort of bad news?'

'It's the lady, sir. She's . . . ah . . . she's done a bunk, sir.'

'Oh, for the love of—'

'I'm most dreadfully sorry, sir.'

'How, sergeant?'

'Well, Sir Hector let us use one of the empty bedrooms upstairs, sir. So we was up there and she starts fidgeting with her . . . with her underthings, and she says, "Sorry, Sergeant, but my corsets seem to have got a bit twisted. Would you mind popping outside while I straighten myself out? Just for a minute, there's a love." So I did. I went out and sat on a chair on the landing, like.'

'How long did you leave her?'

'She was ages, sir. A good few minutes.'

'And you didn't think to check what she was up to?'

'Well, no, sir. Not at first. She was . . . you know . . . she was . . . rearranging herself.'

The inspector sighed.

'But after a few minutes I did knock on the door, but there was no answer,' said the sergeant.

'And when you went in, she'd gone.'

'She had, sir. Out the window.'

'But you took her shoes?'

'Well, no, sir, didn't seem much point. We was up on the first floor. Where was she going to go?'

'Out the window and down the blessed drainpipe,' said the inspector with no small amount of exasperation.

'Yes, sir,' said the sergeant, sheepishly.

'Did you look for her?'

'I had a run round the house, sir, but she'd vanished.'

The inspector sighed again. 'Oh, well, she'll not get far on foot. Get word out, Sergeant, and we'll see if we can pick her up before she manages to catch a train.'

'Right you are, sir. Sorry, sir.' He hurried out.

'I despair,' said the inspector, but unfortunately Lady Hardcastle and I were laughing, so we couldn't commiserate. 'Really?' he said. 'We're laughing now, are we?'

'Oh, come on, Inspector,' said Lady Hardcastle. 'You've got to admit it's rather funny. And poor old Dobson. He wants so much to get things right. He offered to take her to the cells and we knew she was a slippery customer.'

'So it's my fault?'

'Well, if the shoe fits . . .'

'Don't mention the shoes,' he said. 'If he'd taken her blasted shoes, she'd still be sitting up there in her wonky stays.'

We laughed again.

We were still gently chiding poor Inspector Sunderland when Lady Farley-Stroud popped her head round the door.

'Ah, splendid,' she said. 'You're still here. Clarissa is going back to London this afternoon so I thought we might have a little farewell drink in the drawing room.'

'Thank you, Gertie,' said Lady Hardcastle. 'That would be lovely.'

'Miss Armstrong and Inspector Sunderland, too,' said Lady Farley-Stroud unexpectedly.

He and I exchanged puzzled looks.

'You were all involved in recovering the Emerald Eye and I think you all deserve a drink.'

'Thank you, my lady,' said the inspector. 'I should like that very much.'

'Splendid, splendid,' she said. 'Well, come along.'

We went along.

Sir Hector was in the drawing room, looking out of the window. Miss Clarissa was there too, and to my surprise I saw that she was in the company of 'Skins' Maloney and Barty Dunn, the only two members of the band not to be implicated in the jewel theft.

'Clarissa tells me you're fond of brandy,' said Lady Farley-Stroud.

'As a matter of fact I am,' said Lady Hardcastle.

'I couldn't do without my brandy, my dear,' said Lady Farley-Stroud conspiratorially. 'I keep some hidden away in here where Hector can't find it.'

She opened her large sewing box and rummaged around, eventually producing a bottle of very fine cognac, which she proceeded to pour into four glasses.

'Your very good health,' she said. 'And thank you once more for retrieving the Eye. I was quite beside myself with worry, but you clever things have made everything all right.'

'Happy to be of help, dear,' said Lady Hardcastle.

'And what of the murder, Inspector?' said Lady Farley-Stroud.

'Well, my lady, we have a man in custody. The circumstantial evidence – especially some fine work undertaken by Lady Hardcastle here – certainly speaks against him, but we have no proof yet, so my mind remains at least partly open.'

'Oh, I say, Emily. Well done, you,' said Lady Farley-Stroud.

'I can't take all the credit,' said Lady Hardcastle. 'That must go to the inspector for all the painstaking interviews he conducted.'

'You're very kind, my lady, but your song list idea was rather clever.'

'Oh, pish and fiddlesticks.'

Miss Clarissa and the two musicians erupted into raucous laughter.

'None of it appears to have dampened Clarissa's spirits overmuch,' said Lady Farley-Stroud. 'I'm glad she's not distraught, but I confess I was expecting a little more of a reaction.'

'Very robust, the young,' said Lady Hardcastle.

'So it would appear.'

There was a nervous knock at the door and Sergeant Dobson's head appeared around it. He scanned the room, anxiously, until his eyes alighted on Inspector Sunderland.

'You'll have to excuse me, ladies,' said the inspector. 'I think the sergeant wants me. Thank you for your hospitality, Lady Farley-Stroud. I wonder if I might impose upon you for just one more day. I should like to take another look about the place tomorrow morning, if I may. Then I shall wrap up a few local matters and be out of your hair.'

'Of course, Inspector,' said Lady Farley-Stroud. 'You know the way.'

'Thank you, my lady. And thank you both for your help, Lady Hardcastle, Miss Armstrong.'

He shook us warmly by the hand and went out to the corridor where I heard him say, '. . . at Chipping Bevington station? Thank you, Sergeant. Tell them to cuff her this time and get her down to Bristol.'

Lady Farley-Stroud went to the window to talk to her husband. Meanwhile Skins, the drummer, came over to us.

'Wotcha, Lady H.,' he said.

'Hello, Mr Maloney,' she replied. 'Are you well?'

'Not bad, mustn't grumble. We got the word about old Summers and his unrequited love. What a story. A golden idol, its shining green eye . . . I met a bloke once up North. Milton, his name was, Milton Hayes. He writes poems and that. He'd love this one. I might write to him and tell him the story. Might have to embellish it a bit – make it a bit more melodramatic – but it's got promise.'

'Oh, I say,' said Lady Hardcastle. 'What fun.'

'Yeah,' he said. 'Do you reckon he killed Wally?'

'The inspector thinks it likely,' said Lady Hardcastle. 'But his investigations continue.'

'Right,' he said. 'He seemed like a rum un.'

'He did indeed. What will you do now? With poor Mr Holloway gone, and Richman and Montgomery facing charges for theft, smuggling and who knows what else, there's only you and Mr Dunn left.'

'Don't worry about us, Lady H.,' he said cheerfully. 'There's always work for the likes of us. Best rhythm section in London, us. We'll be all right.'

'That's reassuring,' she said. 'And your immediate plans?'

'Well, I don't suppose the Farley-Strouds will want us hanging about now half the band's in chokey. Not sure, really. We could get a train back to London tonight, I suppose, but it's a bit of a schlepp with just the two of us and all our clobber.'

'Oh, no,' said Lady Hardcastle. 'That will never do. I say, I have an idea. I have two spare bedrooms and you shall be my guests for the night. There's certain to be someone in the village who will lend us a cart to get your instruments to the house.'

'That's very generous, Lady H. Very generous indeed. Thank you very much.'

'It's purely selfish, Mr M. I've become rather fond of your ragtime music. We could do with some proper musicians to accompany our poor efforts.'

'You're on, my lady,' he said, cheerfully. ''Ere, Barty,' he called. 'Come over 'ere a mo.'

Skins had only taken a few steps when he turned back and said, 'There is just one thing that never got resolved.'

'What's that?' asked Lady Hardcastle.

He turned to me. 'Did you ever decide what I can call you?'

I smiled. 'You, Mr Skins, may call me Flo.'

Our evening with the two musicians was an unqualified success. They arrived with all their traps just as I was putting the finishing touches to Miss Jones's pre-prepared dinner and they joined us for what they both proclaimed was the best meal they had eaten for weeks.

We adjourned to the drawing room where we pushed the furniture to the walls so that Skins could set up his drums and we had the most enjoyably entertaining time. They proved themselves extremely versatile musicians and managed to turn their hands to almost every musical style that Lady Hardcastle threw at them. By the time we finished, following a spiritedly syncopated version of Chopin's *Nocturne No. 2* which left us all laughing with the joy and silliness of it all, Skins assured us that if ever times were hard, we should get in touch with them. He knew a few clubs, he said, that would 'love a bit of that'.

We were up until the small hours. I couldn't recall a time since we'd returned from India when we'd laughed quite as much. Theft and murder notwithstanding, life in the country could sometimes be really rather splendid.

16

The next morning, we managed to secure a four-wheeler to take the boys and their instruments to the station at Chipping Bevington. They left with our good wishes ringing in their ears and a few rounds of sandwiches in their pockets.

'Well, Flo,' said Lady Hardcastle once they had gone. 'What say we toddle up to The Grange this morning?'

'What for, my lady?'

'The inspector said he'd be there. I wondered if he might have had news of Teddy Seddon's alibi in the Pickering case.'

'Or lack thereof,' I said.

'Just so. We've come so far – we should see it through if we can.'

'Very well, my lady. I shall fetch your hat.'

When we arrived at The Grange there was no sign of Inspector Sunderland. Lady Farley-Stroud was in buoyant mood, though, and invited Lady Hardcastle to join her for coffee on the terrace.

Lady Hardcastle was trying to explain some of the techniques of making moving pictures when Jenkins rounded the corner of the house in the company of one of our friendly local policemen.

'Sergeant Dobson to see you, my lady,' said Jenkins with a bow.

'Good morning m'ladies,' said the sergeant. 'I'm sorry to intrude but I has a message for Inspector Sunderland.' He brandished a piece of paper torn from a notebook.

'He's not here,' said Lady Farley-Stroud. 'Not arrived yet. Have you tried the station at Bristol?'

'Oh,' said the sergeant. 'The message come from there. They said to give it to him when he got here.'

'If he's definitely on his way, I'm sure we can pass it on.'

'If you're sure it's not too much trouble.'

'None at all,' said Lady Farley-Stroud. 'Thank you, Sergeant.'

He knuckled the brim of his helmet and passed the note to her. Jenkins escorted him back round the outside of the house.

'What does it say, dear?' asked Lady Hardcastle.

Lady Farley-Stroud unfolded the paper and looked at it for a moment. 'Just some police business by the look of things,' she said. 'Here.' She passed the note across the table.

'Oh, I say,' said Lady Hardcastle. 'Do you think we might borrow Bert for one last mission?'

Lady Farley-Stroud was suddenly much more interested. 'Certainly, m'dear. It's important, is it?'

'I should jolly well say so. Come on, Armstrong, I think we've got our killer.'

In the car, Lady Hardcastle showed me the note. It was scrawled in Sergeant Dobson's inelegant hand. 'Sgt Hawthorne spk to Dan (Seddon's chffr). Teddy at home on Tue 9th. Drove Ida Seddon to Littleton Cotterell.'

'Ida Seddon?' I said. 'It was Ida?'

'It all fits, dear,' said Lady Hardcastle. 'She's a grubby little woman on the make. She'd do anything to protect her wealth. She must have decided to get rid of Pickering.'

'Why are we not waiting for the inspector?' I asked.

'We're just helping out a little,' she said. 'All the evidence is circumstantial. If I can manipulate her into confessing in front of witnesses, we'll have her.'

'Very well, my lady,' I said. 'You have a plan?'

She did indeed.

When we were about a hundred yards from the house, she had Bert stop the car to let us out.

'We'll wait here for fifteen minutes,' she told him, 'and then go in. You hurry back to the village. Fetch Sergeant Dobson and Constable Hancock. Bring them back to the house as fast as you can.'

We stood hidden behind a large tree beside the road, with Lady Hardcastle consulting her wristwatch every few moments. At last she nodded, and we walked to the gates of the Seddon house. We walked across the drive, then I made my way round the side of the house to the servants' entrance, leaving Lady Hardcastle to ring the front doorbell. I hurried towards the kitchen.

A very surprised Mrs Birch let me in.

'I'm so sorry to intrude, Mrs Birch. The game, as they say in the stories, is afoot. Might I impose upon the hospitality of your delightful scullery for a few moments until the time comes for me to play my part?'

'Of course, dear,' she said, wiping her hands on her apron. 'But what the deuce is going on?'

'All will be explained in the fullness of time, Mrs Birch, I promise.'

I stood by the door that led into the main house, listening to what was going on in the entrance hall. As Langdon had already said, it was difficult to hear much from other parts of the house, but I was certain I'd heard Langdon announcing Lady Hardcastle. After a brief exchange in the hall, I heard their footsteps as they went into one of the rooms. I gave it a few moments more to make sure the way was clear and then slipped out.

'Thank you, Mrs Birch,' I whispered over my shoulder. 'I'll explain everything as soon as I can.'

I tiptoed along the passageway, listening carefully for sounds of conversation. As promised, Lady Hardcastle had made sure her confrontation was in the dining room and I stood quietly outside the partly open door, listening. Mrs Seddon's voice bristled with indignation.

'. . . mean by bursting in here unannounced?'

'I didn't think it could wait,' said Lady Hardcastle coldly.

'Didn't think what could wait? What on earth are you doing here?' demanded Mr Seddon.

'Oh, come, Mr and Mrs Seddon, let's stop playing games. I know one of you was stealing from the firm. Why was that? To try to keep up with Ida's vulgar taste in clothes? I know Frank Pickering knew, too. I know he confronted you. I know you lured him to a meeting late last Tuesday night. I know you got Daniel to drive you to Littleton Cotterell, Mrs Seddon. You strangled Pickering with your scarf. You carried his body to Combe Woods on a handcart you found near the cricket pavilion. I know . . .'

I missed what else she knew because I was somewhat distracted by the distinctive click of a revolver being cocked and the all-too-familiar feel of its barrel being thrust into my ribs. Even through the sensation-deadening embrace of my corset, I'd never forget that feeling.

'I think you'd better join your mistress,' hissed Teddy Seddon, 'don't you?' He jabbed the revolver into my ribs again, propelling me through the door and into the dining room.

'Look what I found in the hall, Mummy,' he said. 'Lady Muck's lackey doing a bit of snooping.'

He waved the gun to indicate that I should join Lady Hardcastle by the dining table.

'Oh, Teddy . . .' said Mr Seddon despairingly.

'Good boy, Teddy,' said Mrs Seddon. 'Here, let me have that.' She took the revolver from her son's hand.

'Ida, really!' said Mr Seddon.

'Just another bit of tidying up to do,' she said. 'Then we can get back to business.'

'Business?' said Lady Hardcastle. 'Murder is part of the shipping business now?'

'Shipping?' said Mrs Seddon. 'You think his tuppeny-ha'penny firm pays for all this?' She waved her free arm to indicate her garish surroundings.

'Does it not?' asked Lady Hardcastle. 'But . . . oh, I see.'

'See what?'

'You're the smuggler that Inspector Sunderland is investigating. He said he was familiar with your firm. So, you underwrite your smuggling ventures by siphoning off funds from the shipping agency? It seems a clumsy way to go about things. One would have thought it would be cleverer to have the money passing the opposite way. Hide the proceeds of your crimes in legitimate business transactions.'

'You're quite the clever one, ain't you?' said Mrs Seddon, all traces of the upper-class veneer disappearing from her voice. 'Yes, we was doing exactly that. But it's a risky venture. Ships sink. Crews double-cross you. Outsiders start operating on your turf, makin' folk suspicious. We had some cash flow problems so I used some company money.'

'And when Mr Pickering threatened to report the theft to the police . . .?'

'Yes, your lady-hoity-toity-ship, I got rid of him. Choked the interfering life out of him with a very expensive silk scarf from Paris and then strung him up in an oak tree. All carefully planned it was. Nothing could go wrong. Not until you started poking your beak in.'

'Excellent work,' said Lady Hardcastle. 'Apart from tying him too high so his feet couldn't reach the log. Oh, and not leaving an impression in the ground from the log. Other than that, an exemplary effort.'

'Details. The police would never have noticed anything like that. You're an interfering snooper too, i'n't you? And I reckon you know now what happens to them.'

'I believe so, yes. But satisfy my curiosity. Even when I realized who had killed poor Mr Pickering, I couldn't for the life of me fathom how you'd managed to get the body into the tree. Even from the handcart it was quite a feat.'

Mrs Seddon looked up at the memorabilia on the wall. Lady Hardcastle followed her gaze. 'Of course,' she said at last. 'The block and tackle. That display isn't asymmetrical by design, it's because there's a piece missing. We should have noticed that, Armstrong.'

'I noticed, my lady,' I said, shifting my weight slightly and balancing on the balls of my feet. 'I thought that's why you wanted your meeting to be in here.'

'Did you, indeed? Well done. Well done. And so it was. And what happened to the block, Mrs Seddon? And the scarf? Why couldn't we find those?'

'In the coal hole till things had quietened down. But I'll have two bodies to dispose of after tonight, so I'll probably get rid of them then.'

'You're a very clever and meticulous woman, Mrs Seddon. I congratulate you on the thoroughness of your planning. Isn't she good, Armstrong?'

'Very accomplished, my lady,' I said.

'Oh, good lord,' said Lady Hardcastle suddenly. 'Outsiders operating on your turf. You knew about Haddock and Richman, didn't you? Did you kill Holloway, too?'

'No harm in tellin' you, I don't suppose. Can't call a corpse to court as a witness. Yes, I killed him, too. I recognized Fishface. You get to know people in my line of work. I reckoned they was up to something. Instrument cases is a good place to hide things. We've used that a couple of times ourselves. Very good. So I had a look to see if they'd pinched anything. That Holloway bloke caught me so I clumped him one.'

'And left him for dead,' said Lady Hardcastle.

'They knows the rules. You don't go round nicking stuff on someone else's turf. Serves him ri—'

She was interrupted by the creaking of a floorboard outside the door.

The listeners at the door realized that they'd been tumbled and began to make their hasty way inside. Mrs Seddon turned towards them, levelling her revolver. She fired at Sergeant Dobson but at the instant she pulled the trigger, my right foot connected with her wrist with a satisfyingly loud crack of breaking bone that could be heard even over the report of the gun.

What happened next has haunted my nightmares from that day to this. Lady Hardcastle's new endeavour meant that I was very familiar with moving-picture projectors. She would often amuse her guests with the flickering images, and one of her favourite tricks was to crank the handle at the wrong speed. Winding it too fast made the people on the screen jitter about comically, while winding it too slowly made them move about with a ponderous elegance, as though struggling through treacle.

My kick had been a fraction late, or perhaps Ida Seddon's aim was a little wild. Instead of hitting Sergeant Dobson as he barged into the room, or loosing her shot harmlessly into the woodwork, she had hit something else. Lying on the floor, blood pulsing from a wound in her stomach, was my Emily.

A week later, on the first day of July, there was a ring at the door. Having reassured the new servants that they would continue to be paid, I had invited them to take some time off and so it was left to me to make my way downstairs to answer the door. There on the step was the tall, handsome figure of Lady Hardcastle's brother Harry.

'Good afternoon, Mr Featherstonhaugh,' I said, with a curtsey. I made my usual point of mispronouncing it as 'Featherston-huff', which in turn drew his usual raised eyebrow and slightly sad smile.

'It's "Fanshaw", you silly girl, as you very well know,' he said, indulgently playing along. 'And how are you, Miss Strong-Arm? Beaten up any sailors lately?'

'No sailors, sir, no. A couple of civil servants who got too lippy, but no sailors.'

He laughed and I invited him in.

'How's the patient?' he asked as I took his hat.

'Oh, you know,' I said. 'Gabbling away as usual. Complaining about her lunch, joking with the staff. She even . . .' My voice cracked a little and Harry put a comforting hand on my shoulder.

'I know, Flo, I know.'

'The stupid old biddy,' I said with a sniff. 'Just careless and rude, she is. Standing in the way of a bullet and then not even having the decency to wake up and tell us she's all right.'

'She will,' said Harry. 'The doctors say it can sometimes take a few days for the body to recover from a shock like that.'

'She'd better,' I said. 'I don't know what I'd do without her.'

He smiled. 'I'm sure I've never met a servant quite like you.'

'I'm one of a kind.'

'That you are. I've never really had a chance to thank you for taking care of my little sister, you know.'

'It's just my job, sir.'

'Harry,' he said. 'After all that you've done for her, I think you really can call me Harry.'

'I'll try, sir, but it doesn't come naturally.'

'No, no, I've noticed that. But I mean it. If it weren't for you, I think Emily would have gone batty years ago.'

'Or strangled herself with her corsets,' I said, struggling to make light again.

He chuckled. 'Or that, certainly. Not the most practical girl, my sister. But over the years you've kept body and soul together and I really don't know what she'd do without you.'

'She might never have been shot if I'd not been there.'

'Nonsense,' he said, sternly. 'You're not to talk like that, d'you hear? I've seen the police reports as well as the medical reports. There's every chance that you saved her life. A fraction in any direction and that shot could have killed her.'

'As it was, it just left her in a coma from which she has yet to wake up.'

'But alive. She's alive. And she's a fighter – she'll be right as ninepence in no time, thanks to you. As I say, I don't know what she'd do without you.'

'Thank you, sir. You're very kind. Would you like to come up?'

Lady Hardcastle had been unconscious for seven days.

While Dobson had placed the Seddons under arrest, Constable Hancock and I carried Lady Hardcastle to Bert and the waiting car. We hurriedly explained what had happened and Bert drove at near-reckless speed towards Dr Fitzsimmons's house in the village.

She was in his surgery for five hours as the doctor worked to remove the bullet and tried to repair the internal damage. He had been an army surgeon in his youth and it had taken all his considerable skill, but he eventually stemmed the bleeding and stitched her back together. After two days he judged it safe to move her back to her own bed but he paid regular visits to check on her progress.

Inspector Sunderland had visited, too. Her predicament clearly upset him and he had chided her for not letting him deal with it. If only we had waited half an hour longer, he said. If only.

Days passed.

Although she remained mercifully free of infection, she had not regained consciousness. She had lain there in the crisp, white linen sheets, her dark hair framing her face, neither moving nor uttering a sound.

I had wired Harry as soon as she was out of surgery, and he had come down on the next train. He stayed at the house while his sister was at Dr Fitzsimmons's and helped to move her home, but he had had to return to London to make proper arrangements for compassionate leave. Today was his first day back.

I spent every waking moment with her, reading to her the telegrams and cards that arrived every day from her friends. I read from the newspapers, too, especially the unfolding story of the fall of the Seddon family and the collapse of their generations-old shipping business.

I led Harry into his sister's room and went to the window while he sat on the bed next to her.

'What ho, sis,' he said, bending to kiss her cheek. 'How's the old girl?'

'She's not getting any better at all,' I said forlornly.

'But she will, won't you, old thing?' he said brushing the hair from her face. 'She'll be right as rain in no time.'

There was a rustle of linen and a croaky voice said, 'I bally well will as well.'

Harry and I looked over in shock at the slowly awakening figure of Emily Hardcastle.

'Now do stop being so maudlin, there's a dear. Would you be a pet and fetch me a cup of tea? I'm absolutely parched.'